THE BLOODY BRITISH

Originally published in German (with some edits) as:
Die Nerven, Die Briten! (Goldmann Random House, 2017)

First Edition, 2019

ISBN 9781706709916 (Paperback)
Audiobook by W. F. Howes
Also available as an eBook

www.Paul-Hawkins.com

Also by the Author:
Humans Are People Too
Avoiding Adulthood
How to Take Over Earth (forthcoming)

THE BLOODY BRITISH

Written and Illustrated and Lived by

Paul Hawkins

Contents

6. At Home with the British

7. Brits Abroad

8. The British Worldview

Epilogue

About the Author   **279**

FOREWORD

Revenge is a Dish Best Served Politely

I woke up, coming online slowly, squinting down at the pale, gangly, startlingly hairless body below me, before blinking in the information that it was presently covered neck-to-toe in right wing nationalist tattoos.

I stared stupidly down at the situation, a sense of quiet alarm rising up inside me, as my tongue simultaneously detected the opposite-of-reassuring taste of hangover all around it.

Oh no… what happened?

I blinked in the rest of the room as the usual smorgasbord of reality consolidated itself around me: my usual girlfriend was asleep next to me; my usual bedroom still looked effortlessly, exhaustingly unlike that of a racist; and outside, the familiar sounds of Berlin's Kreuzberg district still rumbled around my apartment with the usual mix of begrudging hipness and casual menace. I stared at the ceiling while last night's memories finished arranging themselves on the periphery of my understanding.

Then it hit me.

… oh shit.

Like many of my countrymen, I had stayed up all night to watch with increasing levels of quiet unease (and alcohol poisoning) as the United Kingdom, my homeland, voted to leave the European Union, the land where my home is. This morning, waking up to my wife-like girlfriend Linn, a German of the surprisingly inefficient variety, I now felt rather shell-shocked as the slow, creeping realisation set in: I would not be a citizen of the European Union any more. Weirder than that, I noticed with a jolt of cold worry, I would no longer be a citizen of the place that contained the place that contained all my pants.

Like many Brits at home and abroad, I probably wasn't quite as braced for this jarring handbrake turn in reality as I probably should have been, mostly based on what all of the exit polls had been predicting.[1] Indeed, "The Brexit Party" I had attended the night before was a fancy dress event, the hosts clearly believing it would be a relatively easygoing night on the kinds of friendly international people that Hitler would have called "rootless cosmopolitans." Linn even went *as* Europe, dressed all in blue with a halo of yellow stars in her hair, while another of our friends had baked 'brexcuits' for the party. I, meanwhile, had made the increasingly regrettable decision to go as all of the worst stereotypes of a 'Brit Abroad' rolled into one: I wore a baseball cap and white vest (to better show off my sunburn), and branded my whole body with the kinds of tattoos rightly feared by people living in nice, quiet, sunny places everywhere: England flags, British bulldogs, red lions, UKIP logos and the Britain-local mantra of every country's most obvious idiots, "I WANT BRITAIN TO BE BACK BRITISH."

Then, over the course of six increasingly gruelling hours, the humorous (and/or smug, depending on your worldview) element of my costume retreated slowly into a corner, withered away and then promptly died. At 6.15am Central European Time, the result was called: BREXIT. Half of the women at the party – foreigners themselves, or else the native-born partners of bloody immigrants like me – burst into tears, as if some

---

[1] This was way back in 2016 when the world made sense and Donald Trump was just a fat, unhappy man who noticed problems, except loudly.

unspeakably delicate dream of the future had cracked: not what Europe *is*, perhaps, but what it *means*. Shortly afterwards, the party was over, and all that was left was for me to cycle home in the brisk, new light of morning wearing only a vest – a cold, drunk, sad man dressed as a racist. Not since Prince Harry has a fancy dress costume backfired so fully.

And that is how I came to wake up on the morning after "The Brexit Party" in a state of considerable confusion, feeling melancholic and muddled, yet looking, thanks to the inadvisable use of permanent pen, like quite the patriot. I would spend a large chunk of that morning in the shower, lost in heavy thoughts about worrisome futures not yet born, but also, mostly, trying to scrub the words 'FARAGE FOR KING' from my chest.

And as I showered, dutifully removing a layer of epidermis, I expected the news to slowly settle in, and for the initially disorientating impact of it to be replaced, gradually, by the relative calm of acceptance. *Well, that's democracy, isn't it? Things change. Nothing's permanent, not even permanent marker hopefully. Yes: old skin must come off sometimes and then new skin can grow.* Instead, however, the more I thought about the situation, the more I found myself getting increasingly annoyed by it.

It's embarrassing to say it (and sound like one of *those people*) but I will say it (because I was one of *those people*): it was not until *after* the UK had voted to leave the European Union that I immediately began to realise how much I had considered myself to be, and even identified as, a European on some level.

That layer of citizenship, once quite foggy, faraway and abstract-feeling, had to be taken away from me before I truly understood what it meant in real and concrete terms. I was born into EU membership, inheriting many of its personal benefits as a birth-right, and I would grow up unaware that it could be another way. As an adult, I would find myself travelling and working freely within its increasingly generous borders, making friends with the other European people I met there, most of whom seemed suitably enough like me for the whole concept to work. In other words, the European Union *felt* like my country, more and more, in every meaningful sense of that word.

Then, suddenly, it didn't... and the surprising limits of mere nationality threatened to reassert themselves once more, at speed and with force, like the sharp yank of a bungee chord I didn't know was tied to my leg. Overnight, it appeared to me, I had lost 27 *de facto* citizenships in one fell swoop... because of half an island's worth of people *over there*. The British. The bloody British. Perhaps they weren't ever going to use those citizenships... but I was. I had been. *I am?* Wait, what exactly *was* the plan about that, by the way? (Was there one?)

Like many, I had found the referendum debate to be almost entirely confusing and maddeningly light on coherent visions of the future; the only thing I knew for sure from the official campaigning was that both options would definitely be a complete disaster but, luckily, that both options would also be totally fine. Yet this morning, as those two great-but-also-shit possible futures collapsed into one reality, I looked around at the life I had made in the place I was not from, and felt not entirely relaxed to be at the mercy of the winners. When they said *good for Britain,* I wondered, did they now mean *bad for me*?

While I could understand my countrymen's grievances *over there*, I was having my own regrettably incompatible experience of being alive *over here*, where the 27 other member states of the EU had so far only ever extended me hospitality, made my life a little easier and my world a bit bigger. "Hey there, little English man," they had said, "you wanna visit us? Work here? *Live here*, even?* Well, come on in!" The British, on the other hand, now seemed to be looking over my shoulder at those very invitations, like an intrusive parent intercepting my love letters, assessing whether they should tear them up "for my own good."

The more I tried to rationalise this emotional reaction to myself, the more I struggled to. I wanted to be pragmatic and reasonable and graciously accepting of other people's motivations to Leave, but I simultaneously felt very much like a man living in California being told that the United States was now closed to me because Wyoming said so. It *felt*, on some deep psychological level, that *wrong*.

I was an EU "citizen" too, wasn't I? Well, what right did *other European citizens* – especially *other European citizens over there*, a thousand miles away from my pants – have to revoke *that* citizenship from me? The very notion of it, all of a sudden, seemed entirely ridiculous. My passport even says 'European Union' on the very first line in big, bold, gold lettering. Wouldn't it want to keep me too? To protect its half of my dual status as a British-European? To reassure me that I would still get to see both mommy *and* daddy after the divorce? Or did all that big, bold, gold lettering simply mean nothing more or less than, 'oh, sorry, we didn't have any silver. Bit misleading, really. But, yeah, British it is. Just British. So... yep. Good luck with that!'

My future of living where I had always been told I was allowed to live, it suddenly seemed, was now less certain: a poker chip on a negotiating table, conceivably lined up to be lost entirely, or at least gambled with for years and years. And that was a rude awakening: the first time in my life that I was on the complete wrong end of a political event that clearly, significantly, demonstrably affected me. A load of my 'rights' were about to vanish, to be replaced by or compensated with nothing I could readily grasp or understand. It was the moment I felt, as the late, great comedian George Carlin had once warned, that, "rights aren't rights if they can be taken away. They're *privileges*."

Soon after – with the surreal tinnitus of Nigel Farage's apparently-not-ironic 'Independence Day' speech still ringing in my ears – I visited a friend in Spain, who lives on a part of the coastline so full of British nationals that I shall affectionately refer to it as the Costa del Sunburn. It was a place of English breakfasts, pubs called The Old Brown Cow and only very, very British people saying very, very British people things like, "it's too hot."

Yet almost everyone I met during that *too hot* week on the

Costa del Sunburn had energetically voted (by postal vote) to leave the EU, despite – it seemed to me – clearly, significantly, demonstrably utilising their selfsame rights to live in a different (and rather sunnier, I had noticed) part of it. One very, very English man named Keith, indeed, had called this particular British-Spanish settlement his *home* for many years, yet still answered my question about why he had voted Leave with this rather astonishing answer: "well, you know, because of the immigration. That's it; that's the only reason, really. I just think Britain should be British."

I stared back at him – a red and orange man from Roysdon living in the land of flamenco – and waited for even the slightest hint of irony to hit him. And yet, extraordinarily, it didn't. It simply didn't. I even waited a little longer, just to make sure, but the irony appeared to be taking its sweet time today. (Perhaps it was having a siesta.)

Indeed, my *amigo británico* Keith turned out to be so at ease with the idea of leaving the European Union (in which he fully lived, I had also rather astutely noticed) that his total relaxation about the topic somewhat disarmed me. I started to distrust my own slowly simmering Brexit anxieties. *Was I overreacting? Being naïve about the power balance involved? A victim of "Project Fear"? Had I simply read too many articles on The Guardian's website and lost all touch with base reality?* I was curious.

"I don't know, Keith," I said, tentatively. "Aren't you worried about, like, anything? Your pension or your healthcare or needing a visa or something?"

"Nah," he replied, "the Spanish need us."

I looked back at my new mate Keith, cocking my head to the side like a freshly confused Labrador to check if I was missing something, but still his claim looked slightly dubious to me. He was 68 years-old and very, *very* retired. (It's possible, indeed, that no human alive has ever been as retired as Keith.) Yet he also didn't speak a word of Spanish (nor did he, a later conversation would reveal, care much for the culture's local cuisine. "It's all foreign," he explained to me that night, "I can't really get on with it.") In the short time I knew Señor Keith, indeed, I only ever saw him buy PG Tips and Marmite and Heinz baked beans from British-run corner shops, pay other retired British people cash-in-hand for dodgy airport runs, and constantly tan himself towards cataracts, melanoma and the off-brown colour of a shoe, nevertheless believing himself to be a core boost to the Spanish GDP.

Yet I heard many similar variants of Keith's relaxed and cheery optimism echoed back at me that week, over and over again, from other admirably relaxed-seeming Brexit-voters who lived on the Costa del Sunburn. They had voted Leave for all sorts of reasons – some seemingly valid, others seemingly less so – but the central pillar of their present hopefulness for themselves always boiled down to this: that the EU was now going to offer the UK "a very good deal" because of French cheese, German cars and our island's insatiable lust for Prosecco. After a simple, amicable divorce was swiftly taken care of by extraordinarily capable professional British politicians (*ahem*), everything would be better for "Global Britain." We plucky, enterprising, blitz-spirit Brits would finally be "liberated" from the red-tape shackles of Brussels; back in charge of our own, temporarily waylaid destiny, while crazy ol' Europe would remain our closest friend, neighbour and ally, free to pursue *their* own collective destiny of becoming a United States of the Soviet Union of the European Empire superstate thing or whatever. See? *Win-win.* In the end, Brexit would be best for everyone.

I hesitate to admit, however, that this particular brand of optimism looked slightly more worrying to me. Forgiving the not-tiny-irony that ordinary British folks like Keith were now expecting generosity, fairness and compassion from the same institution they had previously (just last week, in fact) accused of being bonkers, out-of-touch and indifferent towards the lives of ordinary British citizens, they were now missing the most worrying potential spanner in the wheels of their cheerful

Brexit thinking.

The European Union – whether it is indeed "good," "bad" or, as I tend to think, kinda *neutral* – is a necessarily self-interested institution, i.e. one that does not, and cannot, want for itself to not exist. It has been built. People work there. There are rooms and people go to those rooms and they order stationery and they use that stationery. The EU *does things* is what I'm saying. If Brexit would really be good for Britain, then other EU countries would obviously be inspired to follow our heroic, trailblazing lead, which could cause a domino effect that would only ever end in the European Union's demise. The EU – in other words – *cannot* "want" anything except for Brexit to be a dismal, echoing failure for Britain – German cars and Prosecco-lust be damned.

Whether the EU can achieve that end or not, I don't know, do I? I'm just a man who is worried about his pants. But the one part of that potentially dismal, echoing failure within the EU's control, at least, was seemingly the deal it would make with the UK upon its departure… a deal which they had every rational reason to want to be at least a little bit sort of rubbish and a deal which they had quite a bit of power to make at least a little bit sort of rubbish, given that there was only one of "us" and twenty-seven of "them." From where I was sitting (in the capital city of just one country bigger than Britain, mostly), the distribution of leverage didn't look quite as encouraging to me as Keith foresaw.

It was around this time, too, that my European hosts – friends, fellow civilians and negotiators alike – looked in sudden need of a little tactical insight into the muddled-seeming mindset of the people who had just chosen to leave them. Well, perhaps I was just the man for the job? After all, it was *my* people that would now carve up the one big team we had both once shared, leaving two teams behind, with them on one side and me stranded squarely on the other. Thus, on that strange morning after the referendum result, the idea for this mildly treacherous handbook to Britishness was born. Between 2016 and 2017 (when this book was first written and published in Germany), I would become a kind of double-agent of toilet book-based espionage, working for the place I lived against the place I was from, exposing the cultural weaknesses, adorable shortcomings and amusing blind-spots of Britishness for my hosts to see. Maybe if I did a good enough job, I reasoned dimly, *they* would let *me* stay.

My countrymen – well, some of them, at least – had just let loose some friendly fire in the rather inconvenient direction of my life, and it seemed only fair and reasonable to send a little friendly fire back. Revenge is a dish best served politely, after all.

To my fellow Brits – Remainers, Leavers and Inbetweeners alike – I hope you can forgive me for this one small act of comedic treachery, so that we can finally look past our divisive political labels once again, and see what still unites us underneath the Brexit tribalism, forever and always: our adorable, eccentric, well-meaning social awkwardness.

Together, my dearest friends, family and countrymen, we will learn how our incredible politeness, innate sense of duty and incredible fear of conflict can be exploited; how our fairness-fuelled, excessively agreeable personalities can be used against us; how peer pressure, awkward silences and our crippling inability to make entirely unimportant decisions without faffing could soon lead to our ultimate downfall. Together, we will squirm in solidarity at the worryingly simple ways that we can be bamboozled, hoodwinked, tricked and trapped by our bloody Britishness.

Please remember, though: I am merely a fish out of water returning to that water to tell my old fish-mates how life in Britain looks, to me, from the outside-in. I offer you only a flimsy and imperfect mirror – made up of my own embarrassment-earned insights and half-baked theories about Britishness gleaned (often begrudgingly) from my time as another place's foreigner. I make no promises about the glamorousness (or, indeed, accuracy) of that reflection... nor whether you, like me, will wish to unsee what you might well find reflected there. However, should something in this little book of wild and sweeping generalisations hit too close to home or otherwise make you cringe with the wide-eyed horror of self-recognition, don't forget: you fired the first shot.

Let's play cricket.

MEET
THE
BRITISH

Chapter One

Meet the British

The day after the referendum result, much of mainland Europe found itself staring at the United Kingdom anew, wide-eyed with nervous curiosity and urgent confusion, as if those previously quaint-seeming islands just past France had suddenly been beamed in from outer space. One question above all others seemed to echo through bars and cafes across the Continent the day after the result: *why?* (Although we Brits, of course, were asking our own equally urgent and confusing question. According to Google's highest ranking search term of the day *after* the referendum, we were preoccupied with the better-late-than-never inquiry, "what is the EU?")

Europe's Europiest Europeans were in a particular state of shock and horror, looking on in transfixed bewilderment and morbid fascination as their next-door neighbour threw off its old, familiar costume and danced around naked in front of them (not in a good way, like a stripper at their birthday, but alarmingly, like a flasher at their grandmother's deathbed.) *What is happening over there,* thought 27 other countries in European unison, *what are they up to now?*

My sense of this aftershock was that many Europeans were perplexed at the first hurdle, by the simple, raw, conceptual layer of *Europeans* wanting to *leave Europe*, the place where Europeans are famously from. (In my experience, Europeans are more romantic about the EU, seeing it less about trade harmonisation, and more as a *so-far-so-good* alternative to us murdering each other non-stop for 7,000 years.) Squinting at the UK from not overwhelmingly exotic places like Antwerp, Frankfurt and Malmo, Europeans hadn't noticed the British seeming particularly different to the other sorts of Europeans you get these days. From the outside, we looked much like an island version of the Dutch (without the ability to learn languages); a slightly more repressed version of the French (without the ability to produce meals with more than two colours); or a politer, faffier version of the Germans (except without the ability to send a short email.)

This was not a feeling that was being entirely reciprocated in the UK, however, as we Brits stared back at our neighbours with vision unfogged by romance, nuance or the hard-won lens of political cautiousness. For we Brits tend to use a far simpler classification system for the world around us: there's *familiar* – a cup of tea, a nice sit down, a well-executed sneeze – and then there's *foreign* – which is everything past Dover.

The Dramatic Limits of Island Life

The British are, of course, an island people. We escape, perhaps a little too often for some people's liking, but ultimately we always come back to the island safety and geography-locked security of our little moat-protected homeland. Indeed, our islandness might explain better than any other factor why we have always had a uniquely wobbly *will-they-won't-they* relationship with the rest of the Continent: we are one of the only chunks of it that have floated off.

While the English Channel is just 21 miles wide, its effects on the British psyche should not be underestimated. Being literally separated from one's nearest neighbours, cocooned by the sea, can do strange and subtle things to a culture like ours. It makes us, in my opinion, a little wackier around the edges than our mainland friends. Around the borders of most continental counties, there's a bit of cultural interaction and feedback that takes place (and maybe even helps stir the European soup) while we Brits stand somewhat more apart and alone (like a bread.) For me, it helps to think about Britain like this: we're eccentric; we're famously, self-defeatingly polite; we're somewhat reserved, modest and isolationist in our instincts; there's fish on every menu and we cope famously badly with embarrassment. We are Europe's Japan.

Our islandness might also help explain how some of the more extreme aspects of our national character developed. Take, for example, the almost existential need for good manners and the accompanying honour-based system of maintaining them. If you had an argument with someone in Ye Olde England, there was only ever so far you could get away from them before you were under water. In contrast, you could be as rude to someone as you bloody well liked in Ye Olde France, knowing full-well it was always possible to climb atop your trusty donkey and get the hell out of there. Ride east of Calais and there's Paris, Köln, Αθήνα, Київ, تهران, 北京市 and กรุงเทพมหานคร. A whole world of enemy-avoiding possibilities. Ride west from Dover and there's Devon.

This water-locked isolation might also explain why our ridiculous politeness comes equally paired with our literal ridiculousness. If our amusing British eccentricities can be accredited to anything of geographic origin, then surely it's the big, wet fence around our garden that historically meant none of our neighbours could peek in and see all of the ludicrous things we were inventing while we thought no one else was looking. How else do you explain croquet, cricket, carpeted bathrooms, cucumber sandwiches and the penny-farthing? Clearly, we always felt relatively comfortable in the privacy of our own cultural garden, wearing our practical bathing suits, eating our bland snacks and playing our dinky and preposterous sports.

However, this relative isolation from our closest neighbours has also meant relative isolation from their constructive criticism and friendly feedback. Perhaps it was all this time marinating in our own juices before phones, televisions and airplanes stirred us more thoroughly into the European mix – but we British still seem to feel uniquely separate, which is why we, unique amongst the Europeans of the continent of Europe, can still say, "I'm going on holiday *to Europe*."

The Everyday Perils
of Pleasantness

Of course, eccentricity needs a certain amount of baseline background comfort to flourish. You can't be as wacky, historically, as the British without first being as comfy, historically, as the British. Hiding safely in the calm of the conquered sea, everything has been relatively "yeah, alright" (or at least "yeah, not bad") in the UK for hundreds and hundreds of years, mostly because our historical solution to most problems was to invade somewhere and steal their solutions. Our national drink? Leaves from China. Our most popular dish? The chicken tikka masala. Our royal family? Germans.

Oh sure, it's not been *all* God-given plunder and glory. There was also a brief historical blip or two, like that century when everybody's children worked in a chimney, or that plague, or that fire, or our compulsory involvement in every war ever. But recent history has been relatively kind to us, nestled as we have been amongst our green, pleasant, tame, safe, fluffy-bunny countryside, while poisonous spiders, huge snakes and dangerous predators roam the rest of the earth, poking their noses straight into other nation's lives and living rooms. In

Britain, floating behind Dover's problem-stopping barrier, we have no greater threats from nature than a bothered wasp, a rogue stinging nettle on a bike ride, or a startled hedgehog falling from some overhead guttering.

As for the more serious tantrums of Mother Nature, we mostly see these kinds of scary events on the news while we sit on our fantastically comfy sofas, sipping our warm cups of brewed Chinese leaves, tutting "dear oh dear oh dear." Our "earthquakes" could be mistaken for the sound of a phone vibrating on a table, our volcanoes are as inactive as our grandparents' sex lives and our "tornadoes" are only going to bother us if we've decided to do all of our taxes and scrapbook-making on the wrong day in a poorly built shed.

In stark contrast to Dover, Calais (where real, proper, actual Europe starts) is undeniably attached to the same fully connected bit of landmass as lions, scorpions, tarantulas, tigers, cobras, crocodiles, bears, hippos, malaria, ebola, Chernobyl and ISIS. It's not the kind of place to hang around in. That's why most of us will only ever go to Calais for a maximum of 40 minutes. You know, just long enough to fill up a van with cheap booze and cigarettes, before we speed back to island safety before we're attacked by the Malaysian pit viper.

The Bloody Weather

Meanwhile, despite 'the weather' topic being a safe harbour from which 90% of all inter-British conversations are launched, the only actually exciting thing about it is how constantly, dramatically mild it is. Insulated by the moderating warmth of the Gulf Stream, everything sits happily in the "alright"/"can't complain"/"mustn't grumble" temperature range almost all year round. We're only lightly seasoned.

Russians laugh at our briefly nippy winters. Australians barely notice our tepid, oh-well-at-least-the-sun-tried summers. For lack of meaningful alternatives, flip-flop season in Britain begins when temperatures hit 18 degrees (and then finishes about 20 minutes later.) Indeed, 'spring,' 'summer' and 'autumn' seem to be unnecessarily pedantic labels to define three quarters of the British year, which would be better described as one slow-motion blur of disappointment wrapped in clouds.

Upon considering this almost objectively dull climatic reality, you might start to wonder why we talk about the weather all day long, all year round, to ourselves, to foreigners, to friends and family, to strangers and to anyone else who will listen. Visitors to the UK, indeed, are often taken aback by our moment-by-moment collective reappraisal of what's just happened and what, perhaps, is about to. "Hm, strange…", non-Brits think as they watch us swap empty weather-based verbiage all day long, "why are they swapping information as if that information was not information that could be as easily attained from looking out a window?" (When on the receiving end of an empty British nicety like, "oh, it's lovely out there today, isn't it?" foreigners secretly think to themselves, "um, yes, I know. I have glass holes in the side of my house too.")

But this, of course, is not how we Brits regard our own situation beneath the rolling skies. We see the weather not as a mild and occasional irritant, but as a great and ever-changing enemy to all possible plans. When discussing the weather, we like drama. Who cares how bloody mild it is all the time? We prefer the epic, romantic narrative of a small yet noble island battling all of the forces of meteorology at once: tidal winds that flank from all sides; seas that lash the shoreline like a thousand angry whips; clouds that smother the horizon in an ever-looming, hope-suffocating blanket of grey.

Oh, and did we mention the rain? *O ye cruel and mighty gods, the rain!* Why, it must surely be that the heavens themselves have chosen us, and us alone, to absorb the indiscriminate contents of the sky. Endless rain, in endless forms – the spits, the showers, the stops-and-starts, the pissing-it-down sideways water-storms

– always trying to batter us down and ruin our chances of a pre-planned picnic. *But will we be defeated by mere weather?* Of course not! We may complain. Constantly, loudly and endlessly, yes. But we will also soldier on. That's the British way. We do not hide in doorways or cancel barbecues like some surrenderable Spaniard who knows the sun will be out tomorrow instead. There is no *mañana* for the British. It's now or never. We will barbecue on the beaches, in the fields and in the streets. We will never surrender, whatever the costs (of trying to cook a sausage outdoors) may be.

The Pleasures of Moaning

On top of dramatising our weather system to ourselves and each other all day (and all year) long, we are also not ashamed of trying to spice up other parts of our mildly inconvenient lives with some extra rhetorical drama. We need the thrill of exaggeration because there isn't much time for real drama and actual calamity inbetween the uninterrupted baseline loveliness of never living more than five minutes away from a Tesco Express.

We may be a nation of moaners (a lifetime of overcast weather will do that to a culture) yet we also have fewer meaty problems to moan about relative to poorer corners of the globe. That's why we've learned to overcome this cruel drama limit imposed by First World life with hyperbole. Suffering is also about perception, of course, and inside every Briton is a reality distortion device I call the Brit-o-matic Reality Filter. This helps transcode all incoming and outgoing communication with a drama-assisting layer of mild and unwarranted hysteria. If it creates an extra two minutes of 'fuss,' 'nuisance' or 'bother,' it's a legitimate candidate to refer to later with the apocalyptic phrasing, "it was a total nightmare!"

For uninitiated newcomers to the national British past-time of complaining, what's important to know is that *we secretly enjoy it*. It's sport to us. A hobby. We not only enjoy moaning actively, but we also love being on the passive, receiving end of a moan, absorbing the harmless complaints of others like a punching bag receives a light massage of trivial punches in a retirement community gym.

Here's an example of a complaint-based British conversation so you can easily see how to merge the conceptually apocalyptic with the totally mundane. (Foreign readers should take note of how the complaining accomplice echoes back each complaint to the complainer, like the backing singer of a blues band...)

"First of all, it took us FIFTEEN MINUTES to find a parking

spot...-"

"... *FIFTEEN MINUTES?!*"

"Mm-mm. Roy was livid, weren't you, Roy? It was an absolute nightmare."

"*MM-MM, ROY, WHAT A NIGHTMARE.*"

"And then – you won't believe this – it rained! Rained!"

"*NOOOO! RAINED?!*"

"Mm, yeah… from the sky! We saw it through the windows first. We both noticed it immediately. *Here we go again*, we thought, *the ordeal continues*. We COULD NOT believe it, could we, Roy? I mean, it's typical, isn't it? The ONE DAY you park on the other side of the car park. Nightmarish, it was. Absolutely harrowing. Like Aleppo, except at Waitrose. Then, you'll never guess what, Jean?"

"*WHAT?*"

"I dropped a box in the supermarket."

"*A BOX?! OH LORDY, LORDY, THAT BOX SURELY NOT GONE FALLED DOWN?*"

"I KNOW! Tell me about it! Sod's law, isn't it? It would happen to me, wouldn't it? Everything always does, doesn't it? Cornflakes EVERYWHERE. Hell on earth. Total nightmare, cloaked in a night terror, wrapped in a satanic sandwich of evil from beyond the wall. Anyway, we were home by one o' clock, then just sat in our pants for the rest of the day, didn't we, Roy? How about you, Jean? How was your morning?"

"MY MORNING? MM-mm. Well, I woke up this morning..."

A World Gone Mad

Unfortunately, the ability to generate more colourful versions of past and presently-unfolding events with our inbuilt Brit-o-matic Reality Filters has made *the rest of the world* (where most events happen) seem slightly more terrifying than it probably actually is. Parts of the big wide world can be *actually* scary sometimes too, sure, but the majority of the big wide world is mostly just people sitting on chairs, eating bread, avoiding the washing up. Filtered through the Brit-o-matic Reality Filter, though, and it can sometimes seem to us like it's a ceaseless, unending hell-scape of wall-to-wall pre-apocalypse doom out there, over the channel and beyond.

Being an "ex-pat"[1] myself, I've experienced this kind of world-weary, tabloid-marinated terror in many a conversation when I've returned home. Sometimes, when I tell British people that I no longer live in fluffy-bunny Hertfordshire (where I'm from) but Berlin (where the Second World War is from), I see them reacting as though the underlying concerns behind their eyes haven't had an upgrade since they last opened a history book at school. *Really?! But, is that… I don't know… safe? Wasn't there, like, well, all that stuff? With the wall? And the Russians? And, you know, the other guy, with the moustache… He-Who-Must-Not-Be-Named?*

I once had a British friend assure me of this curious 'fact,' for instance: "In Germany, if you have an accident on the street and you're not health insured, the ambulances won't pick you up. Seriously. They'll just leave you there to die. *Really!* It's true!" I accidentally laughed, then did my best to explain why that was actually so implausible (specifically, the idea that Germans, a nation of people who wait for the green man to cross an empty road at night, would tolerate an injured person noisily upsetting the *Ordnung*), but she nevertheless persisted in telling *me* that *she* was right. The Fear, it seems, runs deep.

As far as I can tell, this phenomenon is only going to get worse, as millions and billions of camera phones feed an omnipresent

---

[1] When British people leave Britain to live somewhere else, they may not neccessary consider themselves to be immigrants, but "ex-pats." It's important to note the slight semantic difference here: while "ex-pats" are *also immigrants*, there are none of the associated expectations of language-learning, cultural assimilation or contributions to the host economy.

24-hour news cycle with scary footage they can use to chase us from tea break to tea break. "Oh dear, oh dear, oh dear," we'll tut, shaking our heads in utter dismay, "terrible, isn't it? Whatever next, Jean? Dog terrorists? Children made of bombs? You just wonder how it will all end, don't you? I despair!"

Since the average British person can already enliven a supermarket anecdote with so much added rhetorical drama that it sounds like they're pitching *Apocalypse Now!*, it's no wonder the British press are also able to extrapolate an out-of-touch sense of proportion to just about everything they cover too. Indeed, half of the British press (the bottom half, in case you were wondering) operate on something like a *Three-Stage Escalation Scale of Disaster, Dread and Impending Doom*. If it's happened once, it's a trend. Twice, it's a *threat*. Three times, and it's an *EPIDEMIC*.

BROKEN BRITAIN, the news-stands scream at the exhausted British public every day, is a COUNTRY IN CHAOS; a DIVIDED KINGDOM of BREXIT BETRAYAL; an IMMIGRANT ISLAND sinking under the weight of TERRORIST WELFARE CHEATS and TAX-DODGING JIHADI FEMINISTS. It's a TEENAGE PREGNANCY BINGEPOCALYPSE out there, close to BREAKING POINT. And POLITICAL CORRECTNESS HAS GONE MAD too, of course. Has it? Oh yes, you're bloody right it has. *WHAT NEXT?* the papers scream at themselves, foaming at the mouth for blood, *SAFETY-BELTS FOR STEP-LADDERS? WOMEN BUS DRIVERS? HUMAN RIGHTS FOR TOWELS? JUST LET ALL THE BLOODY IMMIGRANTS COME OVER 'ERE FROM BRUSSELS-FUNDED MUSLAMISTAN AND JOIN OUR ROYAL FAMILY? EH? EH? IS THAT WHAT YOU WANT?! IS IT?! IS IT?! IS THAT WHAT WE FOUGHT IN A WAR FOR?!*

With the drip-drip-drip of tabloid doom and gloom (and nonsense), it's no wonder the general British public sometimes feel like the only viable option to survive next week, let alone the next decade or century, is to raise the drawbridge, batten down the hatches, convert London into a nuclear bunker/tax haven and save ourselves. It's us or them: the world's gone bloody mad.

The Yearning for Fortress Britain

Now we've located the lodestar of hysterical British worrying, hopefully we can better understand why the sounds of isolationist drumming seem to get louder and louder these days; not because the world is getting scarier, perhaps, but because it's getting harder and harder to sell newspapers.

Yet, while the world has gone officially mad (or so the papers warn us), Britain's apparent security from that madness still only rests upon a slither of water that people sometimes even swim across for charity. To the most patriotically British of the British (as judged by themselves), the English Channel is our last line of defence – just 21 miles of salty wetness between *the familiar* and *everything that threatens to burn it to ashes.*

Just imagine, dear reader (if you even can), the unending terror-scape of a world in which beloved Britannia had lost her sea border; where she had not one thin slither of distance between her and the rest of the Continent. Once the smoke had cleared and the embers had dimmed in the rubble of such a dark and loathsome world, what would be left of our once great land in the smouldering landscapes of ruin?

France?

It doesn't bear thinking about, the isolationists shudder. Instead, they yearn for work to begin immediately on a kind of *Fortress Britain,* a locked-down Alcatraz island of ultimate safety, a nation that looks out at the world only through a peephole, ignoring the fact that airplanes will continue to exist, and shouts out, "sorry, we're full! No one else is getting in! Good luck, planet!" This unspoken fantasy of island safety, embedded deep within the fear-addled British psyche, is in no way helped by modern science-fiction films, which often cast the United Kingdom (i.e. not France) as the last remaining stronghold of a rapidly collapsing world... one lone, lost island in a sea of troubles; one last well-mannered pocket of humanity making its last stand against the impending apocalypse.

Children of Men (the best film ever made) put our noble country centre-stage in a crumbling world where "Britain alone soldiers on!"; *28 Days Later* chose reliable ol' Blighty as the final bastion of human resistance in the zombie end-times; and *Doomsday* (definitely not the best film ever made) featured our beleaguered homeland once more, with the UK government quarantining Scotland in order to protect itself from a deadly virus that begins in Glasgow. In what must surely be an amazing metaphor for something, they literally build a 30-foot wall to protect all of civilisation *from Glaswegians.*

As for the home-grown British 'zom-com' *Shaun of the Dead,* this film probably best captured our hopes for navigating the impending doom our worst newspapers imply could arrive any minute: the characters' only plan for the entire movie is to barricade themselves inside their local pub, "hole up, have a cup of tea and wait for all this to blow over."

So, if the world at any point looks like it might Donald Trump itself into oblivion, there's nowhere the British would rather be than the British Isles – our safe, North Atlantic archipelago home – preferably wrapped in an impenetrable dome that keeps out scary people, but lets in tea.

The Inconvenience of Emotions

Despite living in a world gone mad, we may seem unnervingly calm and outwardly reserved to non-Brits who have the fortune to meet us. At the very least, foreigners tend to report about our personalities, there are few grand emotional outbursts that come bubbling to the surface of our otherwise stoic crusts. Have you ever seen the Queen belly-laugh and accidentally snort soup off an incoming spoon? No. No, you have not.

If there's a such thing as a poker face, many of us in Britain are playing life with a poker personality. Generally speaking, we almost always prefer the less-is-more approach to navigating the emotional landscape. Being sarcastic almost always trumps being earnest. Feeling quietly guilty about something mostly beats the nuclear option of having to have an awkward conversation about it. And grumbling silently about the waiter will reliably win out over the alternative strategy of confronting him directly about his mistake. (After all, what could be more devastating to an unsatisfactory waiter than a quiet, almost imperceptible yet totally disapproving *tut* noise? That's right! Much better than having to actually tell him that he mistakenly brought you an espresso even though you ordered a steak and chips. *"Tut,"* you'll go, hungrily, quietly, as you sip your espresso. *That'll bloody teach him.*)

In general, if we can solve a problem ourselves first (especially by changing ourselves), that will be our go-to strategy. We just want easy lives, after all, and it's far easier to change our expectations, update our preferences and hide our disappointment than it is to, let's say, keep pursuing a desire for steak and chips at the risk of generating further nuisance in the world. *Real-Time Preference Restructuring* is an elegant, efficient system for navigating the inherent unpredictability of reality: i.e. if we don't get what we want, we simply change what we want on-the-spot and then everything's fine. Or, if it's *not fine*, then we secretly pretend that it's fine, and then everything's fine.

As for our actual hopes, dreams and preferences? Well, why worry about these pesky trouble-making critters when we can bury them alive instead as a token sacrifice to the gods of not causing a fuss? That's it: push them down. Deep, deep into the earth where they can no longer bother anyone. There's a good sport. Personally speaking, as a preference-avoiding veteran of the "oh, well, I don't mind" philosophy, I like to imagine a *Great Well of Collective Shame* a thousand miles beneath the British isles, filled with a million years of compressed blame, guilt, regret and quiet frustration.

When dealing with the omni-flexible nature of our chipper personalities, foreign visitors may find it occasionally alarming, given how few clues we give off about what we really mean, need, want or don't want. *What ominous truths really bubble down there beneath the calm surface of "oh, well, I don't mind"?* they'll wonder. And this disconnect between what might really be going on inside us and what we're outwardly broadcasting to the world is only exacerbated the higher one travels up Britain's antiquated class system. Eventually, past *working-class stoicism* and *middle-class silent, simmering resentment*, one reaches Peak Repression in the form of the much-famed *stiff upper-lip*, that stoic crown jewel of a shiny, waxy, mummy-and-daddy-sent-me-away-but-I'm-ok David Cameron head. Yes: the British *stiff upper-lip* is a kind of psychological botox treatment especially designed for the elite children of the very privileged, concocted with exclusively organic ingredients like unrequited paternal love. It tells the world of problems and preferences, 'look at my blank emotionless face, I went to a boarding school, nothing's getting in.'

However, because there are so few clues about what's really going on inside our heads, this can cause all kinds of problems for non-Brits trying to deal with us through the normal channels of verbal communication, especially for those brave foreigners *living* in the UK who are desperately trying to figure out what we mean, need, want or don't want. And the biggest problem *is* the problem that we might not even tell them there is a problem. (Until it's too late…)

The Problematic Possibility of Possible Problems

Let me give you a small obvious example of this unspoken dilemma from my own life: I hate getting my hair cut, because I never know what I want. I mean, I know what I want, obviously. I want less hair. (More specifically than that, I suppose, I want the same sort of hair, but shorter.) Yet inevitably what always seems to happen is this: the hairdresser asks me something like, "ok, then, what number would you like?" *Sorry?* Or, even worse than that, the cryptic hairdresser offers me some confusing option that I don't have the requisite "giving a shit about hair" to cope with like, "… and would you like a French crop?" *Er, yes? No? I mean, what else is there? An Italian trim? A Slovenian mount? An Austrian flop? Can't I just have* less hair*, please?*

A nightmarish situation to be in, I think you'll agree. I have no idea what this hair-caring person is trying to say to me, do I? Of course not: I am not, as my friends will fall over themselves to tell you, a stylish man. Yet I'm also too ashamed to ask, in case it's obvious what all the bloody numbers and words and questions mean. What if the hairdresser laughs at me? Or posts CCTV footage of my daft question on YouTube? It's far too dangerous to do anything other than smile and nod. Therefore, to avoid embarrassment (the kryptonite of British people), I always seem to mumble back something needlessly obliging like, "ha, yep, sure, whatever you think is best, mate!" Unfortunately, all hairdressers in the known universe interpret this kind of reckless politeness as the grand trumpet call of destiny, summoning them to unleash their inner artisan from the ancient shackles of Beauty School. Inevitably, then, I get a haircut that I hate. Instead of *less hair,* I get some kind of "style," which I loathe. Yet whenever the professional hair-man or hair-woman concludes these cruel proceedings by showing me a little mirror on a stick to inspect whatever Lady-Gaga-chiselled-ice-swan-dada-on-ahead nightmare they've crafted on my poor head, I smile like an idiot and nod approvingly.

They say, "are you happy with this haircut?"

I think, *no! Please, God, fix it!* But what I say is: "Oh my god, yes, yes, yes! Bloody hell, it's wonderful! It's perfect! Très manifique! I'm over the moon! It's revelatory! I must pay at once! And here's an accidentally big tip for you as well, because I don't have the right change and I'm too embarrassed to say it. Good day to you, you artiste! You prodigy! You wizard of hair! Wow, I can't wait to show all of the people I know and will have to see again! *Cheerio!*"

At this point, having ensured the hairdresser will continue their reign of terror on other unsuspecting British victims, I will probably bump into the door on the way out, run home wearing a hat I've wrestled from a homeless man, then cut my own hair again in front of the mirror, weeping.

As far I can tell, people are not having this kind of problem in other cultures. They're simply replying, "yikes! No, no, no, this haircut won't do at all! It's entirely problematic! But, lucky for us, you're holding scissors and I'm paying you, so let's have another crack at it!" (This system, I think you'll agree, is better.)

Needless to say, we do not handle conflict especially well in Britain, which is why we sometimes prefer to pretend instead that problems don't exist. The age-old wisdom that "a problem shared is a problem halved" is not a viable strategy for us, because we feel a crippling terror at the thought of inconveniencing anyone else with *half a problem*. If that person gets given two half-problems, after all, then they would have their own whole problem to worry about, wouldn't they? Then what? Tell them to share it? Nonsense! A problem for a problem makes the whole world problem.

That's why we prefer to suck it up, hold it in and stay silent about our (probably self-caused) problems, at least until the very last possible moment. That way, we can quietly shoulder all of the responsibility ourselves. That's us there, the British, stiff upper-lipped while we nobly carry the massive sofa up the rickety staircase alone, then nobly let it fall down upon us, all without troubling another soul. *For King and Country! Hurrah!*

The Possibility of Conflict (Or Not, Please?)

Perhaps no expression better encapsulates our attitude towards conflict (or its avoidance) than, "let's agree to disagree." It is a neat, friendly and oddly poetic little piece of language, yet it also a miraculously dense blackhole of passive-aggression expressed at its very finest. It still says "you are wrong," of course, but it also says, "you will continue to be wrong, perhaps forever, but unfortunately I've run out of time, energy and patience to unpack your wrongness." What's more, it is both of these devastating critiques, yet lovingly delivered in the friendly tone of compromise, invitation and mutual resolution.

The conversation-ending appeal of "let's agree to disagree" is a wonderful emblem of our ostrich-head-in-the-sand approach to problem-solving. After all, it suggests, if neither party acknowledges that there *is* still a conflict then, well, maybe there isn't one, in which case none of us have to deal with it any more, do we? Nope! Now we can all just relax (neurotically.)

After the surprisingly combative EU referendum was out the way and we all knew exactly what would happen next (ahem), there was a lot of rumour-mongering about when the British government could, would or should "trigger Article 50," the formal mechanism for leaving the European Union's treaty framework[1]. At the time, I couldn't help but imagine the amusing scene of some British diplomat or other actually having

---

[1] In the end, it was decided, we should do it *quickly*, before we had a plan.

to go to Brussels in person to do the slightly confrontational thing, and that, consequently, the British establishment were at levels of panic not seen since the Stalinist Purges about who would have to be the one to go. I presumed then that Article 50 would actually be "triggered" in writing instead – the letter being the last, lone refuge of British bravery – and that the rest of Europe would be spared the sight of a haunted-looking minister shuffling awkwardly into the room, sliding an envelope across a desk, mumbling "sorry" and then sprinting back into the corridor to hyperventilate into a paper bag.

For the most part, you see, we feel that avoiding conflict keeps life relatively simple (and perhaps we're right about that, at least in the short-term.) However, because we tend to avoid conflict, we don't have the cultural toolkit to deal with it (and, because we have to avoid it, we never acquire the toolkit to deal with it. It's a *Catch-22*…) So, we let disagreements slide. We de-escalate confrontation. We let minor indiscretions get swept under the rug. We suffer in silence, we keep the peace, *in public*, and life toddles on.

In private, though? Well, that's another matter. The problem with conflict-avoidance, of course, is that bottled-up negativity tends to go somewhere else instead. That is, rather famously, how feelings work. When a British person gets annoyed at you, you might not find out about it in time to explain yourself, justify your actions or apologise for your behaviour, but that won't stop the issue itself resonating in the other person's mind, bouncing around uselessly in the private space between their ears and last disappointed haircut.

Of course, those people might vocalise the problem they had with you *eventually*… but probably only to somebody else who isn't you, behind your back, hoping it might one day get back to your front once its true origin has been sufficiently anonymised by the Chinese whispers grapevine Tor Network of social gossiping.

Meanwhile, back at the "let's agree to disagree" surface level of British society, passive-aggression is the closest many of us cowardly conflict-avoiders get to openly criticising our friends and family members, especially if that passive-aggression can be delivered in a medium that doesn't require too much bravery upfront. What about, for example, a post-it note left on a bathroom door in the middle of the night?

"Oh, hi Ben! Was just wondering if you'd noticed the towel rack we've had installed since 2002? Just checking, mate! Ha! It doesn't matter really either way, I just saw your wet towel on the floor again, so I just wanted to double-check if you knew about the towel rack. As I said, everything's totally cool – just that it's been there for the entire time you've lived here, and yeah, it's GREAT for wet towels. If you need help finding it, just let me know and I'd be more than happy to go to an opticians with you. Lots of love, Sally. xxx"

That's it: light, cordial and simmering with years of unspoken resentment.

As for face-to-face forms of passive-aggression? Well, there are more rare, but do occasionally come to the surface lightly wrapped in the dressing of "a joke." Luckily, "jokes" are an almost bulletproof passive-aggression delivery system for actual criticisms because the target will either laugh along with your "funny" jesting (and silently correct the offending behaviour privately later) or they won't, in which case they'll be upset but you can pretend the whole event didn't happen by hiding behind your bulletproof shield of plausible deniability ("oh, come on!"

you'll say, as if the person you've just criticised has lost their mind, "it was just a joke!")[1]

Resolving conflicts in Britain – even if a small problem today might mean less bigger problems tomorrow – is just not our cup of tea, thank you very much. It's scary and it's not fun and we don't have to so *la la la it's not happening you can't make us.*

Naturally, I don't exclude myself from this charge of cowardly problem-avoiding procrastination. I hate conflict and confrontation as much as the next British person, no matter how much time I spend in the real-time personality-correction feedback-machine of German society. Sure, I may have written this slightly impolite book about all of my compatriots and countrymen, but I have done so from a thousand miles away, safely hidden behind a bravery-buffer of Belgium, France and the Netherlands. Comedy is confrontation for cowards. *("It's just a joke! Jeez!")*

The Embarrassing Issue of Class

In an effort to reduce potential sources of future friction in the UK, we Brits are always keen to minimise, ignore or brush aside as much of our occasionally embarrassing history as we can. Take, for example, the slightly awkward fact that the entire country (and, ahem, *world*) was run on an elitist and institutionalised class system of some people allegedly being born *better* than other people (when it would later emerge in the 1850s that we all equally evolved, quite embarrassingly, from monkeys. *Awkward.*)

Indeed, what I hadn't fully grasped about the UK until quite

---

[1] Foreign readers need not worry about any of this, as British "jokes" are generally uttered with such a dry, understated and deadpan mode of delivery that it will be impossible for you to notice a genuine criticism has occurred.

recently (when I asked Linn, "what do posh Germans sound like?") is that many other European cultures don't even have 'posh accents' any more, because the aristocratic roots of those societies were pulled out more thoroughly than in Britain via a revolution or two. In contrast, you can still *hear* class in most British voices, echoing down the ages from the times of landowners and serfs like me.

And it's not just accents either, but our unconscious choice of vocabulary too. Quite often in modern Britain, indeed, one misplaced word is enough to give away anyone's native class, even if that person could otherwise successfully imitate the class above them. Whether we say "living room," "lounge" or "drawing room," for example, reliably stores us forever in our correctly assigned *lower*, *middle* or *upper* class boxes. "Bog," "toilet" and "lavatory" are not just words, they'll magic portals that provide telepathic insights into both our bank accounts and about 19 generations of our family tree.

This is an awkward lingering fact of historical Britishness that we modern islanders are dealing with the only way we know how: by trying to pretend it isn't there. (Saying 'mate' a lot to everyone helps. *Yes, mate, we're all in it together, aren't we, mate? Haha, yes, mate! No class differences here, mate. No, mate. Not at all, mate. Ha…*)

Of course, the UK is also making baby steps away from monarchy, aristocracy and hereditary privilege, but our age-old union still holds the title of the world's oldest democracy, a fact which can sound either respectable or alarming depending on the sentence. On one hand, it must sort of work, obviously, since it's still here. On the other hand, it also means there is a lot of old nonsense baked into the system, which is why our society looks increasingly like a magic jewellery shop the closer you get to its epicentre.

The residue of our regal and otherworldly history lingers everywhere, like the charming relics of a stable and enduring continuity or, by a different worldview, the enduring smell of a fart you didn't do in a lift you cannot leave. And, while there is a slow, incremental erosion of this entrenched gold-plated tweeness, it's hard to ignore that we are always having to tweak, patch up and tinker with a model of governance that was, until worryingly recently, a hundred men who met up once a month to discuss poor people while they chased a fox.

(Also, have you ever noticed that our official head of state still wears a sparkly, jewel-encrusted hat and owns loads of literal castles? Yes? Ok, cool, just checking…)

Anyway, to avoid any future friction on the thorny issue of who was and wasn't born divine (in the hope it might quietly go away on its own if we don't draw too much attention to it), most of us generally prefer to avoid embarrassing topics like money and/or how many castles we own.

Of course, this is much easier if we personally don't have any money (or castles) to talk about. However, for any Brits caught in the embarrassing position of having *some money*, the topic gets increasingly awkward the more obvious it becomes, which is why we all prefer to act conspiratorial and strange whenever the topic even threatens to pop up. Even if it's something as innocent as a fellow customer witnessing a fifty pound note come out of our wallets in a coffee shop, we might look around theatrically like we're wondering how on earth it got there before handing it over to the cashier apologetically, as though our wallet is a lost-and-found box of The Economy and now we're returning the currency to its rightful owner.

What's more, all topics that could conceivably be a proxy for personal wealth should also be pussyfooted around, lest they reveal something similarly awkward about our relative position in the wonky hierarchy of public life. It's impolite to talk about our salaries, the fantastic health of our savings accounts and certainly our ludicrous bloody house prices. This is probably, indeed, how they got so high in the first place – all of us just blindly guessing the value of bricks and doors in a total information-vacuum of embarrassment.

This very British inability to openly acknowledge The

Obvious (whose house has a moat and whose doesn't, for example) forces us all instead to self-deprecate about our finances. This is true even of people living dream lives of almost unimaginable wealth. Imagine, for example, you one day find yourself buying a mansion. Perhaps, happy as you are about it (mansions are nice), you might want to tell someone your good news. In Britain, however, politeness would dictate you could only tell someone this by hiding the lurid detail of you buying a mansion in some wider moan about how nightmarish it was to move into your mansion. You can even tell your most broke and destitute friends without worrying. He or she will still respond with (passive-aggressive) sympathy: "oh dear oh dear, poor you! It must have been such a horror moving all of that heavy, gold-plated furniture. Such an inconvenience! How many servants did it take? Gosh, it must been exhausting just watching them..."

Yes: on the awkward topics of money, class and castles, we sometimes have to say and do slightly counter-intuitive things to maintain the surface-level illusion of us aiming to run a fair and sensible society. For probably the best example of this, look no further than David Cameron's speech announcing "permanent austerity" on a literal golden throne after a great banquet in a gilded hall. (*#NailedIt!*)

The Equality of School Uniforms

It is in the name of make-pretend British fairness that Britain's children are sent to school in uniforms. Why not start the theatrics early? After all, it is much easier to blur the embarrassing class boundaries between Brandon Fightstone (son of Sharon and Tony Fightstone) and Millicent Foffington Brumbleberry the 19th (daughter of Millicent Foffington Brumbleberry the 18th and the Grand Earl High Duke Lord of Slothsbury-Mountlollingsforth-upon-Boncelyfoff) when both children must relinquish their class packaging at the gate and proceed as a pair of identical midget businessmen.

And while this may look cute to foreigners – like Hogwarts comes to life twice a day across the country – the subjective reality of being one of those school-uniform-wearing drone-children isn't quite so adorable, let me tell you. The average day of a British schoolboy, at least in my humble experience, consisted of six hours of constant vigilance for fear of being "peanutted" (someone sharply yanking your tie) and/or six hours of constant vigilance for fear of missing out on even one small opportunity to peanut somebody else. It's hard to overstate how life-absorbing this nonsense was; it felt like the main thing that happened in my life for about a decade, lightly sprinkled with maths and acne.

Naturally, the top-down idea of uniforming all British children (to hide their parents' status from each other) also inspires mindless acts of rebellion, with most school-kids trying to undermine the smartness imposed upon them by any means possible. Each and every day, indeed, is like a school-wide competition to see how far one can bend the clothing rules of The Establishment in a mild, sad bid for individuality, yet still stay plausibly within the letter of the law. As a result, almost every boy in my old school looked almost entirely ridiculous almost all of the time: we either had tiny little thin ties (to avoid *peanutting*), short, little fat ones (to look, I presume, like child-clowns), or ties tucked entirely into our shirts, removed or otherwise vandalised. As a show of resistance against The Man, it was hardly a hunger strike. (It was more like a quiet, almost imperceptible yet totally disapproving *tut* noise aimed at a waiter upon realising that the espresso you're consuming instead of the steak you ordered is also cold. '*Tut!*')

Unfortunately, it was too late into my own midget businessman schooldays that I finally realised the simple life-hack for escaping the soft tyranny of school uniforms: ignoring the dress code with total confidence. At some point, I don't remember why, I started going to school dressed in my normal clothes, while acting like it was totally normal to be dressed in my normal clothes. Do you know what happened? Nothing. All of the supposed rule-enforcers and authority figures in the school just assumed *it was normal*. It was like their over-worked teacher-brains, so used to dealing with 2% deviations from the norm ("tuck your shirt in!", "sort your tie out!", "don't peanut me, I'm a teacher!") didn't know what to do with an edge case of 100% uniformlessness. Instead, their minds seemed to invent excuses for you, on your behalf, based on your total lack of shame.

If you dutifully wore your full school uniform but merely forgot to tuck your shirt in, the Feds were on yo' ass like wasps on toddlers. But if you didn't even bother pretending a little bit? Then they assumed you had to leave halfway through the day for a dentist appointment or something. No one ever asked

because, as it turns out, teachers are just over-worked prison guard former-people who used to have dreams, terrified that talking to you might unearth something horrifically above their pay-grade like, "I'm so sorry I couldn't wear my school uniform today, Mr Humphries. I just came from marriage counselling. My parents are getting a divorce. I'm… I'm sad, sir." (*No, no and bloody hell no*, teachers think, in the hope they can go home early, eat sausages and watch Netflix, *I'm not falling for this trap again!*)

For me, learning I could simply go to school wearing my normal clothes (while acting silently smug about it) always felt a bit like discovering some ancient, long-forgotten magic. *You're a wizard, Harry*, I would whisper to myself, in my jeans and T-shirt, stealing glances at the Muggles all around me dressed like shrunken bankers. Indeed, this simple trick – the life-hack of hiding in plain sight – is just about the only useful thing I remember learning in the British education system. School uniforms may be the invisibility cloaks of British upbringings, but confidence is the invisibility cloak of the entire world. If you could survive a British school day in a hoody, you could probably steal the Mona Lisa wearing a high-vis jacket.

The Strange Maths of British "Fairness"

Unfortunately, because of the great amount of creativity that must go into maintaining the illusion of a broadly classless society *in* a society of people literally living in castles, we have been forced to develop our own uniquely wacky definition of "fairness" to sit atop the more universally accepted kind.

That's why we have *the rounds system*, for example, whereby individuals must take turns buying the whole group a drink despite each individual person's drink potentially costing wildly varying amounts of money. It's only "fair." That's why we *split the bill* too, whereby the mathematical formula of *Total Price of*

Restaurant Bill divided by *Total Number of Participants at Restaurant Table* magically equalises the price of a green salad to the price of a tower of pork chops. It's "fair." Finally, it's why we have developed the Great British version of *tipping* bar staff, whereby we all nobly commit to the full and equal treatment of our minimum wage drink-merchants by ensuring everyone gets no more or less than exactly zero. Fair, fair, fair: that's us! Hurray!

The reputation that we have cultivated abroad for not tipping well (or at all) is, by now, pretty well-established. Indeed, I've seen bar and cafe menus in Berlin written entirely in German with just the following few words tacked on at the end in English: "In Germany, it is customary to tip." (OK, ok, so maybe we are not the *only* nationality that can do passive-aggression well…) Let's face it: that swipe is not aimed at the bloody Americans, is it? Every time they sneeze someone gets a tip.

However, while some foreign wait-staff may regard our hesitation, reluctance or refusal to hand over a few extra coins to them as rude, it's actually the opposite. What with our own embarrassingly elitist history (which is definitely, definitely over, *shhhhh*), I think that the whole concept of tipping feels uncomfortably close to us of reminding other people that they are currently our servants. In other words, even if it seems stingy or tight-fisted, it's still less embarrassing than calling the waiter "mate" and letting Minimum Wage do the rest.

The Awkwardness of Being Ourselves

As you can see, our uniquely British definition of "fairness" slots into our slightly muddle-minded society rather well: it is a mere veneer of fairness, after all, lightly draped across a rag-tag muddle of obvious nonsense. In other words: we cannot solve the actual, awkward-sounding problem of "unfairness," so we try to hide it instead.

Our society, much like that of our Japanese cousins, takes embarrassment seriously (by which I mean, *badly*.) We, too, are an island nation of adorably repressed eccentrics and socially awkward but well-meaning oddballs, our brains ever engaged in an eternal struggle to hide our feelings from ourselves while they crunch other complex social equations relating to shame and honour instead.

So it is lucky for us that our semi-isolated island culture didn't also develop its own version of *harakiri*, the honour-restoring suicide, to deal with public humiliations like dropping a jar in the supermarket or having an argument with our partner on the street. Our nearest equivalents – the mopey sulk, the sullen brood, the quiet emotional shut-down – are much less permanent solutions to the problem of temporary embarrassment, which is probably why our culture has made it this far at all. We simply have to carry around the burdens of shame, regret, guilt and embarrassment with us forever instead.

We push it all down or ignore it entirely; we keep our despair private and brief; and we soldier ever onwards with our fingers crossed, whistling to drown out the noise of blame and accusation. In the meantime, we privately hope that one day will come along some particularly awkward British genius who will invent for us a time machine (to be marketed in the UK as *Cringe-Reversal Technology TM*), so that we may finally take our rightful places in the orderly queue of millions of our countrymen – past, present and future – who need a reset button for history.

For now, though, without any means of escape from the inherent everyday awkwardness of having to be ourselves, we suffer not from normal embarrassment – short-lived pangs of *'oh dear, silly me, please pass the sword'* – but yawning epochs of crippling, face-palm, all-day, head-shaking, eyes-closed, toe-curling, wardrobe-hiding, head-against-the-glass-of-a-fish-tank-making-*aaaaaaaahhhhhhh*-noises samurai shame.

The Power of Cringe

To help illustrate my last point (in case it sounded somewhat hyperbolic) I will give you the worst example of horrific and enduring shame from my own life. I call it simply *The Incident*.

Every now and then, I'll be strolling down a street – happy, content, maybe even having the best day of my life – and then *BOOM*. All of a sudden, inspired by nothing, *The Incident* will explode back into my head, like a memory nuke of shame. My eyes wince, my toes retreat inside my shoes, my face scrunches involuntarily inwards like my brain just ate a lemon and I remember *The Incident* with the kind of vivid intensity that other people's minds reserve for the trauma of car accidents that happened yesterday. Except *The Incident* happened in 2007.

Back when I was a student studying Media Nonsense at the University of Poor Decisions, I was tasked by my tutors with completing two weeks of relevant work experience in "the industry." Not wanting to really "experience" any "work" (a goal I have nurtured and kept alive until this day), I asked my cool cousin if I could hang out with him for a fortnight at the cool post-production studio where he "worked" (barely) doing cool TV stuff for cool TV people. In the mornings, I would be a glorified runner, making tea and coffee for cool TV people and, in the afternoons, I would visit a different department each day, learning about cool TV stuff (or, indeed, not.)

I spent an afternoon in the Sound Room, then the Editing Suite, and then the Room with Lots of Buttons That I Completely Understood. It was fun and, whilst I bounced around the building with a job description somewhere between 'coffee robot, idiot and fax machine,' I followed the progress of a TV show called *The Complainers* as a procession of cool TV people did cool TV stuff to it. Naturally, I asked the Sound People if they thought it was any good. They told me it was shit. Then I asked the Editing People and they also told me it was shit. Then I asked the Button-Pushing People and they told me it was shit too.

And so it was, with my conclusion about *The Complainers* pre-decided on my behalf with religious conviction (unshakeable certainty/no evidence) that I walked into a new room the next day to bring two guys some coffee which they'd ordered with a button. One was busy editing and the other completely stopped what he was doing to chat to me and… wow.

He was an *incredibly* nice man. Perhaps the nicest man I'd met all week; maybe even in my entire life. He was open, friendly, grounded, sincere. He was giving off that vibe. You know that vibe? That 'hey man, I get it, we've all been a runner, I respect you as a colleague and a person and an artist, you'll get there, we're all in this together, comrade, nothing's going to stop us now, brother, *vive la résistance*, love lift us up where we belong' kind of vibe? You know the vibe. For me, as a young adult, this was an especially refreshing vibe in a building where 95% of the humans inhabiting it could order warm liquids from me with a button. Hell, the incredibly nice man even asked me about my writing ambitions, totally ignoring that my present role in the hierarchy of life was 'unpaid mover of cups person.' In summary, he was Jesus and we were going to be best friends forever.

However.

That is when it happened. *The Incident.* Not so much a "brain fart," as the cool TV kids might call it, but a rectum-shattering tornado of bowl-collapsing mind-wind. I looked at the fancy monitor behind the very nice man and registered that the editor beside him was working on *The Complainers*. This is the point in most non-anecdote-worthy memories when common sense pops up, right on time, and consequently no anecdote is born. Did it this time? No.

"Oh, you're working on *The Complainers*?" I began, in a tone of voice so innocent that it seemed to suggest that Jesus and I were about to seal our eternal friendship bond over the camaraderie of a shared grievance, "I've heard it's really, really shit."

The kind, fatherly smile on the nice man's face faded, fucking slowly, to be replaced by a blank stare. The editor, who previously hadn't moved, now spun slowly and silently around on his wheely chair, then stopped.

"I hope not," said the nice man in an empty voice, "it's… it's my show."

"… ," I replied, "… ."

Indeed, what followed his reply was an epic, unflinching, astronomically gruelling pause. In my memory – which I feel I can trust with total fidelity – this silence lasted about 9,000,000 days and was comparable only in the resounding depth of its quietness to the endless nothingness of death. The absence of sound was cosmic and deafening. BOOOOOOOOOM! went the silence, echoing around the universe and back again until it had collided with itself and reality was allowed to proceed.

"… ."

However, despite the all-consuming width, depth and breadth of this unfamothable silence, still I failed to fill any of it with an apology, which is what I should have done of course. Perhaps, if I had been quick enough on the draw, I might have even got away with pretending it was some kind of weird internship prank that I was in way over my head with. (*Just kidding! It was only a joke! I knew you were the director all along! Dave sent me to say that, HAHAHA. OH, GOOD OLD DAVE.*)

Indeed, I've been thinking now for about a decade and counting about the thousands of things I could have said in an attempt to retrieve *The Incident* from the clutches of doom and my final conclusion is this: *FUCKING ANYTHING*. Why? Well, because *FUCKING ANYTHING* would have been better than what I actually did, which was stare at the nice man with eyes the size of dinner plates, and then make a weird, high-pitched, almost otherworldly giggle noise, and then stare some more, and then begin a slow pivot on the spot, at roughly the speed of a midnight kebab in the world's saddest town, and then walk gracelessly out of the room in sudden, bizarre silence.

It was utterly, utterly catastrophic. Blood-curdlingly horrific. Like, "I need to go home, learn all physics and invent a time machine" distressing. I don't want to seem like I'm being overly dramatic here but, subjectively speaking (from my awkward British personality outwards), *The Incident* was roughly as bad as the first and second world wars combined.

OK. Now, then. Before we move back to discussing the crippling embarrassments of Britishness, let us pause briefly to recap what happened in the objective world of *The Incident*: I walked into a room, made some small-talk, and then was bizarrely and suddenly rude to an incredibly polite man, by accident, while trying to suddenly and bizarrely impress him, on purpose, with an opinion that wasn't even mine. Probably only fifteen minutes or so passed between me walking through a door into a refreshingly ordinary situation and then walking out of that same door again in a baffling context of wide-eyed dread.

In other words, it could be argued, that *almost* nothing had happened in the great froffing drama of the universe. A fifteen minute blip on the cosmic radar. Afterwards, the nice man would Complain about me (ho ho ho) to my cousin's boss and then avoid me in the building for the rest of the week (including one more particularly harrowing moment when we were *almost* in a lift together but then weren't BECAUSE EYE CONTACT.) Perhaps the very nice man would tell his equally lovely spouse a short anecdote later that day featuring a bit character in his day called Bizarre Unexpectedly Rude Intern Man ("honey, there was a real weirdo today") but no doubt he would soon forget about me, then get on with his life of being a very nice man who may or may not make underwhelming TV shows. (Who knows? I certainly don't. I repeat: I haven't seen it.)

So, yeah. That's what happened. *The Incident.* And now I've typed it out, I need to go lie down in a hot bath with the lights off for about a year.

Staying Safe, Healthy and Sane When Visiting the British Isles

Current Travel Advice Summary

The United Kingdom is a relatively safe and prosperous First World country, but continental visitors should nevertheless take all reasonable precautions relating to visiting an island nation. Once you arrive, do not forget that it will be impossible to leave again without getting wet or enlisting the begrudging help of Ryanair. Be polite and plan accordingly.

Safety and Security

Levels of crime in Britain are broadly similar to those in mainland Europe and visitors are therefore advised to take all sensible precautions against mugging, bag-snatching and pick-pocketing in major cities. Despite the prevalence of crime being statistically similar in the UK to that on the Continent, you may perceive the threat to be higher at times due to the very high numbers of hooded, scowling, shadowy creatures lurking around in alleyways, on benches and at bus-stops who share a striking resemblance to hardened gang-members. Do not worry, these are just children.

Airport Security

Regarding airport security in the UK, visitors are advised to expect longer queues and wait-times in the vicinity of a Wetherspoon's, where local

EU Foreign Affairs Council

Travel Advice for Visiting the United Kingdom

British holidaymakers may be beginning their respective trips with some pre-flight greasy food and/or ill-advised morning alcohol. Give the pub a wide berth and you should make it to your gate on time.

Health

When staying in Britain, visitors are advised to avoid the obvious temptation of trying to "keep up" with the lifestyle choices of British people. While fried breakfasts, casual alcohol consumption and the cultural acceptability of ludicrously un-athletic "sports" like golf, cricket and darts may look liberating, foreign visitors are reminded that the health consequences of Britishness are heavily subsidised for the native populous by the National Health Service (NHS).

The NHS

The NHS is "free-at-the-point-of-use," which makes it one of the easiest health systems in the world to deal with. Simply walk in to a hospital, then walk around the hospital, then ask around the hospital, then shout *"HELLOOOOO?"* in the hospital, and at some point you will find a doctor or nurse (look for tired-looking individuals in white coats, possibly struggling to peel themselves away from a verbally abusive drunk.) While many British hospitals are, in theory, open

Staying Safe, Healthy and Sane When Visiting the British Isles

24/7, please be aware that normal service may be slightly compromised on Friday and Saturday evenings due to Accident and Emergency departments being on red alert to deal with the coming bingepocalypse. If you can, try to break your ankle by Thursday evening at the latest.

Road Travel & Safety

Unlike on the Continent, British motorists drive exclusively on the left hand side of the road (presumably for eccentricity's sake alone) and have an inexplicable fondness for roundabouts. While traffic laws and normal driving customs are widely adhered to across the UK's road network, foreign motorists should take note that wider requirements for social etiquette (politeness, keeping calm, giving people the benefit of the doubt, etc.) are temporarily suspended once everyone is behind 0.5cm of windshield glass. Do not be surprised if you experience "road rage" in Britain (particularly if you're going the wrong way around the roundabout on the right hand of the road.)

Rules for Pedestrians

Foreign pedestrians should be extra vigilant when crossing left hand-sided roads. Luckily, in London and other major cities, pavements in popular tourist destinations are often marked

EU Foreign Affairs Council
Travel Advice for Visiting the United Kingdom

"look left before crossing" to aid foreign visitors in retaining their aliveness. Since these signs have been added, thankfully there have been far fewer incidents of people being ploughed down by black cabs. However, this is mostly due to the increase of people being ploughed down by Uber drivers.

Ideally, pedestrians should always try to cross the road at pre-marked "zebra crossings" wherever possible. Please remember to be polite as you do so: despite British motorists being both legally (and morally) obliged to stop for you, it is nevertheless still customary to give a brief thumbs-up, friendly wave or mouth a little "thank you" to the driver, then jog across the crossing so as not to further inconvenience everyone's day with your inconvenience-causing desire to survive.

Political Situation

The political situation in the UK is likely to remain tense for a great number of years, due to the inherently divisive nature of the binary-choice EU referendum and the inevitable collision of a precarious mandate with the legal, political and economic complexity of shepherding a Venn diagram of legal, political and economic complexity out of a Venn diagram of legal,

Staying Safe, Healthy and Sane When Visiting the British Isles

---

political and economic complexity while trying to keep both Venn diagrams of legal, political and economic complexity roughly intact while everyone helpfully shouts, "just get on with it!"

Unfortunately, despite the baffling tediousness of it all (and seemingly in spite of it), a raging culture war of Very Strong Opinions has been unleashed across much of the United Kingdom. Against all odds, a nation of people who would have previously fallen asleep upon impact with the topic of custom unions are now required, as if by law, to have fanatically strong opinions about them. Foreign visitors are advised, therefore, to tread very lightly around any and all topics even tangentially related to Brexit, such as, for example, anything.

Due to the intractable nature of the central Brexit problem itself (what was promised is undeliverable, what is deliverable is undesirable), the issue threatens to remain inflammatory for many years to come as both sides butt heads over the impossibility of compromise. Luckily for a nation of complainers, though, Brexit offers something for everyone, as the mandate of the referendum was only matched in its impreciseness by its narrowness, whereupon it immediately got fed back into a pre-existing system of duelling mandates between

---

constituencies, representatives, parties and countries within the union. Therefore, due to the complete impossibility of pleasing absolutely anyone, even a little bit, any of the time, all arms of the British state are now devoted to the unenviably full-time task of bungling together an optimally mediated settlement between all possible forms of disappointment.

Political Protest

Despite the increasingly deep-set divisions (and the country's politics seemingly realigning around the goal of hard-won, universal disgruntlement), political protests in the UK remain relatively rare, overwhelmingly peaceful and almost exclusively based on puns. Regardless of the issue's severity, home-made protest signs dominate the crowds of peaceful marches, expressing their owners' frustrations through dad jokes, word-play, innuendos and double-entrendres, whether that's on the environment ("GLOBAL WARMING: ICE MELT THIS COMING"), equality ("GIRLS JUST WANNA HAVE FUN-DAMENTAL RIGHTS") or the criminal justice system ("I DON'T HAVE MUSHROOM FOR YOUR DRUGS POLICY").

DECODING THE BRITISH

LET'S AGREE TO DISAGREE

Chapter Two

Decoding the British

A friend of mine in Berlin by the name of Jan once came to me with a very particular problem.

Jan runs an international company and one of his employees, a customer service representative, was getting a lot of complaints from his clients about her apparent "rudeness"… yet only from the service's English-speaking users, and only ever over email. The German customers? No complaints at all. Phone calls? Fine. Somewhat confused by it all, Jan came to me for help, knowing that I had previously taught English as a foreign language (well, kind of. More on that topic later…)

Louise was, according to Jan, a lovely and normal and friendly and perfectly polite German person. She spoke good English too, he explained, and so it was even more of a mystery to him what was going so wrong in her dealings with the company's English-speaking customers.

Clearly, there was some kind of communication conundrum afoot... but what could the answer be? Why were the perfectly well-intentioned, perfectly well-expressed words of a perfectly polite person bouncing through the medium of email and coming out rude at the other end?

Like a Detective of Niceness, I was called in to investigate.

And the answer, I suspected, lay not with Louise, but with the bloody British. So, I put on my uniform (clothes) and took the case.

The Perilous Obligations
of Politeness

Jan sent me over a few samples of Louise's English language correspondence to analyse in my politeness laboratory (kitchen) and it didn't take me long at all to uncover the source of the conflict.

The problem, as it turned out, was this: the company's English-speaking customers were contacting Louise because they wanted to know things. Louise was promptly and professionally answering those customers' queries, and then telling them exactly what they needed to know.

Do you see the problem?

That's right: Louise was answering their questions directly, WITHOUT including 6 apologies, 4 thank-yous, 8 pleases, 2 comments about the most recent movements of some nearby clouds and at least a decorative smattering of low-content niceties mixed into the word-salad for good measure ("well, at the end of the day, it is what it is, isn't it? Could be worse, couldn't it? Can't be helped. Worse things happen at sea, hohoho. Mustn't grumble, must we? Still, all's well that ends well, I suppose, if you know what I mean. Do you know what I mean?")

You see, Germans don't really do small-talk. In fact, Germans don't even have a word for small-talk. (Or as they would say themselves, *"wir haben kein Wort für Smalltalk."*) We Brits, meanwhile, seemingly don't have the ability to *talk small*. We're a rambly rabble of waffle-blathering chin-wagging chit-chatters who jibber-jabber willy-nilly. Germans send short emails. As for me, despite having lived outside the UK for years, I think I've never sent an email to anyone anywhere for any reason which wasn't at least halfway to being a screenplay.

This missing concept in German of friendly pointless small-talk over email has, historically, been a greater source of problems in international business, politics and intercultural relationships than you might think. Indeed, there's a fantastically compact little proverb summarising this common friction in Anglo-Germanic relations: "the British are too polite to be honest, while the Germans are too honest to be polite." It's a perfect little nugget of wisdom, in my opinion, because it neatly describes how neither side is doing anything wrong, yet how *both sides* mistakenly believe *the other side* is.

And so I went to meet Louise, armed with my handy little proverb, to discover in person what Jan had previously told me: that her English was, apart from its faff-free romancelessness over email, exceptional. It was probably, indeed, almost as good as the English of most of my English friends and definitely better than the English of every single person who has ever left a comment on YouTube.

Thus, in my first session with Louise, I soon discovered that my "job" would not involve teaching her language at all. Instead, I would literally teach her *how to deal with British people*, thus qualifying myself to write this book. I would be, for a time, a kind of Politeness Tutor; a Cultural Ambassador for the Mild of Manners; a one-man Finishing School of English Etiquette for a single student.

As "English teaching" gigs go, it was hard to ask for more. Having a student who already speaks the language better than you do before you start is pretty much the bullseye for a teacher, I think you'll agree. There was no linguistic misunderstandings to solve. But there was a big, fat cultural one.

The Teeny, Tiny Problem of Understatement

The English language, at its politest, contains a lot of what I call "fluff" and what Professor Bousfield, a linguistics academic (described by BBC News as "one of the editors of the *Journal for Politeness Research*"), calls "phatic*"* language. Before we dive into what the word "phatic" means, though, we should first take a moment to appreciate the fact that the Journal of Politeness Research is a real thing that actually exists and, moreover, that it needs *more than one editor.* (What a world.)

Now, then. What *is* "phatic" language, you ask? Well, to put it simply, it is language that doesn't convey 'hard (i.e. directly useful) information.' (You probably see already why Germans aren't so fond of it…) Instead of conveying hard information, phatic language has an entirely separate, softer purpose: for example, in the case of English, it is often there to perform a social bonding function, such as making one's conversation partner feel good and/or sanding down the language's rougher edges to avoid any misplaced hints of passive-aggression.

'Phatic language' (also known as 'irrelevant language' to Germans) is probably one of the hardest things about modern English for non-native-speakers to deal with, since it's often not clear what is even happening, or why. Yet it's important: it's what differentiates, for example, a blunt, simple, rude statement like "I want *that*" from its slightly longer British cousin, "oh, I don't suppose you wouldn't possibly mind just grabbing *that* for me, would you, please? But only if it's not too much trouble, of course. Thank you very much, indeed. I appreciate that, mate. Cheers."

This amusing fluff is confusing stuff. It's why we Brits – in the interest of pretending that everything is always OK even when it isn't – happily say things like "nice to meet you" to obviously massive arseholes, "this was really fun" to family members who have just bored us to tears and "we absolutely *must* do this again" to strangers we're about to emigrate to Australia to avoid, just so we never have to bump into them at a bus-stop again.

In more sensible corners of the globe, you see, *what people say* is quite often *what they mean*. That's no accident. It's often the whole point for them of speaking; the reason they've started moving their lips in the first place; *to communicate*. Words and sentences are – rather famously – a *meaning transfer* technology. For us, however, words and sentences are more like faffy mazes that we have delicately constructed for our conversation partners to aimlessly wander around in (hoping, of course, that they might at some point stumble upon the actual meaning we've hidden in the middle.)

At first, to the sensible foreign mind confronted with British people speaking English (never *quite* saying what we probably actually really mean), this can be like encountering an annoying British code made by British people only for other British people to understand. The keys to the code can prove elusive, especially when the meaning inside sentences comes heavily encrypted with nonsense-level politeness, on top of modern English's other quirks of very non-literal idiomatic phrasing (you don't *literally* "take" a bath, nor "run" it, nor "draw" it) and our frequent use of understatement.

Just imagine, for a moment, that you are a foreign learner of English, hearing a British person say, "oh, there seems to be a little bit of a problem." How are you supposed to know the scale of this "little bit of a problem"? After all, amongst the British, this statement could mean both "oh, there seems to be a little bit of a problem" (literally: there seems to be a little bit of a problem) *or* "oh, there seems to be a little bit of an on-fire helicopter about to crash-land on our picnic" (classic British understatement.)

Perhaps my favourite real-world example of gloriously offbeat understatement came in 1982, when a British Airways pilot named Eric Moody flew a Boeing 747 through a cloud of volcanic ash above Indonesia (not on purpose) and made the following announcement over the tannoy to his terrified passengers, probably the finest example of understatement ever recorded: "ladies and gentlemen, this is your captain speaking. We have a small problem. All four engines have stopped. We are doing our damnedest to get them going again. I trust you are not in too much distress."

Literally speaking, it's an incredible thing to say, I think you'll agree.

Luckily for his passengers (who were presumably not in "too much distress" at this point, as they plummeted, engineless, groundwards, from the sky) we did not have to discover Mr Moody's entry for the World Championship of Most Understated Sentence Ever in the black box of some terrible wreckage, because the "small problem" of there being "no engines" eventually righted itself: by some small miracle, they re-started on their own. As for the unflappable pilot, Eric 'Mount-Everest-is-a-Little-Bit-of-a-Mountain' Moody, he would later make a heroic blind landing of the aircraft through a sand-blasted windshield, guided on to a landing strip in Jakarta by computer instruments and telephone, which I mention not because it's relevant to my wider point, but because I feel duty-bound to mention that he once described said manoeuvre in an interview as "a bit like negotiating one's way up a badger's arse." (My hero.)

Of course, for foreign readers of this book, it may take significant practice and repetitious fieldwork to reach Mr Moody's level of understated mastery with the English language. But persist, dear friend, and one day you'll be able to decode even the most highly encrypted of Brit-o-matic messages, such as: "let's agree to disagree" ("you moron, you're wrong"), "would you mind?" ("do it!") and "hm, that's interesting" ("Christ almighty, you're a bloody lunatic.")

The Slightly Less Honest World of Politeness

In my first "English lesson" with already-English-speaking Louise, I began as if I was trying to talk myself out of the job. I explained upfront how good her English was (she was even able to use English's crazier spellings properly, a feat which still evades many Brits - and all Americans), and how that might actually be part of the problem.

If British people were *assuming* she was British too, which would be especially easy to do over email, then they might also have misguided expectations of her to follow all of the usual faffy back-and-forth politeness rituals of inter-British communication. Not knowing she was German (and therefore politeness-blind), they had no other explanation for why she was so flagrantly disregarding all of the unwritten rules of our crazy language code. Only one conclusion remained: she was rude. I told Louise that she was communicating – i.e. *transferring meaning* – perfectly. Linguistically, no problem. Culturally, though? Well, she was rampaging through the quaint city of Britishness like the German Godzilla of her inbox.

You see, we Brits – so used to couching our simple requests ("I want *that*") in the "oh, I don't suppose you wouldn't possibly mind […] but only if it's not too much trouble, of course" form – are often taken aback by German "directness." To Germans, however, "German directness" is not a thing. (It is more locally known as "getting to the point.")

Our German cousins, meanwhile, have the opposite problem when dealing with us. They get frustrated when we Brits – in our exhaustive efforts to be friendly, good-mannered and politely uncontroversial at all times *say things that are different to the things that we mean*. Germans call this "lying" (which is frighteningly direct of them.) Take Mr Moody's "small problem," for example. If there had been Germans on that flight, they would have continued reading their magazines, ignoring the 'fasten seatbelt' signs, and wondering why all of the Brits around them were going inexplicably bananas. Why? Well, because "a small problem" was not, in the strictest sense of the word "small," *true*. If Werner Herzog had been flying that plane, you'd have got a much more direct announcement instead: "there has been a catastrophic malfunction of the entire aircraft. You must now become alarmed, because our imminent deaths are all but assured." See? More honest; less polite.

Of course, being British myself, I don't, can't and shan't see politeness as a form of lying. For me, it's more like an all-purpose lubricant for social life; something a little sweet to help the medicine go down. However, now I have lived in Germany for some years, absorbing blunt truths, short emails and no-nonsense expressions like "is that art, or can I chuck it?", I am at least slightly more sensitive to German confusion on this point. How *could* they know that all of this fluff is so important to us? After all, you only appreciate the necessity of lubricant if you are afraid of friction…

The Big Burden of Small-Talk

Unsurprisingly, Louise was initially resistant to the idea of typing lots more useless small-talky word-fluff in her job, much like a tea-making person might be annoyed if you told them the only correct way to make a cup of tea was to first rotate the kettle clockwise five times, then walk to the bedroom and back with the tea-bag, then pour milk onto your shoes while singing a magical incantation to the water god of Snarglyblahblah.

When I said to Louise that "a bit of polite small-talk is very important to us," I could see her brain receiving the sentiment more like I'd said, "a bit of pussy-footing awound our licke, ickle feelings is wery, wery important to us (because we are overgrown simpletons.)" Her job already involved a lot of typing and now

I wanted her to type *more*?

Given that Louise was saying the exact same things to Germans *and* Brits in her emails, I suggested the best way to think about the communication-fork from now on might be to imagine she was playing two entirely different characters, depending on the target language. When switching between them, she should take off her "German hat" and then put on her "English hat." (Pretty fun exercise, I think you'll agree.) Our lessons would become a kind of cultural role-play game between the two characters.

Old Louise, with her "German hat" permanently glued to her head, would have said things in English emails like, "as I explained to you before, you have to log in first." (Ouch.) I pointed this example out to her, doing my best to explain that we Brits are quite capable of converting this brief, direct, factual statement into a stereotype-proving German rudeness-bomb. Unfortunately for Louise, "as I explained to you before…" hits the British ear as, "ugh! Can you not see that you are wasting my time? Well done you, you dim-witted island-monkey, now I have to type everything out again while this ridiculous "English teacher" gets paid to explain that he comes from a culture of adult-sized children because you can't bloody read!"

This would be unideal, so I tried to explain how she might express a similar sort of sentiment while wearing her fun new "English hat," perhaps with something more along the lines of this: "oh, I'm sorry, I probably didn't explain myself well enough before, what I actually meant was…" (At this point, Louise looked at me as if I had just suggested the best way of dealing with muggers was shouting your PIN number at them while they run away with your handbag.)

"Um, and why am I rewarding their stupidity?" she asked me, directly.

I thought about it, politely. And, after some soul-searching, research and lesson-planning, I was able to come up with an answer. I call it the 'Paul Hawkins Four-Step Plan to Being Totally Polite'…

The Paul Hawkins Four-Step Plan to Being Totally Polite

(a.k.a. How to Deal with British People)

STEP ONE:
Don't get to the point

To the muddled British mentality, padding out a sentence with empty niceties and luxuriously irrelevant word-fluff often helps soften everything up a bit. Generally, this is done to show the other person that you have the "best intentions" and are not afraid to virtue-signal about it. Mostly, though, it's just another opportunity for some lovely-feeling British faff: why get to the point of your sentence straightaway, after all, when you could have some phatic communication foreplay first?

Thus even "yes"/"no" answers should become far more expansive sentiments of needless faffery like, "oh well, that would be very nice, yes, but are you completely sure that you don't mind?" or "hm, I'm not actually totally one hundred percent sure about that just quite yet. Maaaaaybe, yeah, but, um, well, can I let you know later actually? Is that alright? Yeah? Great, thanks. I'll just let you know later on then (when I have finally summoned up the courage to say 'no' by text message.)"

Incorrect Example: "No, you're wrong."

Correct Example: "Hm. That's a really interesting take on it! Of course you're right to point that out, but don't you think we should also consider [the right answer]? What do you think?"

STEP TWO:
You've only got yourself to blame

In order to avoid anyone else feeling blamed when you talk (which might otherwise cause them to have an icky or unauthorised feeling of some kind), the faffy English of modern Britain commands that everything is/was/will be *your fault* (or at least a lot more *your fault* than it actually was/is/will be.) When speaking, you must appear to take ownership of all possible problems at all times, safe in the knowledge that the British person you're talking to won't let you take the blame, but will also be pre-programmed by the same culture to reply, "no, no, no, don't be silly, it wasn't your fault! It was *mine!*" (This self-flagellation should go back-and-forth for a few rounds, or at least until all insinuations of accusation, motives or intentions have fully dissolved in the politeness soup.)

When playing the no-one-is-to-blame-game, there can be no real "winners" or "losers" *per se*. Instead, it's best to regard the exercise of blame-taking as an ever-present opportunity for *self*-improvement: every misunderstanding or potential conflict should be grasped with both hands as another chance for you to blame yourself for *your* failure to communicate. Hopefully, your partner will do the same too and the whole idea of blame will quietly disappear as if you were a pair of blind-deaf detectives who "witnessed" a murder, but decided the best solution to solve the case was to bury the body together and go to the pub.

Incorrect Example: "As I explained before, I don't understand what you are saying."

Correct Example: "Sorry, I probably didn't explain it well enough before. Totally my fault! Anyway, what *I* meant to say was, well, I'm not quite sure if *I* totally 100% understood what you meant..."

STEP THREE:
Everything is optional (especially if it isn't)

When dealing with each other in hierarchical situations, we must at all times join in with maintaining the long-running nation-wide delusion that everything everyone is doing is ENTIRELY VOLUNTARY. *(Move along, mate! Nothing to see here, mate! Ha!)*

Certainly, no one is allowed to give overt commands in Britain as this would definitely be considered rude, given that the other person could hardly say "no" without seeming rude also. Thus, we politely construct little phatic faff-mazes for each other instead. Even if we are, for example, definitely, definitely in charge of someone else and we are definitely, definitely giving them a command, we must still make that command sound more like it is merely a very polite *suggestion* (even if their refusal would mean them getting fired, killed or locked forever in the Tower of London.)

Incorrect Example: "Get me a cup of tea NOW. Never forget: you are my contractual subordinate!"

Correct Example: "Oh hello mate. Nice socks! Shame about that Arsenal score, eh? Yeah, I know. Nightmare. Absolute horrorshow. Hellish result. Oh, by the way… are you, er, busy at all? I was just wondering – if you wouldn't mind, ah – would you have time, possibly, to get me a little small cup of, maybe, like, tea, please? Just a little one, I mean. No worries if you don't, I'll just catch you later at your annual performance review."

STEP FOUR:
Strike a Vague

Just as it is always polite to self-deprecate in Britain, so is it also always polite to insert extra vagueness into anything you say that could sound even slightly accusatory to someone else's ear, in order to give that person the appropriate wiggle-room to not feel blamed, judged or have an uncomfortable inner experience of any kind.

The passive voice, therefore, is preferred wherever possible to avoid the insinuation of blame, guilt or accusation. See in the examples below how it helps muddy the waters of actual meaning, while emphasising the inherent mystery of motives and intentions involved in all events so nobody can come away feeling stupid...

Incorrect Example: "The problem is obviously that **you** have wedged **your** hand into this railing, **you idiot**. Great, well done... now I need to go and fetch butter to rescue you."

Correct Example: "Hm. Let's see what's happened here. Ah, oh dear. It seems like there is this *big part of an arm*, and this *big part of an arm* is bigger than the *small gap of this railing*. Gosh, and the arm in question seems to be fully attached to your body! What a nightmare. Would you mind if we applied some butter to it, to see if **we** can remedy this mysterious situation?"

The Impossibility
of Short Interactions

There is one other context in which you might hear the term "phatic communication": in the study of our primate cousins, monkeys.

You know when monkeys sit behind each other, combing through each other's fur, picking out nits and eating them? Well, it turns out, rather strangely, that they're not actually picking out nits and eating them, but merely *pretending to*. The elaborate charade, biologists now know, is just a way of bonding with other monkeys in one's own monkey tribe – showing affection, solidarity, friendship, a way of giving off that vibe. You know that vibe? That "we're all in this together, look, I'm eating small insects from your hair" kind of vibe? You know the vibe. It's the monkey equivalent of us seeing our next-door neighbours over a garden fence and being unable to resist saying something lovely and pointless like, "beautiful day again, isn't it, Geoff!" or "yikes… nice weather for ducks, eh, Linda!"

To get a handle on how this phatic communication stuff looks from the outside-in, let's imagine briefly that you are a Russian tourist stuck in a British corner-shop queue and your brief life of tragedy is being interrupted by the inexplicable phenomenon of customers swapping empty verbiage with the shopkeepers, and vice-versa. Well, dear Sergei, I encourage you instead to see these two Brits as a pair of shaved, upright monkeys, dressed in human clothes, pretending to pick nits from each other, except using the medium of word-fluff instead of literal nit-picking. It's all for show. It's theatre.

Let's look at an example. (Would-be tourists should take particular note of the conversation's duration. Plan your day accordingly.) In Russia, the following exchange would consist of a single pack of biscuits being shoved down with a grunt, then a price being grunted back in number form, then both parties trying to survive the winter. In Britain, it looks more like this:

"Hello! Just this pack of biscuits, please. Sorry I'm not buying more things. Thank you."

"Thank you. Lovely/horrible out there, isn't it?"

"Yes, it is. I was just out there, which is why I am presently covered in sunburn/cloudwet. Still, makes a change/mustn't grumble, must we?"

"No/yes. OK, well now we've both mutually agreed on what is simultaneously happening outside all nearby windows, that will be £2.80, please."

"Great, thank you. Oh dear, my apologies, I've only got a twenty pound note. Is that ok? Sorry."

"Oh yes, don't worry! A twenty pound note is valid currency by law. God save the Queen. Oh, but *I'm* sorry, I've only got change. Is that ok?"

"Oh yes, don't worry! Change is also valid currency by law. God bless Her Royal Highness. Thank you."

"Thanks."

"Thank *you*."

"No problem."

"My pleasure."

"Oh, sorry, do you need a bag?"

"Oh, yes, please. Thank you."

"No worries. There you are, then: a bag. There's your one bag. Thank you."

"Thanks."

"Sorry."

"Sorry?"

"Oh, yes, sorry. I've just remembered that the bags cost ten pence now, by law. Is that alright? Bit of a nuisance, I know. Bloody government. Sorry."

"Oh no, don't worry! That's totally my fault: I should have anticipated that already, of course. Don't worry, I have lots of change now, from the beginning of this transaction half an hour ago. Let me just... provide a... little commentary while I...

reach into my pocket… and… find the… aha, got it."

"Oh, lovely."

"Ah, I'm sorry, I've only got a twenty pence piece. Sorry. Is that alright? Sorry."

"Yes, of course! Don't worry. A penny saved is a penny earned, that's what I always say. Ho ho ho."

"Pardon?"

"Oh, nothing. Ignore me, I'm just saying things because of the terror of silence. There you are, then, ten pence change and a ten pence bag. Thanks."

"Thanks."

"Thank you."

"Thank *you*."

"Have a nice day."

"Thank you. You too, mate."

"Cheerio, mate."

"Bye then. All the best."

"You too. Take care, dear shopkeep."

"Fare thee well, noble patron."

"Ta-rah."

"Toodle-pip."

"Tally ho."

"For King and Country!"

"Safe travels."

"See you."

Aaaaaaand… *that's it!* Well done, now you're finally ready to leave the shop with your biscuits. (At this point, you'll probably push a door that says "pull," bump into the glass, crush your biscuits, and then immediately decide to move to another planet so you never have to visit the establishment again.)

The Race to the Bottom

Watching two British people navigate what could otherwise be a tiny, quick, transactional exchange in a corner-shop is one thing. It's the cute, mutual, pretend nit-picking of harmless little monkeys trying to make other harmless little monkeys feel nice. It's adorable, really (and I, for one, wouldn't mind if it caught on a little bit more in Germany, where customers are regarded more as an irritating problem to be solved.) However, these kinds of situation are normally a win-win for both British people. Everyone involved is having an equally nice time (except for any Russians stuck in the queues behind us, slowly dying, wondering if they can bribe their way out of the gibberish…)

Things gets problematic for us, however, when conflict-avoiding win-wins are not possible. Think about deciding who must be the group's designated driver, or whose turn it is to buy the next round when everyone's forgotten whose round it is, or who's going to go through a doorway first when two or more people have arrived at that same door simultaneously. Indeed, watching British people trying to rank themselves by who most deserves to go through a doorway first can be an excruciating thing for foreigners to witness, especially if it happens in a busy context like a train station or airport. For non-British bystanders, it's like watching increasing amounts of vegetables get stuck down a plug-hole.

In zero-sum situations like this, we can even malfunction like politeness robots, getting stuck in an eternal feedback loop of attempting to reassert one's own best intentions over the other. If two Britbots say "no, please, *you* first" at the same time, it's like there's a glitch in The Matrix where all time stands still, and progress in the immediate universe is suspended until the Quantum Error of Impossible Britishness is resolved. Hyper-polite British people have lived entire, unfulfilled lives stuck in corridors; British people have died on the phone, suspended in the "and how are you?" phase; frostbitten bodies have been pulled from the snow outside post offices, hands outstretched, frozen forever in the gesture of "you first... I insist!"

British people are the only culture I know of, indeed, that can get into arguments (by which I mean, *discussions with escalating intensities of passive-aggressiveness*) when insisting upon their own disadvantage. *No, I should miss out! I should eat last! I should be at the back of a queue, I insist!* I genuinely once saw three rounds of increasingly intense back-and-forth between a pair of my friends back home about who should eat the least good sausage on a plate of unevenly well-barbecued sausages. (All of them were fine.) It must have taken an actual minute before one of them finally caved in, and let the other eat a slightly worse sausage. I'm not exaggerating. *A minute.*

God knows how we've made it this long as a culture.

It's lucky, indeed, that we have full access to the life-supporting technologies of modernity. In a state of nature, we'd be moths to the light-bulbs of our own extinction, politely declining the opportunities to be naturally selected with a Hugh Grant-ish wobble of our heads and a quiet mumble of, "oh, gosh, yes, well, we'd love to propagate further, but, uh, well, gosh, only if it's not too much of a fuss, of course, fuf, fuf, fuf."

The Back-and-Forth
of Mutual Burden

Now we have learned the communication model of modern Britishness, I must offer foreign readers a final warning: think very carefully before initiating any provisional conversations with us over email, SMS or social media, as things could very quickly spiral out of control.

While friendliness, recreational small-talk and feigning interest in other people are all good skills for navigating everyday life in Britain, this is especially true for digital forms of communication, where it's easier for sentiments to be misinterpreted as impolite, and therefore why we all turn up our overcautious word-faffing to the max.

So: let's say, for example, you want to borrow a drill from a friend. You decide to contact him on social media, assuming he might possibly have one. Out of pretend nit-picking politeness, however, you must first couch your actual intention in a lot of faffy phatic word-fluff, until the resulting message is an elaborate meaning-maze with a purely ambiguous request to borrow a drill hidden somewhere near the middle. It should look something like this:

"Hey, man! Long time, no see! How's everything going with you? God, it's been ages since we last saw each other. Remember that time at school when we were on that pedal-powered swan boat? Ah, man. Crazy times. Do you still see Dan, by the way? I don't, but we've been emailing each other once a month for eight years. Anyway, I hope you're doing well. Oh, just while I think of it, you don't possibly happen to know anything about drills, do you? I need to buy one soon, but just for a really quick, little, 5-second job. Shame, really, but what can you do? Anyway, no worries if you don't know anything drills, just thought I'd ask on the off-chance. No worries either way. Sorry. And thanks. Hope to see you soon. All the best, Sally. xxx"

Yikes. Now imagine being on the *receiving end* of that message. Not only is it long, but it's also full of things that apparently need replying to. It's an obligation-fest, dressed as friendship. What's more, it's obviously just an emotionally stunted *request to borrow a drill*, and yet it feels much more like a stick of politeness dynamite has been thrown into a Pandora's box of small-talk. Sally knows it, you know it, and yet it's already too late to contain the consequences – *BOOM* – the TNT of obligatory chit-chat has gone off, and now the infinite demons of faff are exploding into your world. You'll feel compelled to respond to, comment on and echo back everything she's said, playing your full, equal and shameless role in a month-stealing dialogue of pointless back-and-forth, even though, worst of all, you've never owned a drill.

As soon as you have noticed a small-talk time-bomb ticking somewhere underneath the hood of your conversation, the only merciful thing to do is disarm it by not replying. Someone has to be the grown-up and put the correspondence out of its misery and, let's face it, you're both secretly hoping it will be the other one. If you feel rude, don't worry: *not replying* is always more of a temporary cease-fire than a permanent truce anyway. You can always restart proceedings any time you want (if you're feeling particularly sadomasochistic) by launching a full and devastating H-bomb of Mutual Burden:

"Oh my god, I'm so sorry that I totally forgot to reply to your last message (polite lie)" – *KABOOOOOOM* – "that was totally my fault (self-blame), I'd lose my head if it wasn't screwed on. (Self-deprecation) Tell me again, how are those lovely children (polite lie) of yours? I have to know! (Egregious lie.) Oh, and also, you don't maybe happen to know anything about spirit levels, do you?"

VISITING THE BRITISH

Chapter Three

Visiting the British

Living abroad can be quite a perspective-changing experience, let me tell you. If you've never tried it, dear reader, then lend me your ear and I'll tell you a tale.

Firstly, you get on a plane.

Then you go on that plane to one of those mythical places where foreigners come from. (You know, where they have weird different plugs and no kettles in the hotel rooms.)

Finally, you get off that plane and become – without filling out a form, passing an exam or even changing your outfit – *a foreigner* to everyone around you. It's magic. Boring, boring magic.

But your exciting adventure into a whole new world of identity doesn't have to end there, because, guess what? You don't see *yourself* as "a foreigner." No, that would be weird. Foreigners are *other people*. When *you* get on a plane and *you* get out of it again, you are still *you*, except somewhere else. Getting on and off a flying metal tube that over-charges you for Pringles doesn't magically rewire your sense of self.

Well, it doesn't for me anyway. I feel normal, except in a place that's weirdly full of Germans. Yet every now and then, I imagine myself being seen in Berlin through the eyes of its more established population: smiling nervously in all directions, wearing a permanent look of innocent bewilderment and effortlessly radiating the exact opposite of localness. I try to remember that while I often feel like fairly solid instances of communication are coming out of my mouth in German, those things are almost certainly hitting everyone else's ears as, "your restaurant is tonight evening open? Exceptional informations! Me is want great dinner from you to have, please, with five friends me also bringing. Thank you, looking to it forward!"

Just as weird for me, though, is "going home" (to the place I no longer live), something you too will get to experience one day if you ever live abroad. Like a liquid poured into two containers rather than just one, you might start to see the true shape of your native culture from the other side of the glass; the way that all outsiders must… from the comfort of a second perspective. You'll break the fourth wall… and Britain itself will start to seem ever so slightly more to you like a strange and foreign land.

After that, dear reader, things abroad stop seeming "weird," just "different." Revisiting your home-town, on the other hand, brings with it a stranger realisation: that "normal" only ever meant "the kind of weird that I was used to"…

The Hidden Oddness of the Everyday

Now when I visit England with Linn, I am part tourist, part tour guide. Sometimes I find myself explaining to her (and, by extension, myself) what had previously seemed to need no explanation. Other times, I'm forced to see something about the UK through her eyes. Places, things and customs I had previously taken for granted (cheddar cheese, pubs, apologising to objects) become things to show off proudly. Mostly, though, a kind of hidden weirdness shines through the surface of the previously normal, and I get irreversible perspective upgrades against my will. Let me explain.

Linn once pointed out to me how strange she found it that

every single window of every single room of every single British house has net curtains. In Germany, windows are things to look out of, hence the glass. In Britain, windows are more like foolish privacy vulnerabilities that must be solved. Ever since Linn made that one small off-hand remark, I now cannot unsee this particular feature of British topography. I walk around my old home, my old street, my old hometown (places that were, for almost all of my life, the most normal places on Planet Earth), and now see endless windows and endless rooms and endless rows of houses, all wearing the building equivalent of a burka. And, all of a sudden, this feature of Britishness seems somehow quietly alarming. What *are* we so afraid of exactly? That our neighbours will look into our living rooms and see us... *doing what?* Sitting on our furniture? Using our appliances? Watching *Love Island?* What great secrets *are* we all hiding from each other?

I also cannot unsee how freaky British postboxes are. You've probably never even noticed them. You probably think that British postboxes are just boxes where post goes. Well, not me. *Oh, no, no, no.* That worldview is gone forever. Obliterated. Now, through my someone-else's-foreigner x-ray glasses, British postboxes are blood red, ominous-seeming pavement-protruding sex toys, covered in the ornate markings and the mysterious, Illuminati-like hieroglyphics of an ancient dynasty of castle-owning demi-gods. They're bloody weird.

Washing-up bowls used to be just bowls that British people put in a sink to do their washing up in. *My god, those were the days.* Now, after Linn asked me just one time, "what's that bowl for? I don't get why there's a bowl inside another bowl," I can't unsee this profound and timeless mystery of British kitchens. Why *do* washing-up bowls exist? *Why?* I used to know. At least I thought I did. But now I have to visit my family in England and constantly walk past a container acting like a sink inside another container that is *literally* a sink. Yet the most alarming part of the sink-in-sink mystery of Britishness is this: everyone else just walking past it as though it isn't even there. They just can't see it.

They are still sleepwalking through the Russian doll daydream of sinky-sinking; still enchanted by its spooky spell. But not me. I... *I* see it. For me, it's like *The Sixth Sense* except about 100% more boring. (I call it my Sink-in-a-Sinkth Sense.[1])

The entire British sink area, indeed, has now become a blackhole of cultural disorientation for me. The hot tap and the cold tap used to be as firm and grounded a feature of my worldview as gravity. But now I've swallowed the red pill of the single mixer-tap, I cannot wash my hands in Britain without thinking woke thoughts like, "the hot stream from the hot tap only goes in the direction of too hot, the cold stream from the cold tap always levels out at too cold, and yet neither is ever the just right, single, steady stream of personally customised lukewarm temperature water that I require for every single sink-related purpose imaginable." *(WAKE UP, SHEEPLE.)*

Of course, I don't even claim to be suffering the full symptoms of this culture shock, as I was at least partly immunised to British eccentricity by growing up in Little England's cocoon before my full and beautiful Continental butterfly form emerged. (I now own a cafetière and can order great dinner in at least one fifth of two languages. *#LiberalElite*)

The Disorientation of Culture Shock

Britain may be the Japan of Europe, but do you know who Britain is definitely not Japan for? The Japanese. Nope. And that's why some small number of our polite, reserved, oddball island cousins have been known in the past to have a uniquely disorientating time when visiting us in Europe, given how alien European culture can sometimes feel for them, yet how familiar representations of it are in their own culture.

---

[1] I don't.

There is, indeed, a phenomenon popularly known as 'Paris Syndrome,' whereby Japanese tourists get overwhelmed by culture shock to the point of having a minor psychological crisis in the middle of their photography tour/holiday. The Japanese Embassy in Paris even runs a 24-hour helpline for potential sufferers of Paris Syndrome, and about 20 people a year reliably end up on its doorsteps feeling woozy, dazed and confused.

This overwhelming disorientation, it is believed, comes from a lifetime of seeing Paris depicted in Japanese pop culture as a common media short-hand for dreams, love, beauty and romance. Then they arrive in Paris and Paris is, well, Paris.

Personally, I think I can relate. When I first visited Paris – my inaugural trip out of the UK as an unaccompanied adult – I stepped out of the Gare du Nord station, inhaling deeply the warm air of a new Parisian summer's evening, my heart swollen with the promise of fresh adventure, my eyes ready to drink in the city that Hemingway called "a moveable feast," and literally the first thing I saw was a man shitting in a bin.

And please don't think I'm exaggerating for comedic effect. I haven't retroactively cut 10 or 15 minutes out of the memory to make it funnier, although that is exactly the kind of thing I would be well within my rights to do. I mean it very, very literally. The Eiffel tower may well have been on the horizon at the exact moment I stepped out of the station, I have no idea, because, if it was, it would have merely been a fuzzy, out-of-focus backdrop to the crystal clear foreground image of the incredibly casual bin-pooing man assaulting my naive young eyes and causing me a considerable amount of disorientation about whether this was a good sign or a bad sign. (On one hand, he was *shitting* in a bin. On the other hand, he was shitting *in a bin*.)

Did I get Paris Syndrome? Well, no. But I'm not from Japan; I'm from London, where I once saw a drunk man on a night-bus looking desperately around for something to be sick into, then, in a moment of divine inspiration, removing his arm from his sleeve, pinching the end of it, then vomiting into his own jumper. It was genius. Disgusting, disgusting genius.

Now, where was I? Ah, yes, the Japanese.

As we all clumsily shuffle towards a post-Brexit Europe, I fear that 'London Syndrome' is soon to overtake 'Paris Syndrome' as the preferred moniker for this specific brand of culture shock, being that it is seemingly caused by the disparity between shorthand media representations and actual reality. At various points before the referendum – presumably in an effort to drum up the prerequisite levels of patriotic spirit needed to attempt the economic equivalent of the kamikaze nose-dive manoeuvre – prominent Leave-campaigners could be heard referring to Britain and the British as "a maritime people," "a buccaneering people" and "a nation of entrepreneurs."

And so I grow worried for the most psychologically fragile of our Japanese friends. As our honour-culture cousins from the East arrive to our humble island home, I hope they will not be too disorientated by the reality they find here…

A Primark people. A pie people. A nation of volunteer police officers trying, and failing, to catch a swan.

The 'Spirit of Entrepreneurship'

If you too are struggling to connect fully with the idea of Britain as a "nation of entrepreneurs" (because you are a normal person surrounded by normal people), perhaps you've just lost touch with the "buccaneering" flagship city of Global Britain: London. My advice would be for you to revisit the financial capital of the world, where said "entrepreneurial spirit" should become apparent to you in the form of a phantom-like presence haunting your wallet; strange, spooky forces endlessly draining the life from your pay-check; paranormal agents causing money to evaporate from your bank account with the quietly alarming effortlessness of ghostly osmosis.

My parents' nearest airport, for example, is London Stansted (which is so not-in-London, it might as well be called London Scotland), where it presently costs £4 just to be dropped off or picked up. Overstay the mere minutes you have been allocated to say farewell to your loved ones before they voyage to distant lands – perhaps never to return – and you'll be fined £50 or have your car towed. *(Welcome to Britain.)* Needless to say, London Stansted airport's drop-off point is the site of some of Europe's least romantic goodbyes. Hell, my mother pretty much pushes me out of the car while it's still moving, then sends me a goodbye text later when she gets home: "Take care in Europe. Lol mum xxx". ("Here I should quickly clarify that my mother has, since about 1998, believed 'lol' to mean 'lots of love,' instead of the more hip and now almost universally recognised 'laugh out loud.' I'm still trying to build up the courage to tell her as the situation becomes increasingly untenable. She once sent me an SMS that said, "granddad passed away last night lol mum xxx.")

Tourists should also be forewarned that London buses have now stopped taking cash entirely, presumably because the wealthy city's transport services don't want to be associated with the same dirty stuff that poor people use to swap for bread. Yuck. Indeed, the entire city of London is increasingly powered by card – contactless card, to be precise – which is a merciful development in many ways, since it helps disguise the fact that £10 is the smallest unit of usable currency within a fifteen-mile radius of Trafalgar Square.

To get around, then, you'll need an Oyster card, which you'll soon get used to topping up, even if you only stay in London for an afternoon. (Best not to think about it as something you put money *on*, like a bank account, but more something you put money *through*, like a shredder.) With your Oyster card in pocket, soon you'll be able to move from Londonplace to Londonplace at roughly the speed of bankruptcy, until it's time to 'do something.' What about an activity of some kind? Oh yes, that sounds funspensive, doesn't it? Indeed. As a rule of thumb, all forms of London-based recreation should be accompanied by a dabble of accidental binge-drinking and cost whatever amount of money is the minimum amount of money a banker would pay to do the same activity regardless of how good it is. After that, what about a few fancy cocktails in swinging central

London to top the night off? That's always a fun possibility (assuming you've recently re-mortgaged your house.)

In summary, an "authentic" touristic trip to London should be an excellently drunken public-transport blur of a contactless card going in and out of your wallet at the speed of a hummingbird, interspersed with you taking photos of old, impressive statues and things that former British people probably once stole. It'll be a day you'll remember forever! (And if not, don't worry! Simply contact the relevant authorities and they can send you a complete record of your day as it was captured on CCTV.)

The Ordinariness of British Towns

Now, I'm no historian (you can thank the British education system for that), but I think that a fairly uncontroversial summary of British history is that the whole country was designed in a pub about 800 years ago. People sat around, drinking warm beer, probably moaning about Europe, and invented Britain.

The positive side of this remarkable origin story is that Britain contains A LOT of pubs. There's roughly one pub every half a mile, which is suspiciously similar to the amount of pubs you'd probably need if you wanted a society where people who like pubs would be able to order a pint, then be able walk to the next pub while drinking it, then arrive at the next pub just in time to finish that pint and immediately order another one.

The downside is that the rest of Britain seems to have been cobbled together as a half-arsed afterthought as the night went on. It's often cramped, confusing and unnecessarily mysterious; an impossible and overpopulated tangle of a million places called Bronglyton-upon-Meed, loosely held together by speed cameras, shame, discarded pint glasses, double yellow lines and the Little Chef franchise.

Indeed, since about 90% of Little England is made up of towns called Boreham, Brimich and Brocklewad, I can take you on a tour of the rest of the country relatively quickly. You arrive via the High Street, the cultural, flagship economic epicentre of the small town; a single line of shops consisting of, at minimum, an off-license, a betting shop, a charity shop, 3 estate agents and a combined chip shop/Indian/Chinese takeaway thing. Finally, there will be an ever-reliable corner-shop or long-standing newsagents, a proud testament to local British industriousness (i.e. probably not run by British people). This core pillar of the community can normally be spotted behind a sandwich-board advertisement for a local newspaper, featuring one of the least newsworthy headlines you have ever seen in your life. This advert for the local paper is updated to a new height of mediocrity every day of the week and can normally be found announcing something of monumental unimportance like, BOROUGH RESIDENTS IN BIN KICK OUTRAGE, or BROMLY TEENAGER ACCUSED OF RE-LOCATING METAL or LOCAL LADY LOSES HISTORIC HAT.

After that, everything else in small town Britain is so confusing that you will have to ask for directions on the ground. Since the UK seems to have been set up by a town planning committee consisting of Picasso, M.C. Escher and J.R.R. Tolkien, nowhere would you find sensible, America-style directions like, "just walk down 43rd Street until you get to 17th Avenue, then get on with your life."

You wish, buddy. Instead, all directions in Britain sound like this: "just toddle over to Littlebig Close. When you see the Y-junction, rotate 49 degrees towards the smallest of the two clock towers, then turn onto Biggleswade Road, follow the first perpendicular alleyway four weeks and a farthingstretch to the ancient ruins of Hogglesmead Lane, turn right on Fivewalls Cross, edge along the hedge, run across the dual-carriageway, solve the forest riddle of the tricksy gnome-king, then hook round the traffic lights, past Paddy Power, then on to Hammercross Path Way Road, mind the gap, then you should see The Badger and Nun and Magic Clock and Crown and Cat pub, which we're outside of now. Then you should ask someone else because I don't know where it is but I'm too polite to tell you. Still, funny weather we're having, eh? It just seems to be doing whatever it wants, just like it always does."

Oh yes, that reminds me: be very careful when asking local people for directions in the UK. Unfortunately, the British urge to be nice (so we can see ourselves as the eternal good guys of every interaction) can sometimes overwhelm other important urges we should have, like the urge to admit that we don't know where something is if we have been asked for directions to it. Be warned: when a British person replies, "hm, I think it might be this way…", they might be acting modest about knowing the way (because they don't want to "show off" about knowing the way) or they might literally be having a guess (because they're embarrassed they can't help.)

The Fun of Foreigner-Friendly English

Given how the rest of the world has become increasingly language-proofed to accommodate our country's most terrible tourists, you might think that we would try to repay the favour with maximum effort when the world, in turn, comes to visit our Old Lady and Big Clock.

However, no matter how much we would like to, we generally don't know how to help. We are famously bad at learning foreign languages, and therefore famously bad at communicating with non-native speakers of English *in English*, because we have so little experience of being in their shoes and therefore what they might find helpful when we speak to them. Instead, we talk fast. We mumble. We use slang, colloquialisms and tourist-tormenting idioms like "taking the Mickey" and "Bob's your uncle," oblivious that these are hardly priority vocabulary for new learners. We make references to old sitcoms, obscure

British celebrities and a million other things that no non-native could possibly have ever heard of. We sometimes say whole sentences (like, "well, you know, it is what it is, isn't it?") that require enormous amounts of the learner's concentration to decipher, yet mean absolutely nothing.

What's more, I'm not really sure that we can be blamed for any of this. We simply don't know much about how the English language works, because we almost always get to play the language game on home-soil, in Britain or abroad, and so our foreign language-learning muscles are adjective-ly flabby. This means we don't know how to simplify things grammatically for non-native speakers. We can't explain to them why something they've said in English is correct or not. We don't have a good intuition for what vocabulary they are likely to know or which words might needlessly confuse them. Combined, these facts mean that we can be both well-intentioned and effortlessly unhelpful at the same time.

Indeed, I regularly hear the complaint from non-native speakers of English that native English-speakers are often the most difficult people in any English-speaking room to understand. While English-learners from all corners of the globe quickly build up an effective toolkit of commonly understood words and phrases that they can use to swap information with each other, we come along, see a group of engineers collaborating to get the engine of conversation running, then throw in a handful of rubber chickens.

Assemble a group of English-speaking Brits, Germans, Italians, Russians, Fijians, Amazonians, Martians, feral humans raised by wolves and a blind-deaf-mute who communicates by mashing *Google Translate*, and it will be us that lets the conversational team down, derailing any hope of common consensus with our "and Bob's your uncle" nonsense. The rest of the world speaks English to be understood by the rest of the world. The English just *speak at* the rest of the world.

As the English language, to the eternal benefit of all British people, continues to cement itself as the *de facto* world language, there's still one important caveat to the commonly held British viewpoint that this is a massively unearned advantage for us. For it seems to me, from my own travels, that the rest of the world basically *caught up* with English, and now, whichever bilingual village I go to, I will always be its idiot.

The Mystery of English Grammar

As for our own village, Global Britain may be small but it is nevertheless able to export quite an impressive amount of idiots relative to its size, perhaps due to our relatively outsized capacity to churn out monolingual citizens who speak no other language than English, and the fact many of us don't even have a particularly full grasp of that. God knows I'm one of these people. I have, more often than I would like to admit, found myself visiting foreign lands and having my own usage of English grammar corrected by *people who learned it as a second (or even third or fourth) language*.

You see, the official educational aim of the British government concerning grammar was, for a time, possible to summarise like this: "meh, don't worry about grammar, everyone else speaks English anyway." Indeed, English grammar was proactively removed from the British syllabus in two recent decades, meaning that many people around my age (a large number of whom, amusingly, are now the world's English teachers) were part of the generation that missed the subject entirely. (Obviously, I don't know what the government at that time was thinking but, if I had to guess, I'd imagine the Minister for Education saying to the Minister for Tourism, "well, there's no point teaching ourselves how our own language works, is there? We already speak it!")

So, what did we do in 'English' lessons instead? Well, all I remember from school was *Shakespeare* ("I don't understand this"), *Media Studies* ("can we watch a film, please?") and every British teenager's favourite school subject, *The Psychology of Emerging Mental Breakdowns in People Who Used to Have Dreams* ("oh, sir! Sir! Sir! I've got a question about Shakespeare! Romeo and Juliet is set in Italy, right? Which is nearer the equator, right? So, if you went there, in Shakespeare's time, would your wife have to put sun cream on your bald patch?")

What's more, those of us who weren't taught English grammar at school probably didn't even know we missed it until we confronted the difficulty of learning a second language later. It was news to me, at least, and I learned it the hard way, in Russia, at the rather unfortunate age of 25. There I was, the only idiot in the room who didn't know what cases, adverbs or subordinate clauses were, surrounded by eager English-learning Russian students trying to explain it all to me. It was embarrassing, anyway, yet it was doubly so because *I* supposed be *their* teacher.

I went to Moscow in 2012 to "teach" (or so I was told) "Advanced English," except without any qualifications, certificates or experience to do so (good old Russia.) My students were wonderful, but it soon turned out, however, that there was something mildly scam-like about the whole arrangement. My students had been told I was a paid, qualified teacher, and I'd been told that my non-paying students would only expect some totally unqualified conversation practice. In reality, they'd paid and wanted to learn things, I had volunteered and knew nothing, and in between a cunning Armenian lady had combined two distant forms of gullibility to create herself a job.

Luckily I was English, so it didn't even cross my mind that this minor niggle (me having never taught anyone anything ever) might in any way deter my success. I spoke English, after all. How hard could it possibly be to teach it? (This naivety will seem either uniquely English or uniquely Arrogantish, depending on whether you once learned at school what an 'auxiliary verb' is, just like I didn't.)

In my first "lesson" as "teacher," then, my complete ignorance about the grammar of my own language hit me in the face like a noun when an earnest student asked me: "Paul, is this sentence in Present Perfect Continuous tense or Simple Past Continuous tense?"

I stared back at him calmly, trying to hide the totality of my confusion as a small man in my mind hit the panic button behind my eyes. (Did you know English has 14 tenses? Did you know it has more than three? I bloody didn't. I pretended he'd sneezed.)

"Bless you, Sergei. Right, I think that's all we have time for today, let's go home, try to survive the winter, and hope we all see each other again tomorrow."

Unfortunately, as I quickly learned through late-night lesson-planning wiki-binging, there is exactly zero crossover between speaking a language natively and being able to *teach* that language to non-native speakers. You cannot just *say things at people* until they understand them, it turns out, much in the same way you cannot *stare at a load of bricks* until they are a house.

And to any foreign visitors to the UK, I can only apologise if the language issue becomes an occasionally frustrating aspect of visiting us. We appreciate you learning our language, we really do. It's just that you have learned our language as it appeared to you in language-learning textbooks… but we never got those textbooks ourselves. So, unfortunately for you, we will be mostly replying in massive, high speed, non-self-aware run-on sentences while making frequent references to *Only Fools and Horses* and Peter Andre.

We thank you for your understanding. (Or not.)

The Bloody Germans

DISCLAIMER: Out of courtesy to my host culture, I must now take a brief hiatus from making wild and sweeping generalisations about the British to make wild and sweeping generalisations about Germans.

Travelling as a German person in the UK may still come – I'm sorry to say – with echoes of historical stigma. While much progress has been made in modern times, it is still possible to encounter old and ugly stereotypes, especially among older Britons who are more likely to hold onto anger, frustration and a sense of grievance towards Germans because of them, in the past, putting their towels on sun-loungers to reserve them.

I don't know why this simple act of pool-side planning has infuriated my countrymen so much historically, but it really has. In one way, you'd think we Brits might appreciate the idea of the towel being used in the morning to reserve a sun-lounger. After all, it's pragmatic; it doesn't involve human interaction (or any of the potential awkwardness that can entail); and it has an undeniable *first-come-first-served* aspect to it, not unlike the British national past-time of queuing.

Yet somehow, when it comes to sun-loungers and towels, we simply cannot get on board with this particularly German brand of *pre*-queuing – presumably because accepting it as a legitimate pool-side practice would somehow involve conceding that the same level of human rights applied to holidaymakers should also be ascribed to towels.

To the British, this idea – human rights for towels – is just not cricket. It's a bridge too far. Towels are *not* people. The whole concept of using an inanimate object to reserve a sun-lounger completely offends our innate sense of sportsmanship, and several times abroad I have spotted irate British holidaymakers removing a German towel in order to relocate the offending sun-lounger as if that towel's human rights were completely irrelevant.

(Of course, if we Brits were the ones coming down earlier in the day to put *our* towels on sun-loungers, we'd probably be just fine with the practice. But, let's be honest with ourselves here, we are spending those precious morning hours nursing a holiday-level hangover or else diluting said hangover in the hotel canteen with a plateful of fried everything.)

Having lived in both cultures, I still have no idea how to bridge this great divide between Brits and Germans (god knows a bit of constructive back-and-forth over email won't help.) But I do, however, have one small idea for any Germans reading: what about buying towels with national flags on them (you know, like we Brits do abroad with our Union Jack towels), *except* only the flag-towels of nations *other than Germany*? That way, those towels can be spread around the pool-side until the hotel looks like the United Nations are about to have their least formal summit yet and the blame will get spread out between the world's nations, while you can still enjoy the cheeky 'Human-Rights-for-Towels' advantages of having slightly clearer heads in the morning. Clever, right? Thanks.

And now it's time, of course, to talk about Hitler.

You see, the other cultural trope not yet fully consigned to the waste-bin of history is British people showing German people their comedic and spontaneously inspired Hitler impressions. However, should you as a German be brave enough to venture into the beer-soaked, pub-wrapped heart of British culture to meet the best and booziest of our friendly society, you might be rewarded at some point with someone swiping their fringe over their forehead and goose-stepping around the place to amuse you. (Sorry.)

I'm not sure quite how much longer this custom of casually invoking the Great Dictator is going to last... because it probably didn't begin when you think it did. It didn't start in 1933 or in 1939 or even in 1945. It started, as far as I can tell, in 1975.

You see, dear German reader, one of Britain's most brilliant and universally beloved TV shows is *Fawlty Towers*, a sitcom about an uptight and grumpy hotel owner who despises most of his customers. (Yep, it's right up your alley.) And probably the most beloved episode of said sitcom is called 'The Germans,' where said uptight, grumpy hotel owner, while suffering from a concussion, struggles against and ultimately fails to hold in a Tourettes-like outburst about the Führer after constantly reminding himself of the instruction "DON'T MENTION THE WAR!"

Today, when we meet Germans in pubs (or, indeed, by the pool-side), we are mostly not thinking about Hitler, Nazis or the war… but there's still a very good chance that we're thinking about Basil Fawlty saying, "don't mention the war!" And from the moment that thought pops up, it's as if a ticking time-bomb of Tourettes has been lit, and it's only a matter of time before somebody is stomping around the pub with two fingers on their upper lip and their legs flailing skywards. It's pretty much unavoidable. You see, the character Basil Fawlty *knew* he shouldn't say anything, and so now we're all thinking about the character that shouldn't have said anything, thinking that we shouldn't say it either. Understand now? It's like a powerful, self-referencing comedy form of meta-Tourettes.

Unfortunately, Hitler impressions may not always be as hilarious in Great British pub-land as they are when performed by John Cleese (of *Ministry of Silly Walks* fame) but by some random pub character called 'Big Dave' (of *Ministry of Silly Opinions* fame.) However, all Germans are faced with a conundrum when confronted with things that aren't that funny because of their reputation for not finding 'funny' things funny. If Big Dave's haphazard impression of a genocidal dictator doesn't tickle their funny bones (for whatever reason), Germans may nevertheless feel compelled to laugh anyway, just in case Big Dave thinks they don't find 'funny' things funny, because they take themselves too seriously, because they're German, and that's what Germans do, because Germans aren't funny. In other words, they're stuck between a rock and a hard place.

Luckily, in my opinion, there's no reason to take offence to any of this as a modern joke-getting German, since there is nothing malicious meant in the *John Cleese-playing-Basil Fawlty-playing-Adolf Hitler* impression. As John Cleese himself once said, "everybody thinks that was a joke about the Germans but they missed it. It was a joke about British attitudes to the war and the fact that some people were still hanging on to that rubbish."

So even if the aforementioned Hitler impression goes down as well as the Hindenburg, the easiest route out of the situation for Germans is simple: you must join in with the joke. (Sorry.) Big Dave is playing *Basil Fawlty*. This is theatre. You must play The Germans.

Turn to someone nearby, perhaps whoever is looking at you most nervously to see how you react, and say in your thickest German accent the next line of the script: "however did zay vin?" (Congratulations! You are now the most popular person in the pub!)

The Seriousness of Queueing

As someone who occasionally encounters the wider world's stereotypes of Britishness, I never quite understood the exaggerated reputation we have abroad for queuing. *Surely*, I thought, *every culture queues? How could you not queue? What other system could there possibly be? Stacking? Bundling? Squashing with intent to proceed? No bloody thank you.*

While I still struggle to believe that there could be non-queuing cultures, I will nevertheless explain why I personally am so fond of the *first come, first served* concept. Firstly, the queue represents the uniform application of mathematics, geometry and effortless non-violence to the intrinsic chaos and complexity of society. It is nothing more or less than the abstract application of fairness to group dynamics. Furthermore, it is easy to learn how to queue: it is, after all, just *counting* and *applied counting*. It is conceptually simple, mathematically precise yet almost always uniformly preferable to a riot; it is as waterproof an expression of fairness as could be imagined. If God is real, God queues.

OK? OK.

Now, having met funny Germans, friendly Russians and Americans who haven't shot me in the face with a gun, I was ready to dismiss the Englishman's "love of queuing" as another amusing but overreaching exaggeration: surely we Brits weren't *really* taking it any more seriously than anyone else in the world, right? That is, until I stumbled across a quote from the late Hungarian comedian George Mikes, who lived the latter half of his life in the UK and explained (in better English than most Englishmen) that, "an Englishman, even if he is alone, forms an orderly queue of one."

That was when I noticed it, and now, horrifyingly, I cannot unsee it. When we go to an empty bus-stop, we do not lean on it, sit on it, climb it, patrol it, circle it in an indecisive dance or begin a picnic, all of which we could do if we wanted to. No: we go to the front, near the sign and face outwards; ready, waiting, informing the incoming bus driver that we have summoned his bus to this precise bit of pavement with our thoughts and now expect the bus doors to open exactly in front of us. In other words: we form an orderly queue. Of one.

The Problem of Evil

In 2015, Linn and I were about to embark on a ten hour bus ride from Vienna to Berlin. Given the length of the journey, we were keen to get the front seats at the top of the double-decker bus – you know, with the leg-room, the view and that little ledge with a place for your cup. It's pimp up there. So, we got up about an hour earlier than we needed to (side-note: I hate mornings) and, sure enough, arrived first. We then proceeded to form an orderly queue (of one, then another one, a.k.a. two.) Soon after we had established the foundational rules of this system, around twenty more people arrived, spontaneously allocating themselves their exactly correct numerical places behind us until a familiar and perfect shape of people had emerged with just two distinct points where the unbrokenness of its simple geometric form ceased: ahhhh, a line! A queue! *Everything was all exactly right with the world.*

And then another woman – let's call her Passenger Number 21 (actually, to make it easier to follow the story, let's call her Demon-Spawned Monster of Cruel and Ancient Evil) – arrived, and do you know where she stood? That's right: in front of us.

"*Ahem*," we said, politely, wishing to draw her attention to the obvious and hilarious mistake she had made... but to no response.

"*AHHH-HEM*," we said, slightly less politely... also to no response.

"Excuse me," we said, approaching the precipice of the politeness cliff-edge... to no response again.

About fifty more increasingly loud, increasingly unpleasant

things we said in all the fragments of every language we could muster... *no response.*

Nothing. Nothing at all.

I stood in front of her. Waved. Clapped my hands, begging for her attention. This woman just kept staring forward, blanking us, blanking everyone, pretending we weren't there. It was infuriating; unbelievable; the rudest thing I think I have ever encountered in my life.

And yet, it seemed, there was nothing Linn or I or anyone else in the queue could do about it. Sure, we could have attempted to relocate the Demon-Spawned Monster of Cruel and Ancient Evil to her correct position in the line with some kind of improvised judo (such a move, I'm sure, would have been greeted with applause) and yet this was clearly not a strictly legal option. Indeed, it was a *rather nuclear option*; one that probably would have endangered our chances of getting on the bus and going home.

Nope. All legal, sensible, normal, moral responses to this monster had been immediately exhausted, and then the bus arrived. Then she got on the bus. Then she sat on the top, front seats of the bus. We could not believe it. I could not believe it. It was like every injustice ever all at once. It was a nightmare boiled in a Glaswegian gravy of diabetic terror poured atop a hellish potato gratin of Stalingrad, and I was seething with repressed British rage. Luckily, Linn and I still got the two seats *next to* the Demon-Spawned Monster of Cruel and Ancient Evil (which is perhaps the only thing that prevented a murder that day) and then our long, long, *long* bus journey together began.

To this day, I cannot think of another time in my life when I have been more shocked, angry or appalled, or behaved more irrationally as a result. (This is no small feat; I once got into a fancy dress street-fight with neo-Nazis while wearing a sombrero...) All I knew was that I was in the immediate presence of the world's worst human being and that this terrible person would have to be stopped. (Part of me also thought, "well, OK, no point wasting too much energy on this situation now, it's over." However, that 1% of me was being drowned out by the other 99% of me which was directly channelling the bloodlust of Genghis Khan.)

In the interests of comedy/therapy, I will now explain to you what happened, even though I'm quite aware that the longer the story goes on, the harder it becomes to see me as a traditional kind of protagonist, as opposed to a deranged out-of-control man-boy who needs to be put on a little time-out in Calm Down Corner.

So, there we are, on the bus, at the top, in the front seats, us, me and her, the Demon-Spawned Monster of Cruel and Ancient Evil. There is one, and only one, thing we share: we are both in the exact seats we wanted in order to have the nicest possible bus journey... yet she has the exact same thing that I deserve and she doesn't. It's not fair. It's not cricket. *It's not bloody on, is it?* And I am all-consumed with a quiet fury that knows no outlet, staring at this woman with the crazed eyes of a voodoo postman gone rogue, trying to magick blackness into her world with only my face. And, in that moment, my malevolence-poisoned being beholds a printed bus ticket on the empty seat beside her with her email address on it.

Oh ho ho, I cackle madly to myself, *now you're gonna get it, lady.* Then, without even a flicker of self-reflective thought that might accompany a healthier mind, all my repressed British anger bubbles over at once and I begin writing her A VERY STRONGLY WORDED LETTER.

I get out my laptop. I move seats. Now I am sat down next to her. She continues to ignore me but a new layer of tension has definitely emerged, and I am pleased about it. My eyes are wide and maniacal. I almost quiver with gleeful wrathfulness, and then it begins.

"Dear Absolutely Awful Lady Who Doesn't Know How to Queue," I type. "Before you entered my life with all the charm of a pigeon to a windshield, I had believed that queuing was intuitive to humans, the way a newborn horse falls out of a mother horse, lands on its face, then immediately starts acting exactly like the 100,000 horses that came before it. Yet here you are – a living, breathing counter-argument to all of civilisation..."

Oh dear reader, I cannot emphasise to you enough how invested in this strongly worded letter I became; how quickly this ill-thought out project spun out of control. I wrote it for literally HOURS with the screen always purposefully angled towards her, hoping that she would read every word of it. And o' how the venom poured out of me. It was as if the gods of outrage and sarcasm had finally tapped that deep, rich, thousand-year-old vein of repressed island rage beneath the British Isles and were now funnelling every letter and comma to the page through my hands. I hammered at the keys like Kerouac; like Wagner in a fugue-state; like Charlie Sheen writes emails to his agent on Day 6 of a Charlie Sheen weekend. It was pure mania.

To add insult to injury, I am normally a chronic procrastinator, yet on that bus journey, in that mind-set of petty vengefulness, I unleashed the kind of raw, laser-driven productivity I have never once unleashed in my entire life (let alone in my "professional" life as a person whose job it is, allegedly, to type things for money...) I didn't notice at the time, so red was my vision, but I had discovered a kind of typing superpower... yet a typing superpower that only became active when the task was even less grown-up than comedy books.

The whole idea of a pleasant bus journey, the one I had allegedly got up so early in the morning to guarantee (and the one I could, in theory, still have), was now cancelled in my mind. Instead, I was now committed with jihadi zeal to wasting these 10 hours of my life just to make sure they would also be 10 wasted hours of her life. It was lunacy. It was psychosis. Whatever the opposite of Zen Buddhism is, it was that.

Back in the present, I just had the thought, *'oh maybe that email might be a fun, light-hearted thing to put in the book! It would certainly get the word count up!'* And so it is that I just re-visited my email account, only to realise how entirely not-at-all-publishable it is.

Firstly, it's 6 pages long(!) Secondly, it's deranged. With sentences like, "you look like all the cruelties of time were gathered into a sack and beaten into the shape of a woman by a thousand angry hands," it almost single-handedly redefines the limits of the word "overkill." In fact, I now realise, the phrase "strongly worded letter" doesn't *quite* capture the full flavour of the email that was sent. It gets really, really *dark* in there, man. It's less "strongly worded letter," indeed, and more "overt attempt to break another person's spirit through the medium of word processing." There are seven paragraphs devoted only to explaining *what a queue is*. SEVEN PARAGRAPHS. That's where I pulled my previous definition of queuing from, word-for-word. And other writers have been asked politely if they would like to spend some time in a mental healthcare facility for typing less insane paragraphs than the following:

"Had you been imparted the knowledge of the 'queue' from whatever feral wood tribe you are presumably the voodoo-haunted spawn of, you would have chosen the back of the queue as the only acceptable location to temporarily park your hate-chiselled skeleton. But you saw that this would not get you the rodent prize of your probing talons. "Me Want Bus," you reasoned, deep in the lightless swamp of your soul. So you *skipped it*. Oh, the pride you must have felt as you hoodwinked all of the other monkeys with your obviously superior cognitive functioning. Oh, what glee must have flickered in the dank, bone-strewn cave of your mind."

At some point (well, on page 4 of 6, to be precise), it became clear that the Demon-Spawned Monster of Cruel and Ancient

Evil was going to try to sleep through the problem called *me* that she had summoned into her world through the Pandora's box of rudeness. (Or, as I actually wrote in my letter, like a maniac, "oh, now what is this?! I don't believe my eyes... are you really blowing your deathly hollow breath into a sad little inflatable pillow? Are you going to try and sleep? To drift off into the spite-free ether and escape the ever-present manacles of your rotten personality? Oh, madam, what a tragic misreading of your present situation you have made!")

So I coughed loudly. I groaned. I cracked my knuckles. I cracked my neck. I cracked every disgusting bit of me that cracks, over and over and over again. I made irritating sounds with my phone. I tapped my feet in constant arrhythmic antagonism. I whistled. Clapped. Snorted. Gargled. Grunted. I made weird squeaking noises with my teeth. I would even pause sometimes for strategically timed intervals, just long enough for her head to lull slightly towards sleep, and then I would start all over again but louder and with renewed vigour (that's a technique I remember reading about from Guantanamo Bay.)

Beside me, Linn watched *Grand Designs*, every now and then shooting me a look of concern. It was the calm, kind face of a loving partner, which nevertheless wordlessly communicated the sentiment, *um, maybe you should stop being an entirely insane person soon... what do you think? Hm? Write some jokes instead? You know, for your job?*

But I was at work. THIS was my life now.

The Demon-Spawned Monster of Cruel and Ancient Evil would nod off. I would wake her. *Nod off. Wake. Nod off. Wake.* Event 1, Event 2, over and over again. Yet I knew there was no way she would be able to connect these numerical dots. After all, comprehending the correct sequence of linear events was not her speciality, which is how we'd got into this bloody mess in the first place. Eventually, she would give up trying to sleep entirely – which, I hope, was the moment when the fullness of her regret became manifest, consumed her being and convinced her never, ever to skip a queue again. She continued to pretend I wasn't there, but every now and then I caught her stealing a peek at my screen until I was eventually forced (by exhaustion) to finish my sad, sad masterwork.

"You created me. Behold the horror of your own creation. You are become death; the destroyer of bus journey. No. Do not look away – this is the seat you wanted, remember? This is the reality you want us all to live in. We are rats in your world. All of us, rats. It grieves me that I must share my planet with you. May a thousand years of shame marinate your lineage.

"Yours for hours and hours and hours,

"Paul Hawkins." *SEND MESSAGE.*

Fortunately (for me – I was knackered), she got off in Dresden. I stuck my finger up at her, cursing her wordlessly as she walked away from the bus, but she never once looked back. Then, a moment later, my phone pinged with the receipt of a new email…

'MESSAGE DELIVERY FAILED.'

I stared at the words, feeling myself slowly deflate like the Demon-Spawned Monster of Cruel and Ancient Evil had given me one last puncture: *I would never get any reward for my efforts* (unless, perhaps, I could hold on to the slim hope that she didn't actually live in Dresden but was forced to eject early to escape the mania-ridden clattering of my aggressive typing.) Then I spent the rest of the journey staring into the distance, forlorn in the twilight of defeat, like a man who'd climbed a mountain to find himself at the bottom of a ditch.

Right. So. Now. Where was I? Oh, yeah, I remember! In Britain, I would suggest you queue. *Aaaannd breathe.*

MINGLING WITH THE BRITISH

Chapter Four

Mingling with the British

There are two things that Continental friends of mine who have lived in the UK regularly report back to me about their experiences there.

Firstly, they say that the UK is an extremely, almost unnervingly, friendly country. Initially, indeed, some foreign visitors are awed by the apparently genuine levels of mutual interest and goodwill being traded between complete strangers all day long for no obvious strategic benefit to anyone. How can someone ordering a cup of coffee have so much invested in making some well-meaning small-talk with the person making the cup of coffee? Why are these strangers so dutiful towards the social aspect of this generic, forgettable, meaningless economic transaction on behalf of the Starbucks Corporation that, in other parts of the world, could be concluded with button-pushing, pointing and grunting?

Secondly, in spite of the unending carnival of effortlessly pointless everyday friendliness in Britain, foreign visitors also report back that it can be a hard place to make friends. This seems strange. Surely, it doesn't make sense that a friendly person could wander through a friendly place and find it hard to make friends, just as it doesn't make sense that a person who loves sand could wander through a desert and complain that it is difficult to find any sand.

Is there, perhaps, another conundrum afoot?

The Friends You've Never Met Yet

Hello. Inspector Hawkins, *Politeness Detective* at your service.

So, chief. Here's the particulars of the case so far: almost everyone in Britain seems nice, right? It's almost the law, it seems. Whether British people know you for ten years or ten seconds, they will generally treat you with the same level of accommodating, agreeable politeness that they would treat a gangster with a gun to their head.

The problem, then, is this: because almost everyone in Britain seems outwardly "friendly," it is hard for non-natives drifting into the UK's polite-o-sphere to get closer to individuals or to figure out which individuals want to become closer with them. They struggle to tell apart friendliness for politeness' sake and friendliness for the sake of "friendy-ness." Or, to phrase it from their perspective: *when is someone in Britain being nice to me because they want to meet me again, and when is someone in Britain being nice to me because they're terrified they will meet me again?*

From the viewpoint of the friend-seeking outsider, the outward cues of our poker personalities can be hard to decipher. Indeed, I have heard us described by foreigners as a "peach people." We all seem soft and fuzzy on the outside, sure... but are we actually soft in the middle? Impossible to know until you've taken a good bite. (Germans, in comparison, are an "egg folk." From afar, all you can tell is that there is an outer shell. Probably it is beige. But is the inside soft and gooey, or hard-boiled and uncompromising? You'll have to start tapping it gently with your friendship spoon to find out...)

In the absence of any kind of culture-penetrating x-ray machine, all I can offer is a few tips and tricks for inspecting the outer skin of the British peach personality to see what clues it might offer to the fruit within…

The Spectrum of Alrightness

Whenever you ask British people how they are doing, how their day was, how their meal is, whether they liked something they just saw in the cinema, or how well things are going at work, nine times out of ten their answer will be a variant of this sentiment: "yeah, alright, thanks."

In terms of helpful feedback, "alright" is a one-word blackhole from which complexity seems unable to escape. Except, in Britain, "alright" can actually describe almost every conceivable emotional state on the short spectrum of possible British feelings (which ranges from "pretty ticked off" to "actually rather chuffed.")

See below, for example, how the simple, surface message ("alright") can be heavily encrypted with other meta-data that other Brit-o-matic Reality Filters can read. If you're British yourself, you should be able to detect the correct tone of each statement in your head...

"Yeah, I'm doing alright actually!" = I'm doing f**king great!

"Yeah, I'm alright" = I'm alright.

"Yeah, I'm alright, I suppose" = I'm not alright.

"Well, I'm alright but..." = My wife's dead, my legs came off in a submarine accident and there's an asteroid the size of Earth heading for Earth.

Obviously, there are very subtle differences in intonation going on here, which can be harder for non-native speakers to pick up on. However, we Brits have had whole lifetimes of practice in which to perfect the art of alrightness, by asking each other, all the time, all day, every day, at every available opportunity, "are you alright? Yeah? Are you alright, though? You're alright, yeah? Alright, mate? Really, yeah? You're alright? *You're sure?*"

Why? Well, despite the near-certainty that the answer ("yeah, I'm alright") will contain almost no useful information whatsoever, asking people "are you alright?" all the time is incredibly important for the functioning of British society, because we generally won't express any of our feelings to each other without an explicit prompt first. This innocent-seeming question, therefore, is actually more like a safety valve on a nuclear reactor. We have to constantly offer each other a chance to release any pent-up frustration that might be quietly building up, just in case. We ask 99 times, for that one time it might prevent Chernobyl. Hidden inside the question "are you alright?", then, is actually this question: "*is there anything you have been repressing for a while? Anything I did to upset you which you haven't yet told me about? Is everything fine? Are you going to blow? I have no idea.*"

It's hard to overstate quite how often this question can come up in day-to-day British life. Take, for example, phone calls. Sometimes after I have asked someone "are you alright?" on the phone, then they've replied ("yeah, I'm alright"), then I've replied to their counter-question ("and you, are you alright?") with how I am ("yeah, I'm alright, thanks"), I even notice, to my absolute horror, that I am asking - *AGAIN* - "...and you? Are you, er, alright?" (*AAAHHHH.*)

When visiting my family in England, Linn is not always entirely sure what to do with the minute-by-minute wellbeing enquiries getting fired at her from all directions, because, as a German, she operates on the far more efficient emotional feedback system of '*I can't wait to tell you if something is wrong.*' One time, when we were both visiting my parents' burqa-curtained house, I was in the kitchen (probably staring in wide-eyed horror at the sink) when Linn came in to the room and told me, "I think your brother just said '*oi*' to me on the stairs."

"Huh? Really?" I asked, scrunching my face in sceptical disbelief, "I don't think he could have said '*oi.*' That doesn't make sense."

Then he came into the kitchen and said, "oigh?"

Aha, of course. Another case solved. "Don't worry," I said to Linn, before translating that my brother was in fact asking her "are you alright?" except crunched into a single, efficient syllable. It was a kind of drive-by inquiry, I explained; a twenty millisecond version of a chat – the minimum viable conversation – in order to puncture the inherent British awkwardness of having to pass someone on a staircase.

The Ickiness of Intimacy

Since we don't exactly have the greatest range of emotional vocabulary for expressing our inner states, concerns and preferences beyond the single word "alright" (and since "alright" and could still mean "not alright" too), this only exacerbates the problem that foreign visitors face when dealing with us in the UK: i.e. *how do you know if a British person really likes you?*

Well, the only definite answer I know to this question is also a rather simple one: we will insult you. *A lot.* If we are constantly teasing you about everything, we probably think you're pretty great.

For newcomers to the custom of expressing affection through the medium of mockery, name-calling and insults, this is probably best understood through the lens of the "doublethink" concept from George Orwell's *1984*: In his book, War is Peace, Freedom is Slavery and Ignorance is Strength, just as in wider British culture, Rudeness is Politeness, Meanness is Friendliness and Cruelty is Love.

As a rule of thumb, the more offensive the insults, the closer the friends, and the more legwork their insults must do in expressing their obvious fondness for each other. Indeed, if you picture the very worst thing that you could ever imagine saying to anyone (words that could only be expressed in print as a "you

****ing ****ing un**** ****ing **** while your mother **** a
****!"), *that* is probably the closest British equivalent to saying,
"I love you and I value our friendship."

Naturally, this custom ("banter" to give it its proper scientific
name) might seem somewhat paradoxical, contradictory or
counter-intuitive to foreign visitors, given that we Brits are
otherwise so polite that we can regularly be caught apologising
to inanimate objects. (I have also apologised to every single
person who has ever bumped into me. Indeed, I would probably
apologise to a bus if it ploughed me down on the pavement.)
So, what is the cause of this strange apparent lapse in manners?

Well, my pet theory is this: insulting people you love might
be the only logical conclusion of a culture that struggles with
earnestly swapping feelings and expressing sincerity. Think
about it: if you live in a society where politeness is the highest
cultural value, where you always have to behave certain ways
to not risk upsetting the powers that be, and where rudeness is
the cardinal sin, this is a bit like having to attend a 24/7 school-
turned-church-turned-workplace event, except the size of an
entire country.

Out there in the busy, hectic, hustle-and-bustle life of our
overcrowded little island home, it's exhausting having to be nice
to everyone all the time even if we don't know them and will
never have to see them again. So it's no wonder that when we
can finally take refuge in the intimate sanctuary of friendship,
all those repressed instincts to call people idiots finally have to
go somewhere. The Japanese of Asia enjoy watching bizarrely
cruel television or buying used pants from vending machines.
We Brits, the Japanese of Europe, insult each other for fun. You
see? It makes perfect sense, you massive idiot. (I like you and
respect your intelligence.)

On the other hand, if no one ever insults you in Britain, this
could be a bad sign: this could mean you are still part of the
giant nationwide *Stranger Zone* of the polite-o-sphere, rather
than working your way up the social hierarchy towards real and

lasting friendships; that the people around you don't yet know anything about you (you're still in the pointlessly nice, pretend nit-picking phase); *or*, worst of all, that they secretly hate you (we are *especially* nice to people that we don't like because there's no better way to annoy them.)

However, before we delve any deeper into the advanced art, craft and science of the *Insult-Swapping Social Bonding Ritual* (or, as anthropologists would say, "before we jump on the banter wagon"), we must understand the British sense of humour.

It is, after all, the keystone of the our personalities.

The British Sense of Humour

To deal with the inherent embarrassment involved in having to be ourselves, we Brits have developed the only defensive strategy one can: a good sense of humour (GSOH). It protects us from ourselves and from each other. We deploy the GSOH System like an ego shield… and so we need to regularly test its strength.

It's easy to see why such a defence would be necessary in Britain. We are, after all, the odd, funny, sweet-natured, homely, frightened-but-brave people that Hobbits are based on. More than that, we're a complain-nation, and we need to be able to bask in each other's enjoyment of misery without drowning in it. We need self-deprecation to diffuse, in response to our loved ones' insults, what might otherwise become self-loathing. We need comedic understatement ("we have a small problem") to deal with a scary world ("all four engines have stopped.") We need slapstick to normalise embarrassment, so we don't die of shame. We need sarcasm to avoid the pitfalls of sincerity. And we need irony to deal with Nigel Farage, a multi-millionaire, private jet-flying career politician whose face appears on television so often you could assume Panasonic and Sony just paint it on in the factory, calling everyone else "the elite."

As you can see, we Brits have a lot to laugh about once we're able to take aim at ourselves. So, no wonder comedy has become one of our most famous exports and why we have become world-renowned for our "good sense of humour." Since it's hard to believe that this reputation was earned through our guilty pleasure of making bad puns (I grew up in a town with a tanning salon called *Tans 'n 'ere*) or through our over-reliance on lazy innuendos that make you groan (that's what she said), I can only conclude that our international reputation for being funny has mostly hitched a ride on the collective coat-tails of Britain's most famous international comedy exports *Monty Python*.

Neil Armstrong once remarked on the linguistic curiosity that people would never say that *he* went to the moon, or that *they* (i.e. NASA/the USA) went to the moon, but that "we" – *humanity* – went to the moon. In much the same way, the average British person is about as responsible for Monty Python as Monty Python are responsible for the fall of the Byzantine Empire, but this certainly won't stop us all from cashing in on their achievements like they were our own. And if the world is happy to think that "the British are funny," then we certainly are too, no questions asked.

After all, it is rare to be given a nice stereotype by the world. In the international comedy roast of cheese-eating surrender-monkeys, obese gun-toting red-necks, and socks-and-sandals-wearing anal-retentives, we are more commonly cast as the dentist-avoiding, Queen-fancying, manners-obsessed, effeminate toffs, prancing around a pub or castle, drinking tea and talking about cricket because we don't know what genitals are for.

A positive stereotype like "the Brits are funny," therefore, is to be defended, cherished and never probed too closely in case it melts under the cruel lamp of nuance.

Indeed, while this book has been written in the light-hearted, soul-healing spirit of revenge, this is the one treasured facet of Britishness I'm happy to give a free pass for purely selfish reasons. I have a slightly vested interest in this myth, since it is used to market my books in Germany the way that Germanness is used to market efficient things in Britain. My German publishers boast of my books "shining with bone-dry British humour" (ORF) the way that Audis in Britain boast of their "Vorsprung durch Technik."

What does the word 'British' add in the phrase "*British* humour"? Nothing, as far as I can tell. *These jokes were made by a man who was born on an island.* Nevertheless, my publisher believes that this label somehow puts all of my half-baked nonsense into the same category of self-evident quality as German engineering, Swedish furniture, French cuisine, Italian grandmothers, American missiles and Russian interference. And I, for one, am going to leave that lovely stereotype the hell alone.

British people: we are very, *very* funny. Trust me.

The Misfortune of Others

We Brits take much comfort in the misfortunes of others. When other British people do things that are clumsy, awkward or embarrassing, we cheer, we whoop and we applaud them. To the uninitiated, this may seem mean-spirited. It is not. We are all celebrating that we are not alone.

Nowhere is this loveable quirk of British culture more on display than when a bartender (or customer) drops a tray of glasses in a pub, where the communal response of the pub, even if the pub is only full of perfect strangers, is always for everyone to stop whatever they're doing and shout a cheerful, celebratory, "*WHAAAAAAAY!*"

When someone drops a melon: "*WHAAAAAAAY!*"

When someone's carrier bag breaks: "*WHAAAAAAAY!*"

When someone trips up a step: "*WHAAAAAAAY!*"

When someone struggling to park a car bumps the curb: "*WHAAAAAAAY!*"

We Brits do not have our own special word for *schadenfreude* (the awesome German word for finding joy in the suffering of others), probably because we didn't know the phenomenon needed a special word; we thought it was just the thing you're supposed to do; the only sensible and natural response. You *have to* be able to laugh at others, because you *have to* be able to laugh at yourself. And if you can't laugh at yourself? Yikes. Then you're never going to survive the everyday indignities of being British *in Britain*.

That's why, to us, there is no sadder figure than a man who slips over on a football and doesn't laugh; nothing more tragic than a woman who notices toilet roll stuck in her skirt then angrily pulls it out without making a stupid face; no weaker character than a person who bumbles, mumbles and stumbles through each and every day of their daft life, without ever celebrating the new heights of incredible uselessness which they have been able to achieve.

The Unimportance of Being Earnest

Sincerity is generally not tolerated in Britain.

Neither is earnestness.

Or over-excitement.

Or too much enthusiasm.

Or *feelings*, of course, which are creepy.

You see, there is a good reason why it is possible for us to constantly insult our friends and celebrate the times when they have had a publicly amusing accident: because taking things too seriously is taboo in British culture. As for *taking yourself too seriously?* That's *the* cardinal sin.

If you want to discover more about this fear of seeming uptight, overly sincere or even pretentious, simply ask a British person the greatest small-talk question of all time: "and what do you do?" To the untrained ear, this might sound like an invitation to start describing one's profession. It is not. It is an invitation to start down-playing, trivialising or moaning about one's profession. To do anything else, indeed, would be rightly regarded as "showing off."

In Britain, you must at all times downplay what it is that you "do" in the knowledge that everyone else will also play down what it is that they "do" and the "equilibrium" of society will be maintained, *wink wink. (There's no leader-board here, mate! Nope. Just lots of people, all in it together, all the same, mate, aren't we? Ha, yeah.)*

So, let's try it. Regardless of how much it might be true, Mr or Mrs Very Impressive Writer Person, you may not answer: "Well, I'm glad you asked, because I'm actually writing a really important novel at the moment. It's an epic spanning three generations, which ties together the evolution of language and the intertwined fate of national identities in a world where we are increasingly defined by the limits of our communication. It's being published by all major publishers simultaneously in 100 languages and then HBO will turn it into a Netflix mini-series on IMAX."

Ahem. No, thank you.

In Britain, the humble island home of self-loathing, saying something "clever" is the absolute height of bad manners and poor form. By being impressed with yourself, you're asking to be taken down a peg or two. The best you could ever hope to achieve with such flagrant disregard for modesty, restraint and the honour of self-deprecation is a bored inquiry about whether your "little book" is going to "have pictures."

A far more British-appropriate declaration would sound like this: "I'm trying to write a, sort of, um, book, I suppose, but I don't know, well, if it'll be any good. Probably not. It's about, I don't know, like, history."

Wow, sounds great! Let's stop talking about it now and get on with our lives immediately! Beer?

The Friendship-o-Meter
of British Banter

Banter, quite understandably, is not a concept that translates equally well into all cultures. Indeed, when Linn first saw my Facebook wall on my birthday, she was so shocked by the floods of well-meaning, horrific abuse that poured in from my nearest and dearest friends that her first reaction was to ask me fearfully if I had done something terrible.

Luckily it can be learned because, underneath the surface irony of expressing something like love through something that looks like hate, British *banter* is pretty much like any other tribe-strengthening ritual in the animal kingdom. It is a subtle ritual of permission-giving, reciprocity, self-abasement and social bonding. Underneath, I think, trading insults shows trust in each other (although admittedly *trust* expressed like a pair of 14-year-old boys giggling in a sex-ed lesson.) Our friends are *allowed* to say horrible things about us, because they have earned that privilege; because we trust them; because we love them; because we can be close, intimate and vulnerable together. (Yuck.)

Once again, savvy readers will notice us wandering back into the maze of phatic communication, except this time with one minor difference: we may *pretend* to pick the nits off strangers but we *really* throw shit at our friends. (If I have learned to self-deprecate and/or insult people well, it is only because most of my British friends are 'orrible savages...)

So, *banter*. How does it work?

First, British people begin by insulting themselves. This act of self-deprecation then gives other British people *permission* to follow suit (while offering some clues about what kind of acceptable insults are freely available in the public domain.) Following a successful act of *self*-deprecation, the same gesture must now be reciprocated, so that both parties have insulted themselves and proven themselves "fair game." If both parties laugh, they have safely navigated the first part of the test (do you self-deprecate?) and can move onto the second (do you take yourself too seriously?) Next, both would-be banterers insult *each other* (which they now have permission to do, in theory.) When/ if both parties laugh a second time, this seals the friendship. The banter ritual is complete.

Now, as both Brits trade ever crueller insults, they can be increasingly sure of an enduring friendship, while the gradual escalation of offensiveness over time will only strengthen the GSOH shield of both parties in unison. Friends that insult together stay together.

Since the *Insult-Swapping Social Bonding Ritual* is one of human society's stranger tribal bond-strengthening ceremonies, we'll now look at it again in a bit more detail. This is why we Brits call our friends "mates." We have to win them first with a curious mating dance...

The Paul Hawkins Four-Point Plan to Making Friends by Insulting Strangers

(a.k.a. How to be Rude, Politely)

STEP ONE:
Insult Yourself

The first step of the banter mating dance is broadcasting that you do not take yourself too seriously, advertising that you have a robust enough sense of humour to handle adult-level banter, and signalling that you can be trusted to "take a joke" without threatening to derail the banter-wagon by getting offended or crying. Luckily, you can prove all of these things at once by making a sufficiently cruel joke at your own expense. Step One, then, is self-deprecation. What's wrong with you? *Tell everyone.*

It's important, however, to leave *some* room for escalation. Do not go in too strongly at first, because this stage of the mate-making banter ritual is more about testing the waters, rather than diving head-first into the deep end. For example: if you've just met someone new for the first time, don't say, "I have control issues, warts and a tendency to self-sabotage in relationships."

As an opening "banter" gambit, this might scare them off. Instead, consider picking some of the more obvious, superficial, low-hanging fruits of your flaw-tree, then work your way up. For example, I have a hairline receding in the shape of the McDonalds 'M,' I bob up and down when I walk (a bit like a chicken-pimp that's pleased with himself), and my beak-like nose has a gently oscillating tip that wobbles comically when I say certain vowel and consonant sounds which prevents my friends taking me seriously when I talk.

Using this kind of gentle banter fodder is often a great way to start bantering, as it immediately diffuses any Tourettes bombs that might be ticking inside people's minds when they look at you, and gives them permission to say out-loud what they're probably already thinking. This helps creates honesty and intimacy, the British way. Of course, if you're totally new to the custom of bantering, you may not yet know how many things are wrong with you (don't worry, you'll find out soon enough.) In which case, start off simple: offer your bantermate a blank canvas for now and we'll try to colour it in later. You could start with, for example, "I'm some kind of a moron." (Good. Fine. Every journey of a thousand steps must start with a single insult…)

Foreigner readers, of course, will have a natural advantage here as they will be something of a novelty by default and will therefore have a rich, untapped history of native stereotypes, prejudices and misconceptions to explore. Where you come from, for example, you might be boring old Günther from Munich but in Britain you can be a one-man self-cannibalising comedian of all German stereotypes. Your self-deprecating jokes about being punctual, rule-following and anal will echo through the ages. Your Hitler impression will live in infamy. Your bad sausage puns will fly higher than eagles. Just remember: don't take anything too seriously and always be a "good sport": after all, the only alternative to laughing at yourself and earning everyone's respect in public is everyone disrespecting you by laughing at you in private. Which is wurst? *WHAAAAAAAY!*

STEP TWO:
Let Them Insult Themselves

Having insulted yourself through self-deprecation, you have extended an invitation to any prospective banter-partners that they may proceed to insult you too, but hopefully they won't… just yet. Always remember: banter is a two-way street. (One-way "banter" is more formally known as "bullying.") Banter custom dictates, therefore, that your prospective bantermate must insult himself first, as a matching sign of self-abasement and humility. This is the British equivalent of returning the Japanese bow. In Japan, you bow to someone of higher status than you to show them your respect. (It says, "I mean you no ill will, sensei-san. With my bow, I make myself physically vulnerable in front of you. Here is my exposed neck. I am at the mercy of your sword.") In Britain, you call yourself a twat. (It says, well, "I'm a twat.")

At this stage, prospective bantermates will hopefully return your bow by insulting themselves ("you're a twat?! Ha, then so am I! In fact, I am definitely quite a massive bellend!"), and you receive permission to proceed further in the friend-making courtship dance of banter. From your side, the only important thing is how well *you* respond to *their* self-deprecation.

Firstly, of course, you must notice that they have made a joke at their own expense. This is crucial. If you respond with sincerity *(shudder)* you will have failed the test. Let's imagine, for example, that your prospective bantermate says, self-deprecatingly, "ack, I'm so stupid!" If you were to reply, from the bottom of your heart, "no, you're not! I think you're really clever!" – this would be DISASTROUS. By appearing to take your prospective bantermate *seriously*, you have lent an air of credibility to the self-deprecation, turning it from a sarcastic, amusing, fun sort of comment into a mere *comment* (which now, awkwardly, needs clearing up.)

In the worst case scenario, the failed banter-givers – the ones who brought up the topic of their own stupidity – will react defensively, as if it was *you* who called *them* stupid, completely unprovoked. By the ancient lore of bantercraft, you have attacked them by *not letting them* attack themselves and thus created good banter's opposite, *seriousness*. "You're damn right I'm not bloody stupid," they might reply, "I got a B in Business Studies, thank you very much. *And* I know how to tie four kinds of knot. How bloody dare you."

STEP TREE:
Let Them Insult You

Assuming you and your prospective bantermate have both now insulted yourselves correctly, it's time for the real test of bantercraft: insulting each other. Let's say you have made the first move, it is now up to you to receive the first insult (with honour.) Bow your head, dig your heels in and brace for impact. Shit's about to get real.

In Step Three, you're trying to show your prospective bantermate that you *trust them* enough to *let them* insult you. Whatever you do, then, you must NOT get offended by their insult, otherwise the banterdance will fail and there'll be samurai shame all over. This would be the worst possible outcome imaginable, as this elaborate ritual has been developed purely to *reduce* the amount of overall embarrassment in society (by bringing potential sources of later embarrassment to the surface *now*.) So, if you *are* offended: keep your actual bloody feelings to yourself. This isn't Italy.

Step Three is about receiving your insult with honour, grace and humility. Luckily, if your prospective bantermates are well-trained in bantercraft, they will know the right level of insult to start at. (If they are unsure, they may echo your original self-deprecation back at you, just to test the waters.) At the beginning of a friendship, it is normal for British people to only insult each other on obviously acceptable or pre-sanctioned topics, before moving into more improvisational territory later. This is the *learning-each-other's-limits* phase of the ancient and noble banter dance. The more you have pre-insulted yourself by this stage, the more categories of insult your partner will have available, and vice-versa. Thorough self-deprecation essentially widens the goal-posts of banter, and makes it easier for everyone to score.

If your banterpartner pulls out the big guns early, insulting you harshly without too much of your prompting, then congratulations! Being subjected to a four-hour tirade of abuse where every single feature of your face, body, personality, worldview and core religious tenets are irreversibly skewered is great news. You're clearly a natural: *a very, very good sport.* To receive such a stream of well-meaning abuse so early on in a British friendship is high praise indeed. You must be a real **** .

On the other hand, the last thing you ever want to receive is a half-hearted, lacklustre and grasping "insult" like, "errr, your fingers are a bit... sort of... short, I guess. I don't know, maybe they're OK. I'm sorry." *Oh dear.* This is bad news: clearly you are deemed unworthy of true banter. If I were you, I'd consider leaving the pub, walking in the direction of the world and not coming back until you have sufficiently developed a personality. Thanks.

STEP FOUR:
Insult Them

The final stage of the banter-mating ritual is responding to your received insults in kind. Your GSOH shield has survived the friendly fire of your bantermate and now it's time to launch your counter-offensive into soon-to-be friendly territory. Let banter battle commence.

Before you launch your own insults, keep in mind that you should be trying to roughly match the strength of what has been fired at you. There are obvious ways to pass and fail this test. You could underestimate the response and insult the other person too timidly. For example, someone calls you "a shit-eating arsehole," then you fire back at them, "ha! Well, you're a very silly sausage!" *Yikes.* This would be a total disaster, leaving any prospective bantermates feeling horrified that they might have needlessly fired a bazooka at a person holding a spoon.

No: bantership is about being well-matched in power and skill. Your bantermate says "I'm so forgetful." You retort, "ha! True! You'd lose your head if it wasn't screwed on!" Yes, that's about right. Nice swordplay, young apprentice. In contrast, if your bantermate says "I'm so forgetful" but you respond, "ha! Yes! And your mother's dead!" then you might have overshot the mark.

BONUS STEP:
Insult Each Other, Forever

Once the mate-making ritual of bantership is sealed – both sides having now offered their trust in each other and both sides having now proven themselves worthy of that trust – the inevitable next step is merciless life-long escalation. Here's a rough guide to the plateaus you may pass together on your journey to the top (or bottom?) of the friendship mountain:

- Cute personality quirks ("you're so clumsy!")

- The entirety of the other person's personality ("your innate clumsiness means a life of even mediocre achievement will elude you.")

- Obvious physical features ("you're bald!")

- Less obvious physical features ("your head looks like a butternut squash even a French market wouldn't sell.")

- Mothers, Beginner ("yo momma!")

- Mothers, Advanced ("your mother looks like a melted walrus candle that a blind person tried to reform in a hurry with their hands taped into fists.")

Good work. As you progress through the hierarchy of British friendship, you should eventually end up in a companionship where each and every piece of correspondence between you both is an ever more creative attempt to break the other person's spirit (see *The Problem of Evil* for further pointers.)

The Insult Forcefield

The more you practice the skills of banter-based self-deprecation, the less easily you will get offended and the less insult-able you will become as a result. To insult yourself and others with increasing intensity (in order to draw out their best insults) is to disarm any actual opponents you may accumulate in life of their arsenal. Insults and name-calling are the weapons of bullies, but *you* can make *their* weapons ever more useless and ineffectual against you. Never forget, brave banter warrior: insults need a target to hit. Self-deprecation shrinks and then finally removes that target.

This is the British equivalent of achieving enlightenment: being able to graciously take any insult from anyone with total equanimity. Taking no offence from anyone, ever. Being essentially un-insult-able. The most enlightened Brits amongst us have teased themselves so fully that they now stand naked before the people who would try to steal their clothes; nothing can harm them any more, it would seem, not even themselves. Fully self-insulted people are thick with armour of their own creation, in heroic defiance of how much that conflicts with the previous metaphor. How do you win fights with people more keen to punch themselves in the face than you are? *Exactly!*

Understanding this timeless wisdom, I hope that the path to a more tolerant world has become illuminated. We must be mean to ourselves, and we must be mean to each other. We must be especially mean to our children – the little British idiots – otherwise how can we ever hope to grow a better world from the soil of their stupid little hearts?

DRINKING WITH THE BRITISH

Chapter Five

Drinking with
the British

Because I am a bloody immigrant (or *e*migrant to you, if you prefer), I am often asked the question, "what is the thing you most miss about home?"

My answer is always the same: pubs.

I bloody love pubs. And – let me be clear here – I am *not* saying I love alcohol. (I *do* love alcohol, but I'm not saying that now.) I'm saying, *I love pubs*. Indeed, more than that, I'm saying this: I would love pubs even if they didn't sell alcohol. However, they do sell alcohol, which is why I *bloody* love pubs. Pubs, pubs, pubs. I love pubs.

Pubs, in my opinion, are Britain's friendliest buildings and probably the finest thing our culture has ever produced. I started working behind the bar of a local pub from the very first moment I was old enough to at the age of eighteen, and continued doing so, on and off, for about five years, during which time I learned almost everything that is worth knowing about life, people, the world, the universe and everything. (Chief amongst these lessons that you can drink beer, make jokes and chat to a myriad of interesting people all day, *and* get paid for it. What a world.)

So, dear reader, I hope I am qualified enough to guide you a little deeper into the workings of these heavenly buildings, and provide you with the inside scoop on the beating heart of British culture. Maybe, if I do a good enough job, you will learn to love the humble British pub as I do too. *Cheers.*

The Communal Living Room

Because I often find myself having to explain (or justify) what it is that I love and miss so much about British pubs (compared to their worse continental counterparts, *bars*), let me tell you afresh about pubs and what is so uniquely glorious about them.

Firstly, British pubs all look almost entirely the same: like charming, old-fashioned communal living rooms that haven't fundamentally changed in style, layout or smell for about a thousand years (except to introduce condom machines, Monster Munch and urinal cakes.) To the uninitiated, this might not sound like much of an advantage, but bear with me.

Secondly, British pubs are *everywhere*. Like I said, a mere one-pint-walk-away in any direction from the pub you are presently sitting in is another almost identical pub you can sit in later.

Thirdly, British pubs are *for everyone*. Where I live in Berlin, there's bars for hipsters, bars for Turkish men, bars for local drunks, bars for tourists, bars for the poor, the middle-class, the rich. In Britain, there's just pubs – public living rooms for the whole of society (*because we're all the same aren't we, really? Ha. Yes, mate.*)

Last but not least, British pubs are *for everything*; for every purpose and every occasion. This makes British social life preposterously easy to navigate. Between the magical, fabled hours of 11am and 11pm (a.k.a. "the day") the humble British pub is a cafe, restaurant, living room, tavern, saloon, social club, community centre, meeting room, dating back-drop, gambling den and gossip hub. It also plays a central role in every stage of the average British life cycle: it's where you go for family meals as a child, where you go when you are coming of age (when using your fake ID first becomes viable), where you go to celebrate landmark achievements in your life (like your 18th birthday, to coronate adulthood with your first legal drink); where you go to meet friends, insult friends, go on dates, develop romantic relations; before weddings, during divorces and after funerals. It's where you go to fill time. It's where you go when you're happy; it's where you go when you're sad (to cheer up, or to have a little public wallow.)

In other words, pubs facilitate almost the entirety of British culture. Indeed, I am even not sure if Britain would be a society without pubs or just a huddled mass of embarrassed, sober people, hiding in our houses, peeking through our net curtains, never leaving our couches except to take the bins out or nip into the garden in a daring (yet almost certainly doomed) attempt to dry the laundry.

The Omnipresence of Booze

Before we spend too much time in the pub, it would be wise to think about the special relationship many of us in the UK have with booze. Being from England myself (a key member state of BINGE BRITAIN), I've certainly grown up gently marinating in a culture of fun-fuelled recreational drinking and its good friend, accidental casual excessiveness. Alcohol, of course, reduces inhibitions. And the average British person is perhaps best understood as one giant inhibition expressed in human form.

We are also, however, a fun-loving and agreeable bunch, which is why we don't mind accepting a little extra chemical assistance in letting our hair down. This is why pubs are the societal bedrock of Britain and why booze is almost compulsorily served to us in every kind of room we are expected to spend more than an hour in.

How many early relationships and formative sexual encounters in modern Britain would remain uninitiated if it wasn't for the liquid bravery that students and young people flush through their bodies to help them approach, grind against and "pull" each other? That's why we sometimes call it "Dutch courage" (although I assume the Dutch, having witnessed a hundred-thousand British stag and hen dos in Amsterdam, do not share this terminology. They presumably call alcohol "British terror.") Other countries may be able to "date" after a coffee and an ice-cream, the freaks, but alcohol in Britain remains a useful tool for nearly every kind of mildly social activity.

For us, it can be used to improve a good evening, rectify a bad one, make a boring person more bearable, help us make friends, have fun, kill time, overcome awkward experiences and conclude any activity whatsoever. For example, if someone is grieving in Britain, you can say to them, "I'm so sorry to hear that, mate. Let me buy you a drink." If someone becomes a parent in Britain, you can also say, "I'm so happy to hear that, mate! Let me buy you a drink." And if someone is about to go home in Britain, having been drinking with you for the entire day, you can still say, "I'm so happy/so sorry to hear that, mate. Just one more then, for the road."

What's more, alcohol is always there for us, like a trusty sidekick, to help us advance through all of the more difficult chunks of our inhibition-marinated lives: for after work, at the weekends, during holidays with friends and Christmas time with family (you know, to make all of those life choices and all of that spare time and all of those voluntary relationships more bearable.)

For the British, ethanol is not just some mere legal drug – a reliable chemical bio-hack for unlocking increasing openness at the expense of coherence – but a reliable and ever-present portal to the Land of a Thousand Great Anecdotes. It's hard not to notice, after all, that no good story starts with an orange juice.

The Stigma of Abstinence

Because alcohol is such a reliable social lubricant in Britain, we sometimes find it's the only drug we can be stigmatised by friends and family for *not doing*. Indeed, abstaining from alcohol consumption is sometimes regarded as a highly anti-social thing to do. Be warned, booze-dabblers: if you *choose* to drink a diet coke or a glass of sparkling water in a British pub (when your fellow pub-goers could reasonably expect you to order a pint), you might be treated like someone who has just thrown a bin through a bus stop window.

Sure, no one in Britain is going to *force* you to drink something alcoholic if you really, *really* don't want to (because water-boarding someone with beer would be considered impolite), but we are certainly not above trying to achieve a somewhat similar result using guilt, shame and peer pressure.

Occasional non-drinkers will be expected, at the very least, to answer a few probing questions about their choices, such as, "why? Is it some kind of wacky new religious thing?", "are you on antibiotics?" and/or "bloody hell, what on earth has gotten in to you today? Are you alright? Have I done something?" The Potential Abstainers must then explain themselves fully, whereupon a final verdict (or, indeed, veto) of their decision can be made by the Peer Pressure Drinking Jury. "Riiiiiigght, ok," we might eventually respond (although in a tone of forced and reluctant understanding) before asking a quick follow-up question, "so... you just want a half then, or what?"

As far as I can tell, the default reaction of disbelief towards non-drinking might be a form of defensiveness on the part of drinkers. Due to potentially high concentrations of passive-aggression particles floating around in the British atmosphere at all times, our criticism detectors are so sensitive they can occasionally pick up a false reading. We hear a British friend say something perfectly normal like, "nah thanks, I don't really fancy boozing tonight," and we wonder if we've been criticised for drinking. If I ask a friend for a beer, then she turns and orders, "one orange juice and one beer, please. Thanks," my first reaction is quiet alarm. My paranoid Brit-o-matic brain has bent itself around a corner to hear: "one normal drink (because I am a grownup and it's the daytime) and one ludicrous drink, please (so my friend can continue destroying his liver, undermining his community and ruining his life.) Thanks."

Now, as you may have guessed, I am a fairly orthodox member of the British drinking community (and also a semi-practising binge-drinker.) I'm not religious about it (I don't go to the Holy Church of Pub *every* Sunday, for example) but I definitely *believe* in Drinking. However, this doesn't stop me from noticing that there are many good reasons to not drink too: health, money, remaining in control, not being a burden on others, blah blah blah. It therefore always seems strange to me that I get to glide through British life being "normal," whereas healthy, wealthy, in-control, independent, boring people have to constantly justify themselves to a self-appointed jury of inebriates like me.

As for actually acceptable reasons for not-drinking in Britain, there are only two known bulletproof excuses: "no, sorry, I would love to but I'm pregnant" (this excuse only works convincingly for half of us, obviously) and "ah, no thanks, I would love to but I'm an alcoholic."

That's it, pregnancy and alcoholism, the only shortcuts out of the peer pressure maze, presumably because the pregnancy excuse can't be received through the paranoid Brit-o-matic brain as a passive-aggressive sleight against drinking generally, and because the alcoholism excuse not only says, "I like drinking too" but also "I like drinking more than you do. Therefore I win and I want an orange juice."

The Intoxicating Effects
of Peer Pressure

When I was at The University of Why Didn't I Bother to Research Any Other Universities Before Applying to University, I remember a few foreign students being perplexed by the attitudes, goals and intentions of their British-born dorm-mates, and vice-versa. Signs would even sometimes emerge of a mild and simmering slow-motion culture clash within our shared halls of residence between two distinct positions: some foreign students, for example, were only attending university in England to do weird, foreign things like "study," while this occasionally disruptive form of behaviour sat very uneasily, of course, with higher native priorities like noise-making, wearing fancy dress at the faintest whiff of opportunity, and investing 90% of all student loans into the long-term future of Tesco Value lager.

I mean, I'm sure you can sympathise with the victims here. Just imagine: there you are, minding your own business, trying to drink a hundred tiny shots of beer within a hundred minutes, wearing a last-minute Osama bin Laden costume made of toilet paper and pubic hair Pritt-sticked to your chin, endlessly singing the chorus to *Tubthumping* by Chumbawumba while some West Country boy with a blue mohican called Wilf (who has only just escaped the stifling vigilance of his helicopter parents for the first time in his life) is beaming 40-foot high pornography onto a neighbouring building with a projector, then there's some bloody Latvian scribbling away with a pen in the corner, making a face at you, because she wants to be a "doctor" or something. It's distracting.

(I mean, don't get me wrong, yeah? I don't mind 'em comin' over 'ere, being our doctors, propping up our economy, funding our retirements, yeah, but, *BUT*... right? I DO think they should integrate, y'know? *Yeah?* This is Britain, yeah? It's OUR culture, yeah? BRITAIN means BRITISH, right? So, why not just put the pen down, yeah, mate? Forget your silly bloody "epidemiology exam" for a minute and drink this pint of Apple Sourz through a traffic cone. That's it, mate. ENG-GAH-LAND!)

Of course, not all foreign students were so insensitive towards our traditions, heritage and cultural norms. However, even for foreign students who *specifically* came to Britain with the intention of binge-drinking (i.e. assimilating), there were still difficult concepts to penetrate, such as *pre-drinking* and *drinking games*. The notion of *pre-drinking* could seem strange to the uninitiated, since the thing that the *pre*-drinking *pre*ceded was always *more drinking*. The prefix *pre-* seemed redundant as in the sentence, "let's *pre*-prepare to get wasted by 8pm." As for *drinking games*, the foreign student often wondered, "well, why can't we just drink without the pretence of a game?" The answer, of course, is that the game framework helpfully removes all forces of responsibility, culpability and decision-making from the equation. Now we are not *binge-drinking by design*; no, now we are following the rules. It's fair. It's decent. It's dutiful. Long live the Queen.

The Local, the Regular and the Usual

Since most pubs in Britain look the same anyway, many of us choose to go to the same one for our entire adult lives so as not to cause a fuss.

This pub we would call *our local*. If we go to our local enough, we are called *a regular*. If we're regular enough in our local, we order *the usual*. If we're locally regular enough to order *the usual*, we may find our *usual* already waiting for us on the bar when we arrive, the bar staff having poured it as soon as we were spotted approaching the pub from afar. As a former barman myself (and one who can still remember all of my local's regulars' usuals now), trust me when I say this: if alcohol is a social lubricant, then the engine of Britain is very well-oiled.

Given the potential simplicity involved in choosing a life-long pub to drink in (which one is nearest?), foreign visitors should be warned that we Brits may not always be overly-descriptive when inviting you to join us for a drink. We will probably just say "*the* pub." Hell, that's if you're lucky enough to get a "the" at all. Ninety percent of the text messages I ever received as an adult living in England were just one word: "pub?"

The challenge for non-Brits receiving such a text message, of course, would be finding "pub," given that each pub in Britain comes straight out of the pub mass production factory and has a name like The Crown and Rose and Hat and Biscuit and Horse and King (which will often be on the opposite side of the road to an identical pub called The Horse and Biscuit and Rose and Crown and King and Hat.) Up and down the country, every half a mile, Queens, Crowns, Lions, Dragons, Swans, Oaks, Cows, Keys, Ploughs, Ships, Bats, Balls, Foxes, Hounds, Pigs, Whistles, Jolly Sailors and Nags Heads, the same names, the same symbols, over and over again, all jumbled up and pulled randomly out of the magical symbology soup.

That's because, in the olden days, pubs didn't have names at all; they just had hand-painted boards hanging outside of them, big pictures atop high posts, in order to advertise themselves to streets full of pre-literate people. The names came after. I think that's a wonderful fact, which perhaps helps illuminate not only how long we've been a pub-going population, but also why pubs are so ingrained in our culture: our society built up around them, using them as the central points of reference for finding each other to hang out. That's why, when we meet at The Crown, we meet at *the crown*. When we meet at The Bull, we meet at *the bull*. And when we meet at The Goat In Boots, you better believe we're going to be meeting each other at the nearest bloody picture of a goat wearing boots.

The Invisible Mind-Queue

Foreign readers who have read this book, perhaps trying to glean from it a consistent picture of how to behave in Britain, may be alarmed by a glaring inconsistency when they first enter (the/a) "pub." Inside the building *something* will be *off*; subtly yet eerily different to all other buildings and all other places in the great wide British world around them. They will look towards the bar area, searching out the appropriate place to stand in order to dutifully *wait their turn* and politely order a warm ale or some fancy crisps, then notice something disorientating: there is… *no queue!*

Oh sure, there are British folks at the bar, standing around, waffling on about Brexit, holding aloft empty glasses, waiting for "a top-up" or another glass of incorrectly pronounced wine ("pee-no grig-e-o, please"), but there's no obvious place to stand amongst them to indicate one's proper numerical position in the queue. *What is this?!*, the desperate foreigner may panic, *can it really be true?! Are they all organised* sideways *now? In a geometric shape with no front or back, only depth? A linear form with no clear numerical beginning or end? WHAT'S GOING ON!? HOW AM I SUPPOSED TO INTEGRATE IF THEY KEEP CHANGING ALL THE BLOODY RULES?!*

Well, don't despair, dear foreign reader, for there *is* still definitely a very polite system of queuing in progress. It's just that pub queues are even more sophisticated than normal British queues: they are, indeed, invisible, special, magic queues that exist only in the shared dimensions of our minds, like in that film *The Matrix*, except not. The barman *knows* the order of the queue that isn't there. The customers *know* the order of the queue that isn't there. Everyone, simply, *knows*. (Oh, sure, the tourists might not know, but they'll find out, won't they, if they try and jump it? Oh yes, they bloody will. *Nobody jumps the invisible queue…*)

If I, as a barman, forgot who was rightfully next in the

invisible queue… do you think I just gave up caring about fairness temporarily and served whoever I wanted to first because it doesn't really matter? No, no, no: I would stand well back, theatrically look from side to side as if all of the customers had become invisible and loudly broadcast to everyone at once, "so…. who's next, please?" Then I would avoid all eye contact until the customers had finished offering the front place in the queue to each other in an elaborate politeness race to the bottom. (No one ever said, "me! *ME!* I'm first! It's my right! Serve *me!*" Nope. All I ever heard was, "her! *HER!* She's next, I promise! I swear to god she was 33 milliseconds earlier than me!")

Yes, that's right: we don't even need a physical manifestation of a queue. We can queue *in our minds*. It doesn't matter how "long" the mind-queue is, how drunk the customers are or how confused the bartender gets, everybody always knows their exact numerical place in it at all times. The invisible mind-queue is sacred and cannot be adjusted for anyone. Well, except in extraordinary circumstances…

The Liquid Trick of British Tipping

There are only two known loopholes to the invisible mind-queue system:

1.) Being a Demon-Spawned Monster of Cruel and Ancient Evil; or,

2.) Being the exact opposite: an Angel-Born Saint of Perfect and Impossible Kindness

As is well-known and well-bemoaned across the hospitality industries of the world, we are not the greatest tippers. This is not necessarily our fault, either: we do not tip bar-staff in

Britain, so it's only natural if we sometimes forget to tip them in the former-Britain of everywhere else.

However, there is one way – a particularly British way – to tip your bar staff, should you wish to show an extra token of your gratitude: *offer them a drink.*

Yes, when we do tip our bar staff, we like to tip them *in booze…* an act of generosity that, due to its relative rarity, will be greeted by the bartender with a level of gratitude bordering on idol worship. Even if you're not in the habit of tipping British bar-staff yourself, try it some time if you want to see what it looks like when pure delight leaks out of a British face. The etiquette is simple enough: order your round of drinks as normal and then, right at the end, finish the transaction by saying, "… and one for yourself, mate."

Congratulations, your bartender will now love you as a dog loves its owner. The bartender may not take the drink immediately (depending on the repute of the establishment, and the repute of the bartender), but may put one "on your tab" to drink later, after the shift ends or for another occasion entirely. The savvy amongst you might have already noticed what this therefore implies: it is essentially just a slightly faffier way to give someone *the value* of a drink, yet not necessarily in the form of a drink. It's credit. It's money. It's a tip. And yet it's a very, very polite form of tip, disguised in the confusing British theatrics of pretending that the economy doesn't exist.

Anyway, if you buy your bartender *"a drink"* (wink wink), the next time you find yourself standing at the invisible sideways mind-queue of a busy bar, you might notice something interesting: a bartender pretending that everyone else in the queue is invisible, except for you. (And I am not saying, by the way, that you have paid a bribe, like a mobster cooly slipping a fifty into the concierge's hand for a better table; I am saying you have thrown bread to a duck and now the duck has spotted you again.)

The Guardians of the Beer

Pubs in Britain generally don't do table service. This means, if you sit in a pub, you are left alone. It's very clear when you want something, because you have to get up, go to the bar and get it. Thus we are all miraculously spared the usual politeness dilemmas of guilt and shame associated with waiters asking us once an hour if we want something, and then continually having to revaluate whether we have purchased enough recently to justify our continued use of someone's else chair.

As a result of this simple role-reversal, bar staff have an elevated social status in Britain: a far more dignified and noble position in our society than in other parts of the world, in my opinion. Bartenders are not people that come to you to ask what you want, like slaves. *You* have to come to *them* to *ask* if you can have something, and hope they grant you permission to drink, like they're the pharaoh (except a minimum wage pharaoh standing on a sticky floor.) This elevates the bartender in pub-based social proceedings. They are the fabled tenders of the till; the holy keepers of the booze; the sacred guardians of the beer. They are the crisp merchants of yore.

You also have to come to them *a lot*, of course, as it is another cultural imperative of British social life that you have a drink in your hand at all times. Finished your drink? Get another. Nearly finished your drink? Queue one up. Queued one up? Queue two up in case you already missed the first bell and might potentially miss the almighty tolling of *the last bell*, which signals the end of the start of the last frantic binge-drink before bed. There's no time to waste: the first bell is at 10.50pm, the last at 11pm, and then there's only half an hour until the staff are jangling keys in front of your face, emotionally blackmailing you with clever lies about "needing to lock up and go to bed." (They actually just want to start drinking themselves, of course. They've got all those liquid tips saved up.)

There's also a long established custom in British pubs that bar staff are allowed to refuse service to any customer they want, at any time, and for any reason. In other words, even if many bartenders, on paper, are poorly paid, squeaky-voiced, mid-puberty drink servants, they still hold within their power the ability to cancel the social life of even the longest-standing community member on a whim.

This is the first thing I was taught when I started working behind a bar: that people were coming into my public *house*, and I could therefore extend them hospitality at my discretion. I didn't have to explain myself, I was told, if I wanted to chuck someone out or "bar" them, just like I wouldn't have to explain myself if some unsavoury, annoying or unfriendly character came into my private house and started constantly asking me to serve them things. (Indeed, my landlord even advised me to never explain myself, especially if my reason was something like, "I'm sorry but your hair looks far too much like a pineapple for me to do my job properly, please get out.")

To illustrate this slightly counter-intuitive quirk of the public house (the customer is never right), I bring you Malcolm, my old landlord – a blunt, impatient man with a handlebar moustache who may well have been born without the ability to feel fear.

One warm day – with sweat on his omni-furrowed brow, a scowl on his ever-scrunchy face and his gossamer-thin patience stretched to perforation point by a beer garden full of people enjoying themselves (the bastards) – I actually witnessed him put a pint of beer down in front of a customer and say, "right, there you go. £3.50, please."

"Oh," said the customer, smilingly, pushing some coins around the palm of his hand with a *whoopsy-daisy* expression on his face, "I've only got £3!"

Malcolm, a man about as hospitable as Mars, stared back at him humourlessly, then picked up the beer he had just put down and took a lengthy swig of it until, I presume, he deemed 50 British pence of it was gone.

"£3 then."

It was an amazing thing to watch. The poor, innocent customer was bewildered. I think I saw on his face in that moment how someone's prior model of the world (*"I am a desired patron"*) can collapse in a second behind their eyes. The man didn't know what to do. Finally, after a very awkward silence, a little embarrassed laugh-thing escaped his mouth, he handed over £3 and then slowly walked away, staring down at his £3 worth of handlebar moustache-brushed beer.

As for Malcolm, he didn't even turn around to see if anyone had seen what he had done. He was not braced for any commentary on his action; it was not done to be witnessed, noticed or retold to anyone later as a funny anecdote in a comedy book. He just thundered off to another part of the pub to carry on his day in what other people are naively calling the "hospitality" industry.

The Free Speech Zone

Pubs should be of particular interest to us on our quest to understand Britishness, because the bar areas of pubs are one of the only places in British culture where it is acceptable to initiate bizarre conversations with total strangers. People at the bar, by virtue of being *at the bar*, have somehow communicated to the rest of the pub that they are open to gossip, joke or small-talk; to the bar staff, to each other and to any other pub-goers wandering into range to order a drink who are deemed temporarily fair-game for some walk-by banter.

Unusual to Britain, conversations in the immediate bar area can be initiated by almost anyone saying almost anything about almost any topic. There are, indeed, seemingly very few rules of engagement relating to context, continuity or coherence. Certainly, bar-based chit-chat is not tethered to the usual timid British conversation-launchers of weather, football and/or how busy the pub is/isn't. The bar areas of lively pubs are *Free Speech*

Zones for political debate; a beer-soaked immune system for our form of civic society. These offbeat parliaments of the masses are places for citizens to moan, to argue, to debate and to air their (probably exaggerated) grievances with everything, safe in the knowledge that everyone's opinions will matter less and less as the evening goes on and all sense gets slowly washed away by the all-forgiving river of drunkenness.

It is around the bar area, for example, that you might hear people moaning most enthusiastically about "BROKEN BRITAIN," that conceptual catch-all of self-deprecation elevated to the national level. Indeed, probably the most popular topic in the beer halls of Britain is *everything that is wrong with the country (that wasn't wrong with it in the good old days)*, a broad topic which includes what our taxes are presently well spent on ("nothing"), which politicians are bastards ("all of them"), who is wrong about everything ("everyone else") and, last but definitely not least, the increasingly sorry state of the NHS. (And what better place to moan about it than in the pub, over a bag of fried, salted pig fat and six pints of lager?)

As everyone involved in this form of part-time politics casually imbibes the Recommended Weekly Allowance of the UK's Chief Medical Officer in a single evening, discussions can get heated between pub-goers who hold opposite strongly held opinions. Indeed, it has been plausibly suggested by anthropologists that this is the social function of "rounds": that the temporary "debt" it creates between people is a kind of pressure valve for friend-based tensions. That's why, no matter how heated a pub dispute in Britain gets ("THATCHER FIXED EVERYTHING!", "NO, THATCHER BROKE EVERYTHING!"), the argument *always* has to be suspended every forty minutes or so by a sacred ritual of gift-giving. You could have a radical communist and a radical capitalist halfway to a screaming match about which one of them BROKE BRITAIN first, and then – mid-rant – the whole thing gets instantly diffused by one saying to the other, "oh, sorry, is it my round? My apologies, where are my manners!

Same again, is it? Ha, no worries, mate. Yes, please, barkeep! Two more pints, please. Wonderful. Thanks, thank you. There you are: that's yours, I think. You're welcome. Right, cheers – to good health! Ah, that's lovely, that is. Um, where were we? Ah yes, I remember. *YOU FASCIST PIG, YOU'RE WRONG ABOUT EVERYTHING!*"

For the most part, this rounds-assisted ability to have good-natured pub arguments is a wonderful feature of Britishness. It might even reflect why and how our politics works in miniature: we discuss our differences openly and thus, by doing so, can always make sure that our decisions disappoint everyone equally.

As is the risk with all *Free Speech Zones*, however, newcomers to British pub etiquette should be prepared to hear some things they might find a little less, um, *palatable*. You'll need a robust and flexible sense of humour, certainly, so don't forget to bring your GSOH shield along to the pub with you.

Remember how I warned German-readers earlier about the possibility of seeing some Hitler impressions upon visiting the UK, for instance? Well, that warning comes specifically from one of the regulars in my old pub, a friendly man named Short Story (whose nickname would probably be 'Big John' if he could get to the point a bit quicker.) Maybe the broad nature of my warning was an over-exaggeration, and in fact German visitors need only be careful in one particular British pub. I don't know. However, for now I think it is safest to assume that there is at least one Short Story in every pub, which is why I have expanded my warning to the national level, just in case. Anyway, *my pub's* Short Story had a particular soft spot for the Hitler impression, as well as a finely tuned comedic nose that could sniff out even the faintest whiff of opportunity to get into character. Whenever any hint of an "appropriate" topic popped up (the connection always seemed dubious, honestly), down would go his fringe, out would spring a comb from his sleeve for use as a clandestine moustache (I never figured out if that was the primary reason he carried it) and soon he'd be marching around the pool table, aiming for at least 90 degrees of vigorous leg extension.

And so it was that when I first took Linn to my old pub to meet this particular group of regulars – my favourite former customers from the good old days of barmanship (ok, *ok*, maybe they bought me some drinks occasionally too) – I had warned her upfront about this potential risk of pub-going, concerned I might otherwise have to spend the whole night worrying that Short Story's Hitler impression could come out any second. Luckily, I was worried for nothing. It came out within the first two minutes.

The High Stakes of Nicknaming

As the cardinal rule of British culture is to mock yourself and all of those closest to you, it won't be long into your pub visit before you are giving out and receiving nicknames as if they were gold medals in honour of your ability to take a joke *and* take the piss. Indeed, if you spend more than five minutes in the *Free Speech Zone* of a pub, it won't be long before your name has been replaced for you by the kind of characters you generally find loitering around the bar area of a pub.

It can happen in an instant, yet it can also last a life-time, which makes it quite a high-stakes game. Here are some of the simplest nickname types – all real examples from my old pub – for beginners to the custom:

1.) The Summary

Is your last name already slightly amusing-sounding? Well, lucky you: that's your nickname now! There's no need for first names like Jack and Michael, after all, with names like Girdlestone and Swingle, is there? Nope.

2.) The Jazz-Up

Our fondness for easy wordplay means we quickly find ways to jazz up even the plainest of first or last names, which is how contact lists across the land are full of Bazzas, Chazzas, Smithys, Shevvers, Jonesys, Wazzles, Dazzles, Hols, Lols, Mo-Mos, Jo-Jos and Jimbobs. If we can jazz you up, by gosh we will.

3.) The Qualifier

In Britain, if two people have the same first name, both must be immediately separated and re-labelled by their most noticeable physical difference. Normally this will lead to nicknames like Big Teresa and Little Teresa or Handsome Steve and Ugly Steve, except mostly applied ironically. (Short Story is not a big man.)

4.) The Unfortunate One That Sticks

When I was at the University of Most People At Least Googled Other Universities First, I lived with two students called Ben. Our building quickly qualified them as 'English Ben' and 'Irish Ben' respectively. Simple. Then, however, a *third* Ben arrived, and an obvious problem emerged. Not only was he objectively more *English* than "English Ben" (he wore ironed trousers and drank more tea), we had now known English Ben for long enough to realise the quality which set him apart from Irish Ben and *New* English Ben (and all possible Bens in the multiverse): his charming and incredible uselessness. The boy couldn't open a tin of beans without somehow exploding a shed. Lovingly, he was downgraded to Rubbish Ben. *Forever.* He's still called Rubbish Ben now, decades later, and I'm reliably informed that the nickname has followed him back from university all the way to his old home-town hundreds of miles away, where it has caught on like a wildfire of descriptive perfection.

Like I said: nicknames are a *high-stakes game.*

Other real examples from just my own social circle include the aforementioned *Short Story* ("because if you ask him the time, it's half an hour before you get it"), *Slow Day* ("in his head, he's chasing a butterfly in a field"), *Guns* (he once said, without irony, "I think I've fired almost every kind of gun"), *Kram* (Mark backwards), *Smudge* (I've no idea why, neither does he; no one does) and, of course, *Nutty Barry* (it's appropriate, trust me. He's really nutty. He once got his head caught in the window of a moving vehicle.) Finally, as further evidence of something (I'm not sure what), I submit to you the nicknames of the only three women that work in my father's predominantly male workplace: Teresa, Gillian and Rachel (who were re-branded by theme, with decreasing amounts of creativity): Teresa the Geezer, Gilli-man and Rachel-bloke.

As you can see, it doesn't have to be big *or* clever, it just has to be *something.* So, if you don't yet have a nickname, it's time to start asking yourself some difficult questions. Are you, perhaps, too boring? Or too uptight? Or, indeed, too terrifying? (I have never once teased Nutty Barry on his Nuttiness, for example, because Nutty Barry once dropped a bit of wood out of a first floor window then fell out of the house trying to catch it. Not since Rubbish Ben has a nickname been so apt. Barry is really nutty. Trust me.)

The Dangers of Rounds

Now you've got a new nickname superglued to your identity, you're probably getting pretty comfortable with the main dynamics of pub-going. You drink, you wee, you have a laugh and you don't take anything too seriously (except rounds.) But, hm, what's that? The slightly elevated feeling wobbling on the periphery of your consciousness? *Merriness?* Uh-oh, could your casual drink be sliding, without protest, into *a binge drink*? Why, that wasn't the plan at all! Oh well, never mind, it's happened before and will happen again. That's one of the main things that happens in the UK: British people go to the pub on purpose but British people get drunk by accident.

There are several reasons why intoxication can sometimes sneak up on us. Firstly, because almost all social interaction in Britain takes place in the pub, there's lots of opportunities for miscalculation. Secondly, because trying to leave a pub before *last orders* is widely seen as anti-social (to be met with emotional blackmail, peer pressure and sobriety shaming.) And, last but not least, because of *rounds*.

At first glance, the round system might seem like a fairly innocent, care-free and relaxed solution to the drink-buying problem. Everyone takes turns ordering; everyone takes turns buying; everyone takes turns carrying the drinks from the bar all the way back to the table (*because there are no servants here, mate, ha.*)

However, the main result of the round system is that everyone involved tends to drink in escalating multiples (i.e. two friends = two rounds, four friends = four rounds), and we also get locked into a timetable of obligation we can't fully control. What's more, the whole group tends to drink at the speed of the fastest-drinking member, because etiquette dictates that no British person should ever have to suffer the indignity of having-nothing-sensible-to-do-with-their-hands. It feels awkward being drinkless, so we don't do that to each other. At the moment someone puts down an empty glass, then, the next round starts immediately.

(Designated drivers should, of course, be exempt from these rules and customs. They should drink for free and be generally treated with the quiet respect of visiting dignitaries. These brave souls have sacrificed enough. They deserve our eternal gratitude, our unceasing admiration and one orange juice per round.)

Like the invisible mind-queue, the round system may look from the outside like another organic, care-free and relatively relaxed British eccentricity. It is not. It is an ever-changing minefield of potential stress and possible social faux pas. Every order is being recorded forever; downloaded onto the *Shame-Guilt-Fairness Drives* of our Brit-o-matic brains, programming our unspoken character profiles of each other. Did someone miss a round? *Recorded.* Was your beer more expensive than mine? *Recorded.* Did I have a glass of tap water in one round and yet this economic data-point was not subsequently reflected in the next round? *Recorded.*

Bundled together, these factors add up to a social reality where we can get drunk entirely by accident, rather regularly, yet are constantly surprised to find ourselves ordering our seventh pint even though we've been saying, "OK, just one more" since our first.

The Gamble of After-Work Drinks

It is easy to slide into an unintentionally long alcohol session after a day of work in a major British city, especially if you live somewhere like London where your work is in the middle, where pubs are, but your home is in Zone F, where nothing is (except crime, fried chicken and your pants.)

Non-Brits, of course, may be slightly squeamish about the idea of 'after-works drinks' beginning at 5pm (which, in other parts of the world, is called "dinner time"), believing this definitely-still-the-afternoon-hour rather early to begin administering alcohol into the human bloodstream. However, non-Brits need only remember this: most British pubs close by 11pm. This means we *have to* start early (otherwise there's not enough time to binge-drink.)

Indeed, 5pm is by no means a particularly early start for us. I have friends in London that regularly go from a "liquid lunch" (a "cheeky pint or two" at midday on a Friday) into early end-of-week wind-down drinks at work ("no one does anything on a

Friday afternoon anyway") before flinging themselves deep into the London evening for pre-dinner drinks, dinner (optional) with drinks and post-dinner drinks. This flows effortlessly into increasingly regrettable pre-Saturday drinks, and often gets wrapped up in time for the last train home. This all falls under the umbrella of what many of us in Britain are still happy to call "drinking responsibly": i.e. we can be completely smashed *and* in bed before midnight, ready for a good night's sleep (so we have the best chance of being fully recovered in time for our binge-drink on Saturday.)

Needless to say, central London in the witching hours of a Friday or Saturday night can look a bit like every Little Englander's worst nightmares of BINGE BRITAIN have come to life; like a terrifying zombie cityscape of marauding kebab-seekers, casual pitch-battles between rival football fans, antisocial street karaoke, embattled Uber drivers, sirens wailing and night-bus vomit-floor terror. If Britain's small town scaredy-cats ever get to build the Fortress Britain of their dreams, they will probably decide to wall up half the capital between Friday afternoon and Monday morning, like a West Berlin of problem drinking.

The Regrettable Need for Sustenance

Some time into your unfolding (yet accidental) bender, you may notice the familiar rumblings of your body notifying your brain that a priority of secondary importance should also soon pass your lips: solids. That's right, it's time to eat. Luckily, you're already in the right place for the job as almost every British pub, no matter how old, dank, dusty or derelict, contains somewhere out the back a versatile food preparation area that we Brits call "the microwave." So, brave stomach-owner, are you ready for some infamous British food?

When we first developed the guiding concepts of our

traditional national cuisine (before we discovered/invented the chicken tikka masala, I mean), our highest priority seems to have been finding sponge-like things to absorb liquids. Sure: decadent, fancy, European things like flavours, colours and shapes were tacked on later, but mostly as an after-thought. Look through your average British pub menu, indeed, and you should only find foods which could be dipped in and out of a bucket of water, leaving the bucket empty.

Pub food in Britain is therefore not a particularly complicated affair, as the planet's age-old stereotypes about us abroad might attest. Most of our "classic" dishes, indeed, follow this simple formula: *thing* plus *another thing*. Done. Fish plus chips. Bangers plus mash. Beans plus toast. Shepherds plus pie. And what about any meal with more than three colours? The humble British roast dinner (ingredients plus oven), for example? Well, because we don't want to look like we're showing off, anything more complex is drowned in gravy until it is back to the single, modest colour of brown.

When our good, honest, decent, unpretentious British food arrives, it is customary, as in most countries, to wish everyone at the table an enjoyable meal. The UK, however, does not have its own version of *bon appetit* for reasons which I fear are self-explanatory.

Indeed, when I first started leaving England to "go *to Europe*" – that exotic, faraway realm of nude beaches, croissants and accordion music drifting on the wind from café to café – one question I was asked over and over again by learners of English before eating was this: "What *do* English people say before they eat?"

"Hm, I don't know," I used to reply in those days, like a bloody amateur, "I think we would probably just say *bon appetit* actually..."

"Oh," my European hosts would reply, in a tone of disappointment, "zat is verwry désappointement!"

Eventually, though, I was asked this question enough times to realise the most polite (and British) thing to do was acknowledge the expectations implicit in the query and respond with the classic self-deprecating quip of my island-folk. So, *what do English people say before we eat?*

"We say 'good luck!' HA HA HA," I say to Europeans now, still as delighted with myself each time I respond with this absolute zinger of an answer as that first time when it accidentally came out as wit, "and 'don't look!'"

"Oh!" my European hosts now reply, in a tone of amusement, "zat is verwry amusément!"

The most important thing to know about proper British cooking, anyway, is that *bloatedness* is always an equally valid goal to *deliciousness* or *responsible nutrition*. Through this lens, all of our most cherished dishes should start to make sense. We blow up the carb-bomb early. We begin the meal with stodge – potatoes, bread, pastry – and then we move outwards in terms of dietary ambition. We ask ourselves difficult questions upfront: could this whole thing be consolidated into pie form? Can this act of culinary terrorism be improved with gravy? Can we put cheese on it? In it? Around it? Through it? How about some mash on top? Some breadcrumbs? Oh, and speaking of bread, what about some bread? White bread? Fried white bread? Fried white bread... *that's battered?*

Add baked beans.

Add coleslaw.

Add more gravy.

Fry.

If all else fails, add crisps and serve.

That's the international stereotype of our food anyway and it's not my job as a humourist, Englishman or traitor to defend it (or to say anything nuanced at all, for that matter.) Luckily, though, no Englishman like me will ever have to reckon with the true reputation of English food, living, as all Englishmen must, under the rainy hat of Scotland, home of the wonderful Scots people, acclaimed purveyors of haggis, the fried Mars bar and that avant-garde masterpiece, 'the scotch egg': a whole boiled egg, coated in sausage meat, then coated in breadcrumbs, then deep-fried, then possessed by the Ghost of Diabetes Past.

As English comedian Marcus Brigstocke once said, "only the Scottish would 'scotch' an egg."

The Merciful Earliness
of 'Closing Time'

Once you have finished eating – and the thing (plus thing) inside your bowel is swelling autonomously with absorbed alcohol like a fast-forward pregnancy of stodge – the rest of the evening stands before you like a mountain of potential, ready to to crumble away in an effortless blur of accidental binge-drinking until the last bell inevitably tolls with a loud, fun-ending, please-go-home-now *klang*.

In some countries, bars close when their customers go home. In Britain, customers go home when the bar closes. It's an important difference, and it's why some foreigners find "the last bell" a particularly endearing and amusing quirk of Britishness. They have noticed (just like we haven't) that we are a culture of people who must be told when to go to bed by the authoritative sound of brass wobbling. They are right, of course: we do. If there wasn't a last bell limit on our most uninhibited of hours, Britain would probably collapse within a week as it accidentally hangovered itself into economic irrelevance. We can't be trusted to set our own bed-times. We're not Mediterranean.

You see, the problem many of us Brits face with alcohol is that we are not very good at recognising, in the moment, the point at which we officially become "drunk" – especially when we get drunk *by accident* (regularly) because we are rarely prepared to admit to ourselves that it happened (again.)

I certainly consider myself to be somewhat *drunk-blind*: i.e. I don't notice that I'm drunk when I'm drunk so I often drink just a bit too much. Indeed, I only tend to find out that I *was* drunk in hindsight, once a hangover has arrived to retroactively confirm the diagnosis. Back when I was a teenage idiot, this involved waking up to the ominous sight of our household's long-established Sick Bucket. *Oh yes*, the bucket would stare back at me with its unblinking judgement, *you were drunk alright, buddy*. (However, if you had asked Drunk Me at any point the previous evening if I was drunk, I would have said, "no, ovcors I'm nod trunk!")

I'm not sure why this is; if I really don't *know* that I am drunk in that moment, or if I *do* know that I am drunk, but am too drunkenly proud to admit it. Hell, I could be side-ways on a roundabout singing *Right Said Fred* songs into a traffic cone, and I would still insist with impressive conviction (and admirable levels of self-delusion) that there was no need to worry about my general constitution. *Yes, offisher*, I would say, *I'm s'totally fine to operadte heavy machinerwy!*

Incidentally, this is not a problem you tend to get in Germany, as Germans are amazing at self-diagnosing their own inebriation. And, by 'Germans,' I mean Linn. She could be four-fifths of the way through her second white wine spritzer when she confidently declares, without anyone having to ask, "I'm drunk now."

Ha! How embarrassing! I think, smashed, before announcing my complete sobriety and ploughing a cement mixer into a lighthouse.

The Collection of Souvenirs

Ding, ding, ding! OK, last bell! The pub's closing! It's time for you and all of Britain's adult-sized children to leave the public house and skip merrily homewards to your private one.

Before that, however, feel free to mount one last charge of doomed resistance against your pub-enforced bedtime with an immature attempt to hide in the corner with your stockpiled drinks as increasingly exasperated bar-staff ask you to "finish up" so they can "go home soon, please" (liars.) When your lacklustre attempt to initiate a "lock-in" inevitably fails, it's time to leave.

Of course, as you are being so unceremoniously kicked out, you are also very much entitled to steal something from the pub as you leave. Perhaps your glass, for example, since it still contains almost all of the last drink you shouldn't have ordered. To any foreigners reading: don't worry. Stealing from pubs is totally normal, as you will notice if you ever visit a British home and discover that stocking up one's private house with objects from one's public house is somewhat of a national past-time.

Raid the kitchen, indeed, of any working-class or lower middle-class home, student house, former student house or bohemian-aspiring middle-class British family abode, and you'll find at least half of the glasses branded with the brewery symbols to prove they were lovingly relocated from the public house to the private house, not only without shame, but often with some obvious pride. Stolen pub glasses are things to be displayed openly and honestly; badges of honour that prove we have been courageous enough to re-purpose a handbag or winter coat for a naff prize in a drunken heist. Sometimes our casually pilfered items may even elicit admiring responses from our friends and families, like: "Oh, that's a splendid glass! Pray tell: where *did* you get it?"

"Aha, a fine thing that you should notice, my dear man. Why, that elegant chalice you hold aloft is from the Stella Artois promotional campaign of 2004, I believe. I "acquired" it, shall we say, at *The King and Cart and Sheath and Shoe* after a rather squiffy night with Big Arms Boris. He could barely carry it, you know, with his tiny arms. Yes, a fine year for pub glasses, that one. Oh, and have you seen my gold-rimmed Cobra glass from the Royal Bengal? A classy specimen it is, indeed. Jane managed to get five of them out of the place up her blouse once, you know."

Yes: we can occasionally be a sticky-fingered people, which we tend to normalise to ourselves by including *the thing we're stealing* in *the price of another thing we've legitimately paid for*. By complaining, for example, that a pub drink is "too expensive" (as if we are forced to buy it through some as-yet undiscovered economic force of pubs), we can thus regard its container as a kind of obviously included freebie, and all of the ethics involved balance out nicely.

"What?! £5.70 for a pint?! Oh wait, I get it! I think what this particular pub is saying is that the pint is *reasonably priced* but it also includes this glass, bar mat, ash tray and dart board. Lovely stuff – everything's fine then. Pass me my rucksack, Boris!"

We don't even really need to want the soon-to-be-stolen thing to justify any risks. A local regular from my old pub called Dave (and here, it's important to add, that I'm referring to a 45 year-old man) once stole one of bar stools, for no other reason than the challenge/thrill of getting it out of the pub unnoticed. ("I just love stealing!" he said on the way out, as I tried a-man-earning-minimum-wage amount to stop him, "I absolutely don't need this!") He brought it back the next day, hungover and sheepishly, before Malcolm told him off with typical brushy-lipped lack of humour.

"It was just a joke," Dave grumbled to me afterwards, "I can't believe he gave me such a bollocking! I've been drinking here for years." I nodded in sympathy, agreeing upon the great injustice that a bar stool should not be included in such a long-running economic partnership.

Another regular (who remains anonymous to this day, so afraid is he of Malcolm's wrath) once stole a large, light-filled plastic snowman around Christmas, then began posting us ransom notes for it from various places in the world, including one particularly glorious shot of it in front of the pyramids wearing sunglasses. And I've even seen a group of people walking down the high street of my own hometown carrying an entire 6-seater pub-bench-and-table combo from a beer garden. (By which I mean, my cousins and I – 21, 23, 24, and 25 years of age at the time – were once caught carrying an entire 6-seater pub-bench-and-table combo by a passing police car, before being politely asked to return it to its previous home.)

And, at this point, it feels briefly worth pointing out why the British police are rightly regarded as the best in the world: they are unarmed. This means they're still forced to deal with hoodwinks, scallywags, rascals, rapscallions and ne'er-do-wells the old-fashioned way; with softer "weapons" like reason, civility, creativity, patience and humour. On this occasion, our spontaneous act of midnight naughtiness was reprimanded as if by an exasperated parent (while, in America, it's all guns, guns, guns, isn't it?) This lovely fact is also why you can push the British police a little bit further than in many other countries, relatively risk-free on the escalation front. Did you notice, for example, that their hats make their heads look quite like boobies? Well, why not tell them? They don't have guns!

The Future of Pubs

And now, British and non-British readers alike, I have something important I must ask of you. As I said before, I bloody love pubs, which is why I must remind you now that they are in trouble.

Despite facilitating almost the entirety of our culture, British pubs are increasingly under threat from a multitude of sources, from up and below, from inside and out: higher taxes on booze, competition from alternative forms of entertainment at home and the circling vultures of property development, waiting to swoop in and gut out historical old buildings just so Saudi princes, Russian oligarchs and Chinese industrialists can have a pool table in their en suite bathrooms or whatever.

27 pubs are closing every week, allegedly, and many British

people – like fish in water that cannot see the water – do not seem to notice the importance of what our culture might lose… perhaps until it is too late. This is why I believe that all pubs should be protected by UNESCO and the Heritage Fund and the WWF (the World Wildlife Fund *and* the World Wrestling Federation) and the IMF and #BlackLivesMatter and NATO and the Fellowship of the Ring and the Intellectual Dark Web and the European Union (even if the timing is a little awkward with that one.) I believe Teresa May should offer them tax breaks, Jeremy Corbyn should nationalise them, Vladimir Putin should move in anti-aircraft missiles and the United Nations should do whatever the United Nations does these days. It's time to get serious about saving British pubs. Hell, maybe we should declare a national emergency, temporarily scrap all of this "Recommended Daily Allowance" nonsense and introduce a Minimum Daily Alcohol *Requirement.*

What's more, it's a problem that risks triggering a bizarre feedback loop of horror. In response to dwindling profits, desperate landlords are employing rubbish gimmicks to try and attract punters back in – theme nights, quiz machines, televisions broadcasting 24-hour news channels, etc. – and yet this clearly cannot be a viable solution to anything because all of those things are shit. When I look around at a charming, timber-beamed building with a crackling fireplace and a homely character that represents a stabilising continuity between past and present, I rarely think, "hm, well, it's almost completely comfortable and wonderful in here, but... you know what it's missing? A bit of Vegas! If only there was a large, loud, constantly flashing, multi-coloured idiot-summoning gambling machine beside me, going *bing, bing, ding-ding-ding-bering, ding-ding-bing, bering-bering, BERING-BERING,DING-DING-DING-DING-DING."*

Worse than that, I recently had a very traumatic experience where I walked past my old pub to see a banner outside of it reading, I kid you not, 'Tarot and Palm-Reading Night.' I'll repeat that again: *TAROT AND BLOODY PALM-READING*

NIGHT.

To me, witnessing this sign attached to *MY* old pub was like being 8-years-old and witnessing the grisly murder of Father Christmas at the hands of the Easter Bunny. We – you and me, dear reader – cannot abandon British pubs to this cruel and twisted fate.

This is not what British pubs are supposed to be. You're just supposed to sit in them, quietly, for hours and hours and hours, drinking weak beer, going to the toilet to make room for more weak beer, and occasionally talking to some guy called Clever Ron as he intermittently gives you his latest 5-second-old opinion from a newspaper which is the kind of newspaper that looks like a newspaper, but isn't.

Everything else is sacrilege.

The 24 Hour News

For me, the worst development of all has been the most subtle and insidious one: the introduction of televisions in pubs playing 24-hour news channels. Nobody needs that much news. Probably nobody *needs* any news. Certainly, none of us need 24 hours of the bloody stuff going *Brexit, Brexit, Brexit, Trump, Trump, Trump,* all day long, and especially not in the one place we visit to get away from the place where our televisions are.

On top of this, televisions have crept into pubs at the exact wrong moment in history when the world has declared itself officially bananas; the era when a globalised, safer-than-ever world suddenly found itself with 3 billion extra camera phones in 3 billion extra pockets, thus ensuring that no preposterous event anywhere would ever be missed by anyone in a British pub ever again.

Let me illustrate why this is such an unmitigated disaster for pubs and pub-going generally. Recently, my old friend Neil and I were in our old local. Neil and I have been friends since we were teenage idiots, but we don't get to see each other as much nowadays, which I blame on him continuing to live where he has always lived, instead of moving to Berlin for no reason like a better friend might. Anyway, despite the fact we don't see each other that much (Neil's fault), I noticed he wasn't listening to me when we met where we always meet ("Pub?" "Pub.")

I looked behind me to see the usual bloody culprit: the 24-hour news, which was presently showing a fireworks factory explode, explode, explode, re-explode, then continue exploding. There I was, trying to tell Neil some exciting story about my incredible ex-pat life ("in Germany, they have three words for *'the'* – *can you even imagine!? It's crazy!*") while next to my head, in his eye-line, there might be a scene from the apocalypse assuming the apocalypse was funded by Disney and directed by Michael Bay.

What's more, if you sit in a pub for long enough on your own, looking around, quietly drinking beer (like you bloody well should), you'll notice similar echoes of this same phenomenon happening all the time around you: people half-listening to their friends, with one eye getting drawn towards the 24-hour news, which is probably showing camera-phone footage of a helicopter crash, a humanitarian crisis, a war zone, a riot or a popularly despised politician falling down a manhole. Our ancient blob-of-steak brains are not designed to ignore such attention-demanding things, of course, which is obviously why the news holds such sway over us in the first place. We can't *not* look at it... even when our friends and families are right next to us slowly dying (from beer and crisps.)

TELEVISIONS IN PUBS MUST GO.

Eventually I got into the habit of sneaking up to the television and turning it off. You know what happened? Nothing. No one even noticed. (Confidence is the invisibility cloak of the world, remember?) If anyone *did* notice, it rarely mattered. If you do anything with enough self-assurance, I find, any bystanders assume you're acting in some kind of official capacity. No one missed the TV. No one moaned. The spell was simply broken

173

and they returned to their friends like they'd woken from a dream. The last and only time I ever got caught turning off the TV by a landlord, I just told him I was turning it off and on again. That's a good cover story if you want to join me in my one-man crusade to save British pub-goers from themselves. Visit pubs. Unplug their fruit machines. Turn off their TVs. If caught, just say, "oh, don't worry! I'm just turning it off and on again. Technical problem. Me and my friend I haven't seen in 8 years could barely concentrate on this unfolding riot in a place we've never heard of. *These are not the droids you're looking for.*"

For a while, moaning about televisions in pubs was one of my go-to pub-rants. Indeed, I talked about it so much that one day Neil met me in the pub and brought with him a little gift that I could use to escalate my ideological war against modernity: a tiny key-ring with a single button labelled *ON* and *OFF*… a universal remote control. *Muahaha,* I laughed, maniacally.

Behind my head, the world was on fire – as bloody usual. (*Tsk,* my Brit-o-matic brain thought, *typical!*) But now was not the time for tragedy and chaos, death and destruction, and the banality of evil punctured with ad-breaks. No: now was the time for fun and insults, banter and bullshit, beer and weeing, so much weeing. I pointed my new secret weapon at the television and – with a quiet *click!* – killed the video stars. Problem solved. Now Neil and I could go back to the good, old-fashioned offline entertainment of my dry, dry chat.

"So, Neil, as I was saying, there's 'der,' 'die' and 'das,' but they're completely arbitrary. 'The' girl is neutral and 'the' banana is feminine. *A banana! FEMIMINE!* It's ridiculous!"

AT HOME WITH THE BRITISH

Chapter Six

At Home with the British

About two thirds of British people buy houses compared to only one third of their mainland counterparts. That's quite a staggering difference, I think. We Brits, it seems, have become uniquely invested in our houses and the very notion of home ownership as a central tenant of adult life.

On one hand, this is understandable. Houses are primarily, after all, a weather avoidance technology.

On the other hand, what can seem strange to our continental counterparts is the large amounts of personal debt we're willing to shoulder at a young age. You know that old expression, "an Englishman's home is his castle"? Well, they think it's a metaphor. As far as they can tell, an Englishman's Home is his Massive, Massive Mortgage.

To continental Europeans (who only rent properties for a place to change their underwear without getting arrested), our obsession with buying houses seems particularly bemusing, as though the main goal of our lives is trying to negotiate the longest, most expensive slave contract we can with the bricks we use to store our family members and tea bags in.

Oh, we think in return, *you silly, flippant Europeans – with your wine at lunch and your techno-pop and your wonky-eyed philosophers and your day-time naps and your sexy-sex – you just don't get it, do you?*

The Housing Crisis

If you want to understand the British home-owning fetish, you must first, of course, understand that a house is not a house but an *investment*. Britain is full, remember? Too many immigrants. Not only that, but there's not enough housing stock; the construction industry doesn't have the manpower to keep up with demand. Not enough immigrants. Anyway, there's no need to think about that or any other issue in a deep and nuanced way here, just trust me: it's all a bit of a nightmare. (Unless you already own a house in Britain already, of course, in which case you won't be able to hear the problem over the soothing sounds of your walls whispering *cha-ching.. cha-ching.. cha-ching..*)

The other benefits of home ownership are obvious: after just 25-40 years (merely half a human lifespan!) of paying to live in an Investment, hunkered down in the snuggly warmth of a life-smothering loan, you'll earn yourself the following exciting opportunities. You can either:

a.) keep living in it, "rent-free";

b.) not live in it, but rent it out to other British people in an attempt to get back some of the money you paid for it;

c.) not live in it, but sell it for more money than the smaller house you could have lived in all along;

d.) live in it until you get old and sick, using it to pay your nursing home bill (until all of the money is gone almost immediately); or

e.) die and give it to your (otherwise doomed) children.

Just think of all those exciting options you'll have in just 25-40 years! Life's too short, everybody! Let's buy!

The Renting Crisis

Britain doesn't have a very good rental market, so British people mostly buy houses. Because British people mostly buy houses, Britain doesn't have a very good rental market. Do you understand? There's no hope.

The strong rental controls and prevalence of unlimited contracts in places like Germany make renting more appealing, especially for couples like Linn and I who are shambolic human beings. And because our landlords are never getting us out (except with claw-marks along every door, floor and wall), we have turned our rented apartment into a *home*.

As for rented flats in London, my similarly aged friends mostly consider them to be temporary off-beige person-storage units. They keep water out. They keep secrets in. But a bulldozer driven by a Saudi prince, Russian oligarch or Chinese industrialist could arrive any moment, so it's not worth putting up any decoration with a nail or screw. *No, no.* Best to use blue-tack and keep a packed suitcase near the door, ready to flee to the next 6 month rental contract when the oil barons roll in to buy the neighbourhood for a place to store their ill-gotten gains.

No wonder, then, that renting in Britain is seen only as a temporary solution to the housing/weather-avoidance problem, and why many young people decide to skip this stage altogether by staying in their childhood bedrooms (while saving up for a deposit) until the age of 38.

That's because attempting to get on the Great British Housing

Ladder nowadays is like arriving three-quarters of the way through a giant, rigged game of musical chairs without music or chairs or hope. Indeed, one's only chance of actually "winning" the game, as far as I can tell, which is if your entire ancestral heritage perish simultaneously in a bus accident *and* you inherit some free houses (instead of their remaining debts.) Not ideal.

What's more likely, anyway, is that their houses will keep rising in value and they will only ever cash out for a round-the-world retirement cruise (whereupon you'll be swindled out of any remaining share of the inheritance by the quick work of a charismatic cult leader, lawyer, loan shark or Nigerian email scammer.)

While the generation in charge of most things in Britain – the baby-booming voter-block drifting ever upwards through the population pyramid, voting for themselves and hoovering up resources as they go – keep squatting atop the country's wealth, younger people have been left with a housing situation resembling the *Swedish Cake Dilemma*.

In Sweden, when someone brings cake into the office, it is considered rude to take the last slice. What you can do, though, is slice that last piece of cake in two and then take half of that. The next person, too, can do the same, slicing it again into quarters, and eighths, and so on, and so on, until what everyone is finally doing in their unending sugar-lust is not cutting cake but splitting atoms.

Due to overcrowding and mass immigration on our tiny little island home, a similar thing is arguably now happening to the heavily strained British housing stock. Soon, an Englishman's house will no longer be his castle, but 1/32nd of someone else's former castle, to be paid off for an entire life-time only to be further split, at the exact millisecond of death, into 32 "cosy maisonettes in Camden" (more continentally known as "cupboards.")

The Stressful Etiquette
of Being Hosted

If a British person ever invites you into their investment opportunity house, it's important to know the right etiquette once you have walked through their well-tended yet entirely pointless front garden, wiped your feet on their multiple consecutive doormats, and then crossed the metaphorical drawbridge into their mortgage castle.

Firstly, of course, you should compliment the decor of the house immediately, as if the porch, doormat collection or merest teasing glimpse of hallway is enough to ascertain that you are in the direct presence of interior design greatness. Secondly, you should ask if this is a "shoes-on" or "shoes-off" house. The answer to this question can be important in Britain. After all, there is a chance you might be entering that legend of all legends, the All-Carpeted British House, complete with carpeted bathroom, that holy grail of curious British comfort (which is only gross if you think about it, which, we've proved, you need not.)

If you are arriving to the house for a large family gathering or other similarly awkward British "party," this may require a more advanced test of your politeness stamina. There could be gathered in the hallway a group of people who have all got up from their seats and stood in a welcoming formation to greet you. I call this a "Hello Tunnel."

Take a deep breath – one last swig of calm before the politeness storm – because you are about to battle your way into the living room through a relentless bombardment of smiling niceties (*hello-mate!-you-alright?-hey-how's-it-going!-yeah-you're-looking-well-hi-yes-lovely-alright?-no-yeah-oh-good-thanks-no-yeah-how's-it-going-hello--darling-y'right-yeah?-not-bad-alright-mate!-hello-hi*) and charming physical awkwardness (*failed hand-shake, half-cuddle, high-five-meets-fist-bumps, one-kiss, two-kiss, three-kiss-collision confusion.*)

While we Brits can get through an entire Hello Tunnel in a single breath without collapsing, those new to the custom may require some additional stamina training in order to compete in the Politeness Olympics of a British social gathering. In particular, foreign guests should practice *asking for permission* before entering a British home.

"Should I take my shoes off?"

"Can I put this wine in the fridge?"

"Shall I sit down now?"

We Brits ask each other for permission to do *everything*. Of course, this is mostly just good manners and how one might expect any guest in any culture to behave. What seems to be uniquely special about Brit-on-Brit hospitality, however, is how much we *keep* asking each other for permission, even long after the answers have become completely bloody obvious. It doesn't matter if we've been in someone else's home for an hour or a month, we will always err on the side of cautiousness, checking in with our hosts constantly to avoid any risks of presumptuousness about we're allowed to do.

"Could I just nip to the loo?"

"I couldn't just grab a glass of tap water, could I?"

"Is it OK if I breathe this oxygen? Great, thanks."

The Death-or-Glory of BBQ Planning

We have invented many eccentric things over the years, from Marmite to Morris dancing, from penny-farthings to cucumber sandwiches, from week-long games of cricket to the heroic pointlessness of all the front gardens in all the land (acres upon acres of immaculately tended lawn-space upon which no one has had a picnic, built a shed or sun-bathed ever.) However, one invention stands out in its eccentricity amongst all others: the *All-Weather Barbecue*.

Since "changeable" is the primary adjective applied to British weather in the springsummerautumn disappointment period, we can't wait forever for that oft-fabled forecast of a reliably sunny weekend. At some point, we have no choice but to scribble those three fateful letters in our diaries: … *B… B… Q.* We gather up all of our courage, throw a dart at the calendar, send out invites, cross our fingers and hope for the best. We pray and we stockpile frozen burgers. After that, it is up to the gods.

As the Day of Reckoning approaches, non-stop small-talk weather-fretting reaches frenzied new heights of worry, speculation, intrigue and rumour-mongering. For days and weeks, we look with anxiety at those three ominous letters in our diaries, muttering incantations under our breath every time we look out at the garden (*"please, oh please don't let it rain!"*) As Zero Hour of B-Day approaches, we don't relax our guard or allow ourselves to slip into false hope even for a second. There might be bright blue, cloudless skies in all directions the hour before… but British weather can *never* be trusted.

You probably think I'm exaggerating. How can weather be *that* changeable? Well, I'm not. Picture the scene: it is the part of springsummerautumn that other countries call summer. My extended family are at my parents' house, in my parents' garden, where invites to a Caribbean-themed barbecue have long been sent. We are all wearing colourful hats, flower wreaths and tropical shirts (but they wouldn't stop the coming bruises…) The clouds gather. The sky rumbles. Ice cometh.

For evidence of the All-Weather Barbecue phenomena, Your Honour, I submit to you video of my stepdad Roger, the last man yet to retreat into the house, pioneering with the heroic undertaking of the legendary *Outdoor-Cooked Sausage* while under constant bombardment from hail-stones the size of mini Mozzarella balls. He nevertheless soldiered on with true blitz spirit, cowering from the *thud-thud-thud* of summer sky-ice underneath a giant Fosters pub umbrella (that was once included in the price of a drink, *ahem*) while my mum screamed at him from the kitchen, "just leave it, Rog! We'll put it in the oven! *Save yourself!*"

The Excesses of the Festive Season

As for our mid-winter celebrations, thankfully these are a lot easier to rely upon. In modern times, Christmas in Britain lasts roughly from the middle of November (at the latest) until the middle of January (at the earliest) and could be neatly summarised as the official season we let ourselves indulge in all of capitalism's and consumerism's most questionable excesses. Indeed, for many of us, the Christmas season doesn't even begin in our minds until we have seen "the Coca-Cola advert," whereby we are given official notice by our friendly neighbourhood Coca-Cola Corporation that *"HOLIDAYS ARE COMING."* (Still, at least this is an improvement on our old system of official notification, which was waiting for our grandmothers to first tut, "I can't believe it! It gets earlier and earlier every year! Christmas stuff in the shops already! It's only June!")

As for Christmas Day itself, this lands somewhere in the middle of the expansive Christmas season and can be readily identified from space by our entire population's unflinching devotion to wearing a crappy paper crown for one whole day. Then, for 24 hours, everything is done in the spirit of greed, excess and unlimited growth. We eat until it hurts. We drink until we nap. Fun and games are crammed into every available minute of the day until it's hard to find any spare moment in the schedule to enjoy them. Children are showered in sugary foods, unearned lavishment and as much unsustainably colourful Chinese plastic as can be crammed into an absurdly over-sized decorative sock. All of the adults, meanwhile, give each other a Fitbit (*faster! better! more productive!*) and Grandma Norris is topped up with sherry until she nods off and the rest of the day is spared her adorable brand of war-winning nostalgia, casual backwardsness and sweet-natured racism.

As for all of the nicest things about the British Christmas – thankfully inherited from more traditional, pre-consumerism Christmas times – we seem to have borrowed them from even more Christmassy places. London's flagship Christmas tree is from Norway, our Christmas markets are from Germany (the International Home of Christmas) and, much to the chagrin of some UKIP supporters, it has even been suggested that the whole thing was originally inspired by events involving a bearded guy from the Middle-East.

Anyway, as far as I can tell (from about 9 seconds of research), all British culture has contributed to the global Christmas party is the Christmas cracker, although even that was heavily inspired by the French bon-bon sweet, except with the uniquely British twist of adding a little "gift" of disposable plastic nonsense, destined for the throat of a sea turtle. (*Ho ho ho, Merry Christmas!*)

As the years go on, the humble tradition of present-giving is growing increasingly out of hand, thanks to the ludicrous arms race of trying to exceed the crazy new heights of expectation set by last year's gifts. "Christmas shopping" is no longer done in bouts, but in sprees; our affection for one another getting expressed through the medium of spending noticeably more cash than last year, *credit card debt be damned*. Indeed, I fear, the runaway culture of excessive present-giving might one day become so pervasive that Boxing Day becomes a 24-hour period spent *boxing* up duplicate gifts so they can be pawned (or a day of boxing. Literal boxing. All of us just hitting each other for more and more of each other's stuff.)

Anyway, if the EU really wants to hit the UK where it hurts during the Brexit negotiations (and help those poor sea turtles, full to bursting with useless mini-combs, paperclip puzzle things and tiny screwdrivers), they could consider trade sanctions upon novelty goods from mid-November until mid-January when all of the forced festive momentum fizzles out, decorations are finally removed, the last morsel of turkey ends its journey in a sad little sandwich and the holiday is turned off like a big switch labelled "Christmas." (Until next June.)

The Crippling Inability to Inconvenience

When I first moved to Berlin, I stayed for the first week with a German CouchSurfer called Marie (who I had previously met in Dublin) and her Argentinian husband Emie (who I was yet to meet) in a "one-and-a-half room flat."

Now, I'd never heard the term "one-and-a-half room flat" when Marie had first sent her invitation by SMS. Perhaps you haven't either. (To be entirely honest with you, I didn't even know rooms could come in halves, only multiples. Having grown up in the *Swedish Cake Dilemma* housing culture, I thought dividing one room made it into two rooms and doubled the price.) Anyway, to cut to the chase, there was a kind of storage area next to Marie's bedroom, behind a thin pseudo-wall and a curtain, and in this narrow, windowless compartment was a cleverly constructed high-bed so that couchsurfing guests could climb a ladder, crawl from the bottom of the bed to the top and sleep – quite comfortably – in the same "half-room" as clothes, boxes of photos and a vacuum cleaner.

So, that's where I was, sleeping, up there and back there in the pitch-black half-room high-bed, when I awoke suddenly in the middle of the night, and noticed something slightly awkward about my situation. I couldn't move.

When I tried to move, a sharp, short, stabbing pain shot through my back and legs. If I was completely, totally still, the pain disappeared. But when I tried to adjust my position, I quickly realised it was almost impossible. (And at this point, it's probably good to add that I was naked. Like, full-on, no pyjamas, no pants, European naked.)

As the magnitude of my "slightly awkward" situation (near total paralysis) began to set in, I struggled to find my clothes at the bottom of the bed with my toes in the darkness, to see if there was any way to hook them upwards towards my arms. *Ow, ah, ow, ow, ow, ah...* shit. There wasn't. That's because they weren't at the bottom of the bed; they were at the bottom of the ladder. Shit.

I mustered up my courage and set forth timidly on the great adventure of trying to fetch them. I bum-shuffled and elbow-squirmed and hip-wriggled my body slowly down the bed, as blind and limp and graceless as a sad worm on a moonless night, wincing constantly from short, stabs of pain, like another worm getting a tattoo from a third worm who isn't qualified to do tattoos. It took, probably, 20 minutes. I wiggled and winced and wiggled, then waited and wiggled and winced, inch by painful inch in a ladder-wards direction, then step by painful step down the ladder until eventually I got to its bottom, whereupon I realised I couldn't bend down to pick my clothes up. The stabs of pain were now so bad after my wormventure that I literally couldn't bend, squat, lunge or shuffle my further in any direction. I tried to move my toes, in an effort to begin the provisional groundwork of the taking-a-step procedure, but they wouldn't peel themselves from the floor without a flash of pain shooting up my back to stop me.

Checkmate. I was stuck.

In the understated terms of my island-folk, it was at this point I realised that *slight awkwardness* had developed into a full-blown *little bit of a problem.* I needed help.

However, I couldn't entirely figure out just how much of a traditional "emergency" this really was: if I didn't move, everything was kind of, sort of, almost fine, I suppose. Given the totality of the circumstances (quick recap: blind, motionless, silent CouchSurfer standing naked in storage at 4am with a sudden mysterious case of harmless total paralysis), I didn't know how to *start* asking for that help.

I couldn't think of anything to shout out through the pseudo-wall quasi-door Curtain of Awkwardness that seemed appropriate. Every option that crossed my mind seemed either too weird, confusing or creepy. I also couldn't think of anything to say (shout? whisper?) that suitably explained the whole of the situation without seeming overly-alarming (yet still seeming alarming enough.) What expertly chosen string of words would prove itself reliably coherent to a person who was *just* having a dream yet who was now suddenly awake, hearing a disembodied Englishman behind a bit of fabric ask for assistance with an unspecified problem at 4am?

I just needed to say something, I realised. *Preferably something short and succinct and not-insane that nevertheless covers all the key points.* At a minimum, I reasoned, this would have to include: *please wake up... don't panic!... it's just me, Paul, your stranger from the internet... I have a problem... I'm sorry to wake you... it's about 4 o'clock I guess... I don't know, I can't see... I'm behind the quasi-wall fabric-gate of room-dividing pretence... everything's OK, yeah, I just can't move... can you call someone? ... I just might be a bit paralysed, that's all... no, no, I don't want to cause a fuss... please don't come in... I can't move... I don't know why... I need help... everything is blackness... not yet... I'm naked... please can Emie put pants on me?... sorry...*

It was a tall order, I noticed, and I wasn't totally sure how I should begin. It all seemed terrible and cringe-worthy, and all of the options swirled around my head, chased around by the unhelpfully sarcastic inner narrator of my Brit-o-matic mind.

"Hello."

No way, that's crazy, I thought. *They're asleep. You can't say, "hello."*

"Hi!"

Nope, too cheery. You are paralysed, you fool.

"Hello?"

A question? Really? A riddle? You're not lost in a magic cave.

"Sorry."

No, too weird.

"I'm stuck."

Bonkers.
"Are you awake?"
Seriously? You're going to question them awake?
"Help!"
You can't say "help!" you lunatic.
"Guys?"
Oh yeah, great idea. "Guys." Jesus. What are you – American?
"I'm hurt!"
Ugh. Way too much.
"Um."
Um, not enough.
"Marie, I've had an accident."
Bloody hell. "An accident"? "AN ACCIDENT"? You can't say "an accident"... have you lost your bloody mind?

Round and round my mind went, lost in crazed self-talk, offering up ideas and suggestions to itself, only to be sarcastically shot down again by itself. *NOTHING* seemed appropriate. There was just too much to explain, yet too few words to explain it. I mean, what would *you* have done in my situation? Begin telling a really weird story to people who aren't yet conscious and hope they come to and catch up? Get their attention first? Then what? Invite them ominously into your "room" (their cupboard) to talk? Wait nakedly in the silent, shadowy abyss of shelving for them to arrive, then blindly hope they don't freak out and throw open the curtain holding a baseball bat? *HOW THE HELL DO YOU START?*

I couldn't think of anything at the time and – in stark contrast to the ever-lasting omni-trauma of *The Incident* where hindsight later revealed *FUCKING ANYTHING* to be the optimal solution – I still can't think of anything now.

So, dear reader, this is what I actually did instead. Are you ready? I stood there. I just stood there. Unmoving, wide awake, at the bottom of a ladder, eyes open, with the hoover, in the naked man quiet of an insincere "room," *FOR HOURS.* Just standing. Upright. Half a room. Eyes wide open in the pitch black darkness (imagine an LSD-addled badger getting caught by a night-vision camera and you get some insight into how I probably looked in that moment.) I was bored out of my mind, cold, with one arm resting on the ladder and a wall about 10 centimetres from my face, looking like a temporarily paralysed human signpost.

It was fully depressing, like Morrissey had taken over as the chief thematic writer of my life. It was, quite literally, a night of darkness, silence, loneliness and pain. I was bored and sad and increasingly annoyed with my own bloody Britishness, knowing already that the first thing Marie and Emie would inevitably say to me was, "why the hell did you *wait* to wake us up?"

Yet, in my head, I wasn't *waiting all night* for them to wake up. That would be preposterous. I was *deciding how to wake them up*, which just happened to take *all night*. A far more sensible explanation. I was, I knew, very busy thinking, planning and pro-actively solving the internal conundrum of what word or phrase I could say, shout or ominously whisper through the curtain that my brain would consent to releasing from my mouth. And then, finally, after night-time had fully ended, they both stirred. '*OH THANK YOU, GOD!*', I thought, at last. They kissed each other good morning. And then they kept kissing each other good morning. *And then they kept kissing each other good morning. AND OH F*** YOU, GOD.*

And just like that, it was already too late.

Darkness, sadness and pain were about to do an encore, except now with an increasingly embarrassing soundtrack. On top of that, I seemingly now had a new problem too: not only would I have to explain all of the same stuff to them as I would have had to five minutes ago; now I would have to explain further why it was that I stood up for half the night in a self-imposed prison of blackness looking like a sad, shit tree *and then even longer whilst they were having European sex one meter away from me.* (Oh… and did I mention I was naked? OK, great. Just checking.)

Luckily, the universe threw me a bone at this point (no pun

intended, you cheeky reader) because their alarm clock went off with the glorious tinkling sounds of interruption. As soon as I heard it happen, I straightened up (*ow*) and realised this was my last chance: *it's now or never!*

"Marie...?" I said, in my out-loud, useful, external world voice.

"Paul...?" she replied, confused and cautiously, "... is everything... are you... OK?"

"Oh yes," I said, "but, um, I have a little bit of a problem."

"... ok.. do you... want to tell us?"

Yes, please. I then proceeded to explain what had happened in one giant run-on sentence that included, I hope, some of the more relevant data-points. When I finally finished talking, there was a good long pause and then they both started laughing hysterically. (What can I say? I'm gifted.) After they asked me the inevitable ("why the hell did you *wait* to wake us up?"), they called a house doctor, put me into a dressing gown (thanks, Emie) and then retold my story in German to an increasingly delighted medical professional, who laughed along with them at my utter ridiculousness while she prepared to stick a needle into me, giggling with unrestrained delight the entire time with her face one inch from my now exposed arse. Finally, she was able to pull herself together enough to give me a jab at the site of the pain and the problem was gone within the hour.

And that was that; the morning I learned three valuable lessons. Firstly, that British people, even at home, may need guardianship and constant enquiries about whether they are alright (we might not tell you until it's too late); secondly, that British politeness can be as debilitating a condition as temporary full-body paralysis; and, finally, that morphine is really fucking excellent.

The Disappointment of Mornings

After you've had a Great British night's sleep (preferably in a comfy bed, not a self-imposed prison of deep black sadness), hopefully you'll wake up fresh and rejuvenated to the twinkling morning sounds of birds singing and/or bin-men spitting.

Waking up in the UK, however, optimism, delight or gratitude would be inappropriate ways to greet the new day. We are not entirely fond of mornings in Britain, of course, for the obvious reason that mornings are how awkward, disappointing British days always begin. *Oh here we go again*, we grumble silently to ourselves as we blink in the first worrying wink of Nigel Farage on morning TV, *it's all down hill from here, I guess…*

Luckily, starting the day with a slightly gloomy outlook (which, admittedly, should recede gently with every passing cup of tea) can also bring with it a silver lining, upon which we can base all of our remaining hopes.

As Frank Sinatra once said, allegedly, "I feel sorry for people who don't drink. When they wake up in the morning, that's as good as they're going to feel all day." Well, indeed: this is exactly the kind of lovely sounding, self-deluding bullshit that we Brits are happy to throw our weight behind. However, since it's impractical to wake up with a hangover *every* day of the week, our culture has invented similarly rude awakenings as a fail-safe, such as the weather report, the fried breakfast and the traffic jam. It's all part of our rationally pessimistic philosophy for framing the upcoming day. After all, things can only get better if you start the day wrong.

Checking the weather in Britain is one of the quickest routes to reliable disappointment. Simply walk past all of your windows to your television, turn it on and wait for a qualified, polite person to reveal the varying forms, intensities and durations of upcoming mild which are about to descend in and disappoint you from all directions. At this point, you can already begin to make a few brief mental notes for your upcoming day of possible small-talk ("it seems like only six months ago, the weather was totally different!") and then you're free to plan the necessary, practical arrangements for the tiny bit of outside-ness you may experience between your home and office. Regardless of how much you can minimise your exposure to the elements, it's best to prepare for all possible conditions, just in case. Bring your umbrella, sunglasses, coat, flip-flops, sun-cream, emergency tent and scuba gear, and you should be equipped for the average British afternoon.

Next up is breakfast, where it would be hard to find a better way to start the day wrong (nutritionally speaking) than with that most heroic of breakfasts, *The Full English*, a morning meal rightly regarded across the planet with equal parts admiration, horror and disbelief.

It's not only that the fry-up is greasy and stodgy, of course, but that is greasy and stodgy and *early*. (It's not exactly the kind of light breakfast that begs to precede a yoga session or a light jog on the beach, is it? No.) Indeed, in a modest breakfast world of yoghurt and fruit and muesli, few other cultures have summoned the morning courage required to drag one vegetable and half a farm-yard through a lake of hot vegetable oil, and then organise the result into a crude, glistening pile.

To remind any non-Brits reading what we Brits sometimes ask our internal organs to process shortly after emerging from the dream state, let's quickly recap the terrifying majesty of the Full English breakfast: eggs (fried), bacon (fried), sausages (fried), black pudding (fried), hash browns (fried), tomatoes (fried), mushrooms (fried), baked beans (microwaved and/or fried) and perhaps even some chips (fried) to round it off. Only then, finally, can we throw some bread into this gaping nutritional void: toasted white bread with butter on, for example, or fried bread (which is bread... but fried.) As for sauces, if that seems at all necessarily, these traditionally come in two exciting varieties, with only the ominous-sounding local descriptors of "red" and "brown" to tell them apart. "Red sauce" is your basic, no-thrills tomato ketchup affair. Nothing to write home about. As for "brown sauce"? Well, no one knows what "brown sauce" is, not even the people who make it.

The Full English breakfast is, of course, delicious (as you would expect any meal to be that simultaneously shaved a year off your life expectancy), but, believe it or not, the utter madness of it all doesn't even have to end there. For if you want to disgrace yourself a little further before you've even had a chance to brush your teeth, you could always waddle over England's northernmost border to Scotland once more, where it's possible to add one more final layer of breakfast insult to breakfast injury: for the 'Full *Scottish* Breakfast' also contains haggis, which is everything the English won't eat boiled in a sock.

BRITS
ABROAD

AFTER SUN!

Chapter Seven

Brits Abroad

Generally speaking, we Brits have a pretty underwhelming reputation abroad, perhaps because the grisly notoriety of our namesake breakfast precedes us, or perhaps because there are still many of us whose idea of a perfect holiday is going to a place that is exactly like Britain, except with sun. (Or cheaper beer, a Red Light District and night-life that continues past 11.31pm.)

And then, when we get there? Well, we're not exactly famous for our ability to *blend in seamlessly*, bless us. We are, however, famous (or, indeed, infamous) for our amusingly alcohol-inspired exploits, our tendency to travel in large, unruly packs, our aversion to local tipping etiquette/dogma, our difficulties with speaking a second language well (or at all), and our inability to resist novelty-fuelled transport options such as the Beer Bike – scourge of the modern metropolis. Add to that the simmering possibility that one person in our large travelling group might do something wholly inappropriate by accident – perhaps leaping into a war memorial fountain while dressed as a sexy lifeguard, for example – and it's no wonder we Brits regularly top opinion polls for the world's worst tourists.

As someone who has spent a lot of time outside of the UK

– both as an "ex-pat" (a.k.a. immigrant) and a *Brits Abroad Pack Member* of various stag-dos (my eternal apologies to Amsterdam, Bratislava and Ibiza Town) – I've always found something both cringe-worthy and hilarious about the way holiday destinations seem to get divorced in our minds from the normal rules of everyday life: like they're not real places where real people really live, but interchangeable backdrops for our banter-wagons to roll through; country-sized Disneyland play-parks without limits, borders or closing times that we assume much stop existing once our holidays are over.

Before a Great British holiday begins, the chosen destination exists only as an idea; a myth; a dream. We talk about the upcoming trip in reverential times, like we're visiting Narnia. (*3 more sleeps! 2 more sleeps! 1 more sleep!*) When we finally board the plane, we cannot help but be excited: we're leaving the island! We're crossing the sea! We're visiting the *rest of the world!* A flight is no mere air-bridge from our home islands to any of the other spots on the same globe where all of our footballers come from… it's a magic portal to a parallel universe.

Yep: watch out, world. The bloody British are coming.

The Export of Stag and Hen Parties

The myth-like nature of holiday destinations is particularly true for British-launched stag and hen parties, where the goals of the trip are best imagined through the eyes of the best man or chief bridesmaid.

They do not need art and architecture, culture or cuisine. No: they need robust infrastructure a ten minute walk from the hostel that can absorb an almost uninterrupted chain of ridiculous behaviour and good-natured carnage without the host country declaring a national emergency.

Of course, this can sometimes cause a bit of a culture clash, but that's hardly our fault, is it? As far as we're concerned, it is merely an unfortunate coincidence that many of these places *also* happen to be actual real places where actual real people live and do actual real things like work and commute and get annoyed at groups of kinky British chav angels throwing a giant inflatable penis into the pathway of a tram. What can we do about that? If you can't take a joke, maybe you shouldn't have an airport.

Indeed, if the occasional bit of friction arises between us Brits Abroad and our native hosts, it tends to come from this entirely understandable mismatch of intentions. When groups of 16 British men/man-boys (wearing identical T-Shirts with the slogan "Cock-Block Colin's Stag!!!") get hungry abroad, they do not imagine themselves to be crash-landing in the same kinds of restaurant where local couples – weeping child between them – are negotiating their divorce. Nor, when we gumption-filled Brits are drawn like moths to the guaranteed banter-flame of a hired Beer Bike, do we imagine our pedal-powered fun-mobiles to be sharing the same road network that local people are using to drive pregnant women having babies to hospitals.

HOOOOOOOOONK, they notify our beer bike of their impending emergency, yet in an easily misinterpreted gesture of seemingly high-spirited noisiness.

"*WAAAHAAAAAY!*," we shout back cheerily, with a thumbs up and a friendly wave, "that car loves it! She was a good egg, that woman. I love this place, wherever it is. Everyone's so friendly!"

Yep: the Great British holiday destination exists only temporarily, like a detail-rich video game level for us to navigate without consequences until we go home. With that in mind, we hop from bar to restaurant to bar to club to bar to hostel to bar, generally causing as much casual mayhem, commuter panic and cultural confusion as possible (while injecting just enough money into the local economy that the UK passport hasn't yet been banned as a global safety precaution.)

Finally, after the stag or hen party is finished, the foreign place-as-myth collapses once more. Finally, the time spent there is written into the annals of friendship lore, whereupon great fables of stag heroes and hen legends will live on in the pub-tales of infamy, like that mythical time that Mud Flaps (Tom), Chunder (Adam) and Dr Mong (Dave) got stuck in a wheely bin outside the Bratislavan Houses of Parliament and had to be rescued by the fire service, or that hallowed time of yonder when Sambuca (Samantha), Chops (Charlotte) and Have-a-Banana (Hannah) miscalculated escalator etiquette at 1pm in Prague's central station and everyone got temporarily held on terrorism charges. *Ah, legendary!*

The Difficulties
of Inter-British Diversity

Because we Brits sometimes behave on holiday as though our destinations will stop existing the moment that we leave them again, we're not always super attuned to the touristic reputation we might also be leaving behind us in our wake. This is not necessarily a problem for us personally, of course, but might well be a problem for future Brits who come along after us and inherit our banter-fuelled legacy, for good or ill.

Sometimes when travelling, for example, I can feel this reputation-by-proxy preceding me. Sometimes it compels me to double-down on being as humble, respectful and polite as possible, in order to try and re-balance some of the more negative stereotypes associated with my countrymen. Other times, the winds of expectation blow in the other direction, and I feel my newfound foreign friends will be disappointed in me if I'm *not* drunk, disgraced and dancing naked on a church scaffold within 45 minutes of landing. (In which case, of course, I feel it is my patriotic duty to oblige.)

What's more, these expectations, preconceptions and prejudices may only be getting more unwieldy for us to manage as flights become cheaper than the average British bus or train ticket. In earlier times, it was only a certain kind of posh, slightly otherworldly British traveller that would traverse the European mainland, perhaps by rail while wearing a hat, in search of its scenery, cuisine and culture. Now, though, thanks to Ryanair and EasyJet, every corner of Europe now faces the strange new threat of us all being able to reach them for a tenner. There's no hiding anymore. It doesn't matter if your country emerged from the iron curtain five minutes ago, we've got to have our stag and hen parties somewhere.

Sure, there was time when places like Amsterdam, Barcelona and Hamburg bore the brunt of the onslaught of Britain's least charming export. But they at least had the necessary infrastructure in place to deal with us – kebab shops, Irish pubs and go-karting – to safely absorb menacingly large group of Brits shouting "FUZZY DUCK" over and over again in a quiet plaza at 4am.

Now, however, almost nowhere is safe from having a red, white and blue target painted on it. Stags and hens – like the brave pioneers of old – have discovered all of the quieter nooks and crannies of the Continent, and are bringing their disorientating regional accents along with them. As RiotOnAir and QueasyJet join the dots on the map, many Europeans are getting their very first taste of Brummies (Birmingham), Scousers (Liverpool), Geordies (Newcastle), Mancunians (Manchester) and Neanderthals (Glasgow)[1] – British folks that sound so unlike the voices on English-learning audio-tapes that locals meeting them might feel like a portal to Middle-Earth has suddenly opened up in their capitals.

Luckily, as terrible British tourists go, the very worst offenders amongst us are still relatively easy for native Europeans to spot from afar, as they tend to leave our Country of Origin pre-packaged in an internationally recognised uniform of nuisance-making: Union Jack shorts, England Football shirts and the arm of a semi-unconscious friend used as a scarf. When combined with a sunburn, a seemingly bottomless beer superglued to one hand from 10am onwards and maybe a bum-bag for your passport (can't trust those hotel cleaners!), this get-up should be heeded like those labels you get on tobacco products. *WARNING: BRIT ABROAD.*

No wonder some of our worst tourists are feared across the Continent as they tumble out of budget airlines like recently released inmates on a jail-break, immediately befriending other Brits in the holiday, then loudly blundering around the place with all the subtlety of people who still think they own it. Oh yes, the British Empire may be gone, but it is not yet fully forgotten...

The "World Language"

For a mix of reasons relating to Hollywood, The Beatles, Microsoft, Netflix, The Very Hungry Caterpillar and the rampant, sea-faring expansion of the British Empire to almost everywhere that didn't ask for it, the English language has

---

[1] Sorry

become the *bona fide* "world language." *Hurrah for us!* This means two main things:

1.) Very little "foreign" cinema, TV, music or literature penetrates our comfortably insular cultural bubble (especially because we're all also already drowning in the abundant cultural output of the USA); and;

2.) Today we Brits can go to almost every major city in the world, bump into the beautiful, young people we find floating around there and apologetically use our own native tongue to explain that we are lost, cold, confused, hungry, thirsty or stupid. Thanks to everyone else doing exactly all of the work of understanding us, we'll probably survive to go on holiday again. The world has become relatively safety-proofed for us to move around in.

While Slovenians learn English to talk to Spaniards in Sweden and Slovakians learn English to talk to Serbs in Switzerland, we just turn up on holiday, mumbling. In this sense, native English-speakers *have* won a kind of language lottery without even having to buy a ticket. While the world's peoples all work hard to understand each other, *we* mostly get to freeload on *their* efforts. The planet is, in some small way, already a Global Britain.

Typically, there are three attitudes that we can employ to deal with this colossal windfall of pure good luck:

1.) A kind of undeserved, self-entitled smugness;

2.) A kind of unearned, self-inflicted shame; or,

3.) A kind of hard-won, self-defeating attempt to actually learn another language.

Having thought about it, it's not immediately obvious to me which one of these approaches makes least sense. The first option, as we have discussed, almost always sounds like this: "well, there's no point learning another language, is there? Everyone else speaks English anyway, and they love to practice, don't they? So, actually, we're just helping them really."

These oh-so-charitable Brits float through the world imagining themselves akin to volunteer aid workers, treating encounters with the locals as if they've given the gift of English-practice each time they ask someone where they can rent a Beer Bike from.

As for the second attitude, this is a quintessentially British combination of shame, self-deprecation and quiet, sad, purposeless grumbling, all rolled into one distinct sentiment. It sounds something more like this, of course: "oh, it is bad, isn't it, really? Everyone abroad speaks such good English, don't they? We can't speak bloody anything, can we? I had French for 9 years of school and all I remember is the word for pencil case. We're useless. *USELESS.* Shame on us."

While this attitude is infinitely more shame-filled than option one, it also has roughly the same result. We suffer through the embarrassment of not knowing another language, yet we also know there's no point really trying to do anything about it. That's because, underneath the self-flagellation, we're still secretly thinking, "well, there's no point learning another language, is there? Everyone else speaks English anyway, and they love to practice, don't they? So, actually, we're just helping them really."

And finally, there is option three: that admirably brave, well-intentioned and endearingly hopeless attempt to actually learn another language at the last minute. Some of us embarrassment-laden British tourists do, of course, *try our damnedest* to learn a little bit of the local language of the place we're visiting as a token gesture of goodwill. And, by god, how adorably we fail.

Still, our hearts are in the right place, so let's look at option three in a little more detail…

The Paul Hawkins Three-Stage Brit Abroad Language-Speaking Plan

(a.k.a. How to Blend In, Obviously)

STAGE ONE:
Say Nothing

Stage One is quite easy to achieve: it involves either speaking only English, except slightly louder, *or* speaking only English except occasionally punctuated with a few innocent, well-meaning phrases like "Gracias, Señor" or "Gutentag, Frauline" to the waiters and waitresses (to assure them that we have correctly identified their genders, perhaps), then the noise "um" and then everything else in English, with charades.

STAGE TWO:
Say Anything

Stage Two is more advanced than speaking English loudly while over-gesticulating. It is probably best summarised as a cobbled-together attempt at making some kind of foreign sense using whatever miscellaneous scraps of *foreign language* we have readily available in the *abroad* section of our brains (regardless of the language of origin), plus lots of English words mixed in, except we have lightly repackaged those English words with foreign-sounding articles first ("Can we have *le menu*, please? *Le menu*? And *le winelist*? Gracias.")

Normally, what happens in Stage Two is a fairly well-intentioned brain-spasm, where our eagerness to show the locals we're making an effort to communicate quickly overtakes our ability to do so. A particularly successful example of a

Stage Two sentence, therefore, always sounds like the love-child of a phrasebook and a neurological disorder; something like: "HOLA, MADAME, WO IST... er... *the toilet?*"

You know: definitely wrong BUT NICE AND LOUD.

STAGE THREE:
Say Something

Finally, there's Stage Three: if willpower, devotion and last-minute use of a language-learning app on the plane are applied, we may just be able to muster up the locally translated equivalent of this glorious effort: "Hello. I'm sorry. I don't speak *[Your Language]*. Sorry. Do you speak English, please? I'm very sorry."

We cultural aficionados who reach this esteemed level of foreign language acquisition are normally so enormously proud of ourselves that we will then spend the rest of our trip using "please," "sorry" and "thank you" interchangeably, at all times and in all contexts, like a talking toy with a broken pull-string that gives the same response no matter what happens.

Finally, having asked someone abroad in their local tongue if they speak English (and after they've replied with a modest, humble, total under-exaggeration like, "yes, a little bit"), we will then proceed to talk at them with the same speed and complexity of English we would use if we had just encountered them on holiday in our country. Luckily, in spite of our best efforts to challenge them, they'll probably pick up the slack with their impeccable English (they love to practice, don't they?) and we can feel ashamed of ourselves while we follow their perfect directions to the nearest beer bike.

The Fear of Foreign Menus

Given this state of affairs, it's clear why the whole world has rolled over and accepted English as the 'world language,' drawing up all of its cafe, bar and restaurant menus accordingly. Don't have pre-translated English menus somewhere out the back (with an emergency bag of frozen chips)? You're only punishing yourselves.

On top of being able to slightly inflate the prices (to include the tip we probably won't leave at the end), cafe and restaurant owners should also consider simplifying their choices preemptively in advance. This is because we Brits secretly see any complex restaurant menu as a sign of weakness. To us, menus are not mere lists of options, but the starting point of a negotiation…

"Oh, bonjour, señorita," we say to the unsuspecting waitress (*a woman!*), "I'm ready to order, ja. Could I, um, could I possibly get the beef goulash, potato dumplings and red cabbage, please? Dankeschon. Oh, but, uh, can I maybe get some sort of, like, coleslaw maybe… instead of the red cabbage? Is that possible? Sorry, por favor, I hope I'm not being a total pain. Oh, and – sorry – instead of the dumplings, could I possibly just get some chips? Chips? You know? CHIPS? *CHIPS?* That alright, yeah? Oh, grazie. That's all, then, thanks. Oh, except instead of the goulash, with the beef… can I have the beef, but in a lasagne? Lovely-jubbly. Mercy bo-coup."

Ah, perfect.

This style of ordering food abroad is pretty special, I think. It's like the chef, whose life's work is cooking, has only designed the menu so far like a scribbling toddler who couldn't keep within the lines. Indeed, I would recommend to any restaurant-owners reading this not to waste your time giving us menus. You might as well just give us a list of ingredients you have in stock and let the haggling begin.

What's more, we do not only haggle with our waiters and waitresses; we must also haggle with each other (and ourselves.) Knowing what we would want to eat is one thing (if only the world were so simple), but first our Brit-o-matic brains must run a few parallel calculations to make sure our choice would be socially acceptable. Outwardly, we might all be saying diversionary things to each other like, "oh, it all looks good, doesn't it?" But inside? We're furiously crunching those numbers.

Will my meal take too long to cook? Will I look greedy, tight-fisted or out-of-touch with modern culinary etiquette? Will I pay too much and not eat enough? Will I eat too much and not pay enough? Can I ask what meat is in schnitzel, or is it totally obvious and I'll end up going home with the nick-name 'Schnitzel-Mystery Mark'? Oh bloody hell, I better wait for other people to start ordering first, just in case. Maybe if I keep saying 'oh, it all looks good, doesn't it,' I'll buy myself some extra menu time…

The Patience of Waiters

The first time my family came to visit me in Berlin – ten of them, all at once, as a surprise trip for my mother's birthday – Linn and I tried to take them to the sorts of "authentic" places where local people eat. One of our favourite little restaurants, for example, is an Italian place in our neighbourhood which prides itself on being good, reliable and simple: they just do pizza and pasta, red wine, white wine and beer; the waiters just speak Italian back to you like they can't be arsed with running a restaurant; and the "hospitality" element of the experience consists of items being slammed in front of you by fast-moving, sweaty people swearing at each other. It's "authentic."

As soon as my Brits Abroad family pack bundled onto the restaurant's biggest table, however, Linn and I realised the colossal magnitude of our mistake: there were *(of course)* no English menus(!)

Brits Abroad Language Panic set in immediately, with my

family looking desperately from side to side for help whence no help would come. Eventually, Linn and I were forced to stand up and translate the entirety of the massive menu out-loud, broadcasting long lists of ingredients to half the restaurant while my family (who are a predominantly naughty bunch) interrupted with constant jokes, funny insults and sarcastic questions. This was in equal parts amusing and stressful, since their total immersion in holiday bantertainment mode meant we had to repeat the menu *twice*, all the while dragging the "authenticness" of our fellow diners' experience down a plughole of noisy British holiday touristic chaos. On and on, it went, the ordeal, while my face turned red from the warm glow of unwanted attention. "Ham, onions, horse meat…" *Horse meat?* "Yes, horse meat. Mozzarella, tomatoes, basil…" *Horse?* "Yeah, horse. Peppers, mushrooms, tuna…" *But, horse?* "Yeah, I know, but they eat horse, don't they. It's like a pretty cow for them or something. Artichoke, egg…"

Eventually, Linn and I lost all semblance of direction or control, and could do nothing more than watch on in helpless, paralysed terror as my family started engaging directly with the waiters. Confusion reigned. Cultures collided. We couldn't stop it.

At one point, I saw Linn on the other side of the table, looking like a medic in a battlefield, desperately trying to explain to my uncle for the second time that, "they only have red wine, white wine and beer." My uncle nodded, made a hopeful-sounding 'um-hm' noise, then four seconds later tried to order a vodka and diet coke.

"No, scusi," the waiter replied, Italian-ly.

"Aha, OK, no vodka-diet coke?" said my uncle, nodding at the waiter, looking back down at the little book of squiggles once more, perhaps forgetting he couldn't read it. Undeterred, he tried again: "what about a vodka… *normal coke?*"

On the other side of the table, probably looking more like a firefighter in a nuclear war, I was desperately trying to explain to my step-dad again that "they only have traditional Italian pizzas." At which point, with a horrifying innocence, he tried to order a Hawaiian. The waiter said something back in Italian (which I can only assume was, "we only have Italian pizza. Hawaiian is not a kind of Italian pizza. It's from Hawaii.") Nodding in feigned comprehension to the Italian man, my step-dad then asked him if the chef wouldn't mind just adding some pineapple to one of the Italian pizzas – like the ham one, for example?

My toes curled towards my ankles in retreat, as the waiters crowded around our table like perplexed mechanics around a smoking engine. While my family kept asking them unflinchingly earnest questions in English ("like meat… *from a horse?*"), Linn and I ran around, trying to intervene, help or at least contain some of the faffiness we had unleashed upon the restaurant and its waiters. By the time everyone had finally ordered, we were sweatier than they were.

The Tricky Business
of Splitting the Bill

There's only two systems of bill-payment method available to British people in restaurants, at home or abroad. Either one person in the group makes a martyr of himself and pays for everyone's everything, saying something along the lines of, "nah, don't worry, guys, I'll get this (because I'm very impressive.)" *Or* everyone at the table decides to split the bill equally, no matter the price of what each individual had to eat or drink. That sounds more like this: "right, so, that'll be £108 each – yes, of course that includes you, Hungry Tom, you salad-munching, glass-of-water, vegan bloody tight-arse. You're not getting out of paying your fair share again just because you live in a bin."

The elusive "third option," European readers might notice, is the one they're probably most familiar with from their more sensible restaurant-going cultures: eating what you want, drinking what you want, then paying for what you ate and drank… an extraordinarily simple, fair and surprisingly air-tight system of splitting a bill, which the British nevertheless reject, dismissively, as "going Dutch."

According to one theory I've researched (for 30 seconds), the origin of the phrase "going Dutch," a.k.a. *being stingy*, dates all the way back to 17th-century hostilities in the period of the Anglo-Dutch Wars. The phrase entered into common parlance in England, apparently, as a way to badmouth the bill-splitting Dutch and, by extension, make ourselves feel morally superior to them. It is, in other words, a relic of patriotic, oldy-worldy war propaganda: the British equivalent of Americans renaming French fries, after France Frenchly declined to join the invasion of Iraq, "freedom fries," or their previous rebranding of *sauerkraut*, after Germany Germanly started the First World War, "liberty cabbage." (God bless Americans, they're so adorable sometimes!)

Anyway, as George Orwell once wrote, foolish language leads to foolish thinking, which is perhaps the best explanation we're ever going to get for why we restaurant-going modern Brits are still denying ourselves the simpler, fairer and entirely superior system of "going Dutch" out of ancient peasant pride.

Instead, we have cobbled together our own ridiculous system of splitting the bill "fairly" in defiant opposition to Dutch people 400 years ago. We split everything right down the middle, tipping unanimously based on whatever amount of tip the most forceful personality in our group has suggested we leave behind. Then, quietly, we internalise the great unfairness of it all.

From the very first moment we open our menus, then, our Brit-o-matic minds are crunching the numbers, trying to anticipate any potential pitfalls or social dilemmas that might cause possible embarrassment, guilt or shame later on when the bill comes. *Is it fine to get a starter? Can I get two side dishes or will that seem greedy? Am I allowed to order a large wine if Jim only had an orange*

*juice, even though Karen paid for the taxi, but Karen helped Jim move house
and I've never owned a dog?*

Oh sure, we Brits *looove* to pretend we're not secretly crunching
those numbers (while saying casually outrageous things like,
"of course! Don't be silly, have whatever you want!") But, let's
face it, no table of Caesar salad-nibblers are going to magically
forget that you ordered a lobster on truffle tartar mixed grill
medley with a tankard of Dom Perignon. No: that sneaky order
is getting stored forever on the Collective Mind Tab, isn't it? (Oh
yes, it is; there's no 'I' in 'TEAM,' you bastard.) Of course we
will all pretend that it's ok for you to get "what you want," and
yes, we will all still dutifully split the bill anyway (saying ludicrous
things like, "no, of course it's fine! Forget the mathematical
reality, we're on holiday!") Rest assured, though, our Brit-o-
matic shame-brains are writing you out of the will and dis-
inviting you from Christmas, you cheeky bloody pisstaker.

Because we all know in advance that we will have to equally
contribute to the total cost of a final bill that we cannot fully
control, this gives us two main choices upfront when it comes to
ordering our own food and drinks:

1.) The Split-the-Bill, Halve-Your-Dreams Model

This is a kind of mutually prescribed race-to-the-bottom
where none of us dare get what we truly want because we're
too worried about seeming greedy if our friends don't roughly
match our level of spending. The *Split-the-Bill, Halve-Your-Dreams*
model is essentially there to save us from any possible sources of
embarrassment when the bill arrives; to ensure that it doesn't
read like an itemised list of perfect restraint, modesty and
economic fellowship, stained only by one great mark of Wagyu
burger shame (with your name on it.)

The worst case scenario we're trying to avoid is this: your
friend orders some kind of modest jacket potato affair, selflessly
thinking of *your* budget. A wonderful, dutiful, classic British

friend. Oh, but what's this? *Whoops, big mistake, buddy!* you think in return, like a bloody psycho, because, in spite of your friend's honourably modest decision, you have decided on the mega seafood platter mountain of dreams, and now, unswervingly, you're going to order it because there are no rules in the cruel, imaginary universe of this hypothetical scenario. Now, they have to watch you eat lavishly expensive food pile, saying nothing in protest, regretfully poking around their sad baked beans while bits of lobster tumble grotesquely from your chin, all the while knowing they will have to subside your disgraceful behaviour. (*Still, at least you won't call them Dutch...*)

No, that wouldn't do at all, you shudder. Of course you can't actually *take* the real-life discounts offered by the mutual responsibility fund of British friendship — that wouldn't be British at all. Well, don't worry! Luckily, the *Split-the-Bill, Halve-Your-Dreams* model is here to help.

This is how it works: you want the seafood platter but your friend, in a sudden moment of unexpected Dutchness, orders the jacket potato. You, dreaming only of crab, are momentarily caught off-guard by the potential price discrepancy between the two dishes, and quickly rescan the menu as you quietly put a pillow over the mouth of your actual preferences, and now, guess what? You're ordering a jacket potato too. That's right: it's baked beans and friendship all round tonight, comrades.

2.) The Split-the-Bill, Share-the-Pain Model

This option is less like a race-to-the-bottom and more like an arms race to a bill of total insanity.

In the *Split-the-Bill, Share-the-Pain* model, the proverbial gloves come off early: some hungry, thirsty character on one side of the table orders a starter, a main, three sides, a half-litre of beer *and* a jug of wine to share. No one complains, of course; nope, not so much as a peep of passive-aggressive dissent is heard. There's just complete silence and stunned complicity from the other side of the table (apart from the private screeching sounds of each discretion getting etched onto our Mind Tabs forever, of course), and now that's the new economic reality from which no one at the table can escape. We're sharing that bill, aren't we, no matter how we might really feel about it.

So, how do we respond? That's right: irrationally. Now that the Pandora's box of decadence has been prised open with a crowbar, the rest of the group scramble to keep up, lest they get stung with an unfairly equal share of a bill they didn't equally indulge in. Imagine a game of poker where everyone calls on every round, regardless of their starting cards. *Fun?* Maybe. *Wise?* No. Every cocktail ordered becomes a round. Every naan bread or pita bread is called, and raised. Every escalation in chicken wings or hummus is matched with unilateral, terrifying confidence by all parties at the table. Perhaps you recognise the internal logic (yet dangerous implications) of this strategy? That's right, it's the *Mutually Assured Destruction* approach to dinner.

Not only is it impossible for a poorer, more financially cautious, more Dutch co-diner to prevent the unchecked proliferation of the final bill... quite often there are subtle, retaliatory measures involved too. Sure, you'd think we might be able to see the self-sabotaging aspect of the *Split-the-Bill, Share-the-Pain* model, but unfortunately it seems to be impossible for us to escape the siege mindset once it has taken hold of us. Instead, we abandon reason and accept the gauntlet that's been thrown down, all the while thinking passive-aggressive thoughts like, *oh, you're having the friendship-subsidised Black Forest gateau for dessert, are you Stingy Mark? Well, in that case, mate, I'm ordering a double scotch to sip while you eat it. How do you like THAT? Oh, and what about this slightly more expensive single malt whiskey? Oh ho ho ho yes, that will do just fine, I think. Enjoy your cake, you bastard.*

The Surprising Niceness of a World Gone Mad

Despite any cluster-bombs of awkwardness that might inadvertently go off in my "authentic" Berlin neighbourhood, I love it when my friends and family come to visit me. Indeed, once Linn and I had figured out the life-hack for dealing with the problem of *Brits Abroad* food-ordering faffery (take them only to massive, sprawling, tourist-ready restaurants where the chefs have no fixed belief in their work), everything else about hosting British people is simple. British tourists, indeed, are probably the most easygoing in all the world.

Firstly, even when we are abroad, we're far more likely to be drawn to a good bargain than a famous landmark ("yeah, sure, the Colosseum *looked* interesting in the tour guide, but it was also 2-for-1 on ham toasties at the Irish Pub.") Secondly, we will always report back to our host culture's representatives that everything is "fine," "alright" or at least "not bad," whatever it is they're showing us (as long as there's alcohol, chairs and ketchup.) Finally, our whole personalities are almost custom-designed to make us ideal tourists: we're the perfect mix of polite, agreeable and dutiful. We'll follow our hosts anywhere and do whatever they suggest without introducing any complicating factors (like our own preferences.) This keeps things simple. "It's up to you!" is more than a platitude; it's a state of mind.

Probably my favourite feature of our *Brits Abroad Mentality*, however, is this: we tend to express our surprise, affection and enthusiasm for nice things on holiday almost universally through the lens of our relative disappointment that the UK cannot have nice things also. It's like an amusing form of self-deprecation, except elevated to the national level and done on behalf of our entire society. Let me explain: our foreign hosts tell us the price of a beer, and we reply, *"cor blimey, that would be double the price in England!";* our foreign hosts explain to us that the metro system doesn't have barriers, and we reply, *"holy moly! You'd never be able to trust people like that in England!"*; our foreign hosts explain to us that we are allowed to buy alcohol in the cinema*(!)*, even during the daytime*(!)*, and we reply, *"shit the bed! Seriously?! In England, there'd be a riot before the credits!"*

In other words, we Brits do not celebrate nice things abroad; we lament only that we cannot have nice things at home. We look at anything vaguely pleasant a foreign land can offer our hope-filled eyes – a bit of street art, a community garden, a recycling bin – then tut and shake our heads, before commenting on it wistfully: "oh bloody hell, would you look at that? Never in a million years would *that* happen in England, would it? Shame."

Once again, the narrative of BROKEN BRITAIN – a society imploding under the weight of disappointment in itself – rears its head. And as for me personally, these two-sided observations function as wonderful reminders, not of what I've left behind, but of what is also nice here. As Berlin makes its unceasing transition from *different* to *normal* in my mind, it's great to see little details like these through the fresh eyes of my most easily impressed British friends and get reminded why I like it here too. And the smaller the 'nice thing' my British friends are lamenting they can't have themselves (an un-vandalised bench, some matches being given away for free on a bar, a phone-box that hasn't been recently used as a urinal), the more lovely it becomes when they shake their heads at me in Berlin and say, "see? *See?* Now why can't we just do that back home? We're totally crap, that's why."

Probably my favourite example, indeed, came when my good friend Gordo looked at a blanket on a seat outside a Berlin cafe on a cold day and asked me, quite earnestly, "Paul, what's that about?"

"It's a blanket," I replied, "in case people get cold."

He looked at me, seemingly struggling to process the answer I had given him. Apparently finding the explanation lacking, he persisted, "yeah, I know that, but… like, who put it there?"

"The cafe did," I said. Gordo still looked suspicious of my grip on reality, so I tried to clarify the concept a little further, "you know, in case people get cold."

"Wow," he said after a while, nodding slowly as if a tiny key was jangling somewhere near a padlock in his mind, "but that's crazy. I mean, you can't imagine that in England, can you?"

Well, can you? Honestly, I don't know anymore. Perhaps Gordo's implication here *is* right: maybe you *couldn't* leave something as inherently valuable as a cheap Ikea blanket exposed to the outside world in sticky-fingered Britain without nailing it down first or attaching it to an angry guard dog. Hell, in BROKEN BRITAIN, you'd probably have to chain down the table and chairs too, and the ash-tray and the coasters, and maybe even the customers, just to be safe. (The world's gone mad, don't forget.)

The Zoning Genius
of "English Pubs"

In 2015, my dear friend Gordo (real name Adam) made his second odyssey to Germany, but this time for an unrelated stag weekend in Hamburg with his colleagues from the place he works, which is one of those banks you might read about in the Panama Papers. Linn's from Hamburg, so we took the train up to say hi.

Gordo, he'll be pleased to know, is one of my favourite people in all of Christendom – a kind of lovely, stylish, music-obsessed idiot-genius with a brain that affords him the superpower to recite an entire jukebox worth of obscure lyrics and tell you what year any film was made (hence the genius), but a mind that would *use* that superpower to recite an entire jukebox worth of obscure lyrics and tell you what year any film was made (hence the idiot.)

His work colleagues, however, were *not* my favourite people.

(Sorry, Gordo.) I don't know the quickest way to summarise everything that was entirely wrong with them, so I'll just say this: they were all *EXACTLY* the kind of people that would work in a bank. Does that help? Excellent.

On the first day of their banker wanker stag weekender, then, Linn and I met them around midday, whereupon we found them all already in a state of drunkenness they seemed to have achieved half a day ahead of schedule. Gordo himself was glassy-eyed and slow to react to human-talk, hiccuping constantly at me while slurring the words to some rare Bob Dylan b-side, a thick smudge of leftover sun-cream on his nose only emphasising his transformation into some kind of midday hipster booze vampire. As for the Stag himself: he was, it seemed, beyond hope. Imagine a zombie eating a human brain from its skull, then swap the skull for a cardboard box, then swap the human brain for some chips, and you should have a rough idea of how well he appeared to be doing at this particular juncture of history.

Sure enough, as is often British holiday custom, the group had started drinking as soon as they arrived in the airport of departure – middle of the morning be damned – and had not stopped lubricating their innards ever since.

Indeed, the pre-flight, pre-holiday, pre-drinking custom of British holiday boozing is such a proud tradition that the last time I was in "London" Stansted, I spotted a Ryanair poster that read, "One Last Pint Before You Fly?" This is a baffling question to be asked by an airline poster, which broadcasts its advice (to drink *at least* two pints) indiscriminately to an airport's worth of people 24 hours a day, no matter morning, noon or night.

Inevitably, Gordo and his underwhelming workmates soon declared sobriety bankruptcy and headed back to their hostel to sleep through the remainder of the day, while Linn and I agreed to meet them all again later when they vaguely resembled people again.

Eight hours later, they finally sent us an address and we headed off in the direction of a pub they themselves had chosen, which was called – *imagine yourself a little drum-roll, please* – "The English Pub."

That's right: "The *English* Pub."

They had booked flights, researched accommodation, packed suitcases, ordered taxis, converted pounds into euros, then been flung through the sky in a winged metal bird powered by 100,000,000 year-old compressed-liquid-dinosaur-juice and scratch-cards, then visited the only pub that looked exactly like the one they had just left in the airport.

As for the Stag, he was conspicuous in his absence, having passed out before he'd gone out to *The English Pub*, the first casualty of his own supposed celebration. This is another British stag do tradition: that the person who the party is ostensibly *for* does not have to make it out to witness it, having long been put into the fast-lane to zombiehood from the first moment they arrive in the airport to the last moment they stagger past the "One Last Pint Before You Fly (Into Catatonic Oblivion)?" poster.

And so we stayed with the group for the whole night in the English Pub – THE ENGLISH PUB – without moving to any other places that the city of Hamburg, Germany, Mainland Europe, uniquely had to offer that might be a little less, *oh, I don't bloody know,* ENGLISH.

The next night, we sent Gordo a message again to find out where we should meet him and his rubbish friends for the second (and last) night of their big weekend away from England, only to have those three bloody words come back at us again. We could not believe it.

The English Pub.

… THE *ENGLISH* PUB?

… *THE ENGLISH ****ING PUB?!*

Upon our second visit to Hamburg, Germany's English Pub, 'The English Pub,' Linn and I quickly decided this madness had to stop. Given that the Stag wasn't present (again), it seemed like Gordo was under no obligation to hang around with this crowd of massive bankers, so we stealthily moved him in the direction of a cash-point instead, then kidnapped him. We whisked him away to a friendly little bar with a jukebox (which was called, if I remember correctly, The *Not-The-English-Pub* Pub), and before long he was doing his best Mick Jagger impression in the middle of a dance-floor to a crowd of local admirers. We loved it. He loved it. And at the end of the night, he said, "wow, you'd never get a place like that in England. I wish the rest of the group had come here too."

To which Linn replied, with all the wisdom of a Hamburger, "but this place wouldn't be this place if those guys were in it."

"Fair," Gordo agreed.

And right then, in that very moment, I realised the hidden genius of *The English Pub*. It's like a quarantine zone that all of England's worst tourists endeavour to impose upon themselves. Merely by luring the kind of English people that want to go to *The English Pub* to *The English Pub*, the kind of English people that want to go to *The English Pub* are not anywhere else in your city causing a nuisance. You don't need barricades to keep them out; you can use *Sky Sports* and 2-for-1 Jager-bombs to keep them in, voluntarily confined to a small, safe, manageable geographic area of Englishness.

The Bloody Americans

When I said that we Brits are *often* voted the world's worst tourists, I neglected to mention the other nationality which sometimes narrowly clinches the top prize instead of us: that would be our good friends, the bloomin' Americans, wouldn't it? Yee-ha.

The USA and the UK have a "special relationship," of course. It is also, as we are often reminded, a mutually beneficial one (i.e. you scratch my war, I'll scratch yours.) But it is also – let's be honest with ourselves about the realities of the modern world – not a *fully, totally, 100%* equal partnership any more. The Americans know this. The British know it too. A huge, glaring and increasingly difficult-to-ignore disparity exists between us. It is that we Brits (in spite of more superficial trivialities like the United States now having a navy that could defeat all other navies in the world combined) believe that we are secretly, quietly, um, *better*. Ahem. Yes, you heard me. This is why we can't help but treat our American friends with a mildly patronising haughtiness, like they are some buffoonish, embarrassing stepson we are forced to keep bringing to the family BBQ, even though last year they ate all the burgers and launched a missile at the buns.

Of course, one is not supposed to make sweeping generalisations about whole countries and cultures, or judge any group of people based on the individual traits of some of them. No: that is an overly simplistic view of the world's peoples and communities reserved for demagogues, populists, racists, fascists, authoritarians and comedy writers. However, even the most wise and mild-mannered of us in Britain are willing to make a teeny, tiny exception for American stereotypes because, deep down, we still believe that Americans are all still *baaaasically* British anyway, except we sent them off a few hundred years ago with a Power Rangers lunchbox, passed on the baton (or truncheon) of world policeman from us to them, and now watch like hippy parents from afar as they blunder through the world like a fat kid on jelly.

But we're not going to interfere, we think. *No, we have to let them make their own mistakes…*

This gently patronising attitude we Brits sometimes exhibit towards our, well, *less civilised* American offspring is encouraged by our plentiful second-hand exposure to their culture of purely American phenomena (like pre-sliced rubbery "cheese," Scientology, free bullets with all Happy Meals, automatic cars and their choice of leaders.) On the other hand, we're not shy of taking credit for the Americans either. When they're stupid, it's because they're American. When they're great, though, it's because they're our brainchild.

Of course, this self-judged superiority remains almost entirely unspoken in British culture. Naturally, we would be far too polite to bring it up to their faces (what with all their nuclear weapons) but, rest assured, it's in there somewhere, bubbling away just under the surface of our stoic, emotionless crusts. And, occasionally, a little bit of it might even seep out, like a short burst of hot steam, at the mention of the three remaining, entirely acceptable-to-say-out-loud prejudices:

1.) Sitcoms

We Brits do not even need to watch the American remakes of our beloved home-grown sitcoms to know instinctively, and without evidence, that they have been "dumbed down." Our perceived superiority in humour – as judged, again, by ourselves – is perpetuated by how easily we can watch *Friends* and *Seinfeld*, laughing along, if we so choose to, at all of the funny noises the characters make, whereas, on the other side of the pond, American studios invest billions upon trillions of dollars recreating "our" shows from scratch, shot-for-shot, should one character, once, mention a roundabout.

2.) Language

British people, especially the bloody English, still sometimes cling to the outdated and spectacularly irrational notion that English, the language, is somehow "*our* language." What's more, we have even been known to demand upon occasion (lunatics that we are) that "if the Americans aren't going to use it properly" then "they should bally well get their own!" It is, I think you'll agree, an amazing thing to say. Especially in a language that comes from German.

For us, of course, no greater foible exists with Americans "borrowing" "*our* language" than their constant, flagrant and intentional misuse of the perfectly simple word *football* (which should, of course, be exclusively reserved to refer to the game that is not called *soccer*.) Unfortunately, no matter how many times we insist upon reminding them, the bloody Americans continually insist on using the word "football," foolishly and embarrassingly and wrongly, to refer to that other game where almost no one uses their foot to kick anything (apart from occasionally that thing that isn't *really* a ball.)

It won't be long, indeed, before everyone in Britain condescendingly refers to American Football as *handegg* – because, on top of "stealing" "*our* language," we also secretly believe that the Americans have "stolen" "*our* sports" too. And, well, are they at least using them correctly? No, of course they bloody aren't, you know, because of their tiny, half-time, quarter-time, weak-beer, release-the-multi-ball attention spans. Baseball, we constantly remind them, is just rounders for show-offs. Basketball is netball with ADHD. And don't even get us started on the ludicrously overlong distraction-festival of *American Handegg* because everyone in Britain, despite not understanding a single rule of it, dismisses it as "rugby… with pads."

3.) Tourism

Despite we Brits being notorious worldwide for naughty touristic behaviour (especially our world-renowned hooligans' behaviour after *football* games), for the 8 years that George W. Bush represented the world image of the United States, American tourists were expected to visit the United Kingdom somewhat apologetically, as if they now had to be both ambassadors for their country *and* the ownership of a brain. That was, of course, until Obama showed up on the scene, with his comparatively magical ability to form coherent sentences.

Then all of a sudden, after the Brexit vote happened, it looked like the tide of haughty superiority against Americans might turn once more. For a brief historical moment, there was Obama, the rational, capable technocrat, on the rubbery not-real-cheese side of the Atlantic, while, on our side, there was a clown-bus driven by Boris Johnson going *honk-honk-honk*.

Luckily for the UK's ego, though, this lopsided phase didn't last long, as very soon afterwards the United States (and Russia) chose to elect a man called Donald Trump, whose only qualification for the job was that he asked for it and half the country went, "oh, ok then. Can't see any glaring personality flaws to worry about, what have we got to lose?"

Yes, "The Donald," as he was lovingly known to the people racing head-first to be on the wrong side of history, seemed to have been magicked into the universe just to make George W. Bush look wise, qualified and statesmanlike in hindsight. Yet no country benefited more than jolly old Britain from the screeching diversion of the entire world turning its head westwards at the same moment it asked itself what a Brexit is.

Once again, the United States of Formerly Britain had proven itself to be our great dyslexic stepson and ally, by making a massively distracting noise at the pivotal moment of our own historic national crisis, not unlike a rotund boy with a personality disorder on a diving board shouting "MOM! MOM! MOM! LOOK AT ME! MOOOOM! *WATCH THIS!*"

An Invasion of Football Fans

There was a great amount of irony to be enjoyed in the run-up to the 2016 In/Out referendum. There was the irony of Britain – of British Empire fame – saying, "we don't want to be ruled by other people!" There was the irony of Britain – of Royal Family fame – saying, "... because we never elected them!" And then there was probably the greatest irony of all:

the nightly news having to cover the highly charged issue of *free movement of people* during a month when literally hundreds of thousands of England football fans were marauding around France for the Euro cup, many of them smashing the place up.

It seemed at the specific historical moment, you see, that if anyone had a right to be anxious about *free movement of people* in 2016, it was actually any other European country brave enough to host the championships in a year that England managed to make it through the qualification round. *(Ahem.)* With only a small bit of water between us and them (and no possible visa regime to protect them), France was overrun in a week by legions of flag-waving British foreigners.

And yet, as of now, there is absolutely nothing the Continent can do to stop it potentially happening again; nothing theoretically protecting them from almost unlimited amounts of beer-fuelled, rowdy Englishmen descending upon the tournament to cheer on England (apart from the performance of the England team itself, of course.)

Every night in June, you could switch on the news across the UK and hear someone from the Leave campaign trying to make their case about the problems free movement causes, then the next report would be some embarrassingly repetitive scenes of England fans, covered head-to-toe in England flags, re-enacting Braveheart on the cobbled streets of some pretty European town. And, if they weren't literally fighting Russians or rioting, they were running around in large, drunken groups with their shirts off, endlessly chanting – with an optimism unrestrained by data – about England *winning*(!) Yes: whenever you hear a crowd of people endlessly singing *"FOOTBALL'S COMING HOME, IT'S COMING HOME!"* you are witnessing the fascinating scene of collective self-delusion called 'England fans.'

It was, it seemed, the second Migrant Crisis of the year. Of course, no one wants to give ISIS ideas but, well, if they had been paying close attention to the England Fan phenomenom, they might have noticed the most effective way to cause mass carnage and terror at the Euros was to open a Free Beer Tent in the vicinity of a chip shop.

In fact, England fans behaved so badly in neighbouring France that our national team was even threatened with expulsion from the tournament entirely. At which point, the official British Football Association, in an act of desperation and questionable decision-making, resorted to dragging Wayne Rooney in front of a television camera to appeal for calm. For those who don't know him, Wayne Rooney is a kind of human fight in football shoes. It was the sporting equivalent of dragging out Pavarotti to appeal for diets.

Luckily for France, then, that England were not in the tournament for very long (*ahem*), which is probably the only reason the British weren't politely asked by Europe at the time if we wouldn't mind Brexiting ourselves for their benefit.

Anyway, the new hot topic amongst the post-Brexit British Brexit people of Britain is a points-based immigration system, just like that of our other slightly wayward stepson, Australia (you know, that place we used to export our people *to*.) If the EU casts its mind back to the 2016 cup, it might do well to consider a similar system in relation to us too, perhaps using alcoholic units instead of points. For example, if inbound Brits are found to have had more than 3 pints at their departing airport, their visa could be conditional upon them eating a sandwich first.

THE BRITISH WORLDVIEW

Chapter Eight

The British Worldview

Clearly, we are discussing the topic of Britishness at a pivotal juncture in our long and faffy history, right at the highly charged and precarious-seeming moment that our countrymen have started arguing over what exactly that identity means (or should mean), and what we will choose, together, for it to mean in the future.

So, as we near the end of our time with the bloody British, it's interesting to ask the question: what next for them?

Uncertain days lie ahead, certainly. Indeed, never in my lifetime has it seemed harder to predict what might happen next in these strange, confusing and often reliably boring times. Clearly, the United Kingdom (which feels more accurately like a *Divided Queendom* as each day goes by) is at a unique and precarious impasse.

Are we plucky Brits, as some think, heading for a bright and glorious future, with all of our energies and eccentricities unshackled from the stifling bureaucracy of Brussels? Are we ultimately destined to lead the world once more (in glorious service industries, like insurance)? Or have we, as others argue, shot ourselves royally in the foot? Are we destined, instead, to annoy ourselves and every other nation in lorry-driving distance as we lose our economic lifeblood to Dublin, Paris and Frankfurt, until we eventually complete an impressive nosedive into historical irrelevance?

Politely, I would like to suggest: who the bloody hell knows? I certainly don't. (And I suspect we, as a nation, haven't quite reached the *Let's Agree To Disagree* stage on this question yet...)

Since the *British Problem* seems destined to remain in the international headlines for some time, it is interesting to wonder where we might go next as a country, possibly having a whole new world of opportunities right in front of our door and/or possibly having done quite an impressive shit on our very own doorstep.

The best place to look for clues, I think, is in the British worldview: after all, people's beliefs, as they profess them, are often the best guide we have for anticipating their actions. And so, if there are any clues to what Britain's future might look like, perhaps we shall find them in Britain's past. Let's try, then, to diagnose just what exactly might be going on underneath the hood of the British psyche, using sweeping generalisations and a patchy view of recent history as our guide. What strange genius or common madness drives us?

A Long-Simmering Identity Crisis

Britain has – for almost the entirety of its existence – been suffering from a long-running and ever-mutating identity crisis.

Firstly, there's the surface-level labelling problem that every British person must face when they look into the mirrors of culture, countryhood and citizenship: *what am I?*

For example, I'm English because I come from England. But I am also British because I come from Britain, which contains England. Geographically speaking, though, I grew up on the island of *Great* Britain, which also contains Scotland and Wales (which have their own devolved parliaments, while England, in order to further confuse matters, does not.) Legally, though, I'm a citizen of the United Kingdom, also known as the United Kingdom *of Great Britain and Northern Ireland*, which contains the country (province? territory?) of Northern Ireland, which is on the island of Ireland but not Irish. (Well, sort of.) The island of Ireland contains both Northern Ireland (which also has its own devolved parliament, but only *sometimes* – don't ask) and the Republic of Ireland, which were once both known together as the Kingdom of Ireland, until becoming part of the United Kingdom of Great Britain and Ireland which used to be British (and, before that, All-Irish, obviously.) Together, and sometimes apart, and sometimes controversially, all of these countries together are known as the British Isles (or 'the British Isles and Ireland') – that is to say, the North Atlantic archipelago (of technically 6000+ islands) upon which I was born... although there's also the not un-tricky issue of the "crown dependencies" (e.g. the Channel Islands and the Isle of Man) and the British overseas territories – those other technically British, but strangely un-British-looking places, in surprisingly un-British looking parts of the world, like Gibraltar and the Falklands.

In other words, Britishness is a bubbling Venn diagram soup of legal overlaps, cultural headaches and sports teams mash-ups that contains something to offend everyone. It is also, of course, the only constitutional sands upon which any kind of Brexit Sandcastle can be built because there is also – just in case the news hasn't reminded you in the last five seconds – the not-small issue of the (ahem) *European Problem.*

While the British joined up to (and arguably helped create) a Union of European nations in the 1970s, there always seemed to be some level of simmering domestic confusion about what exactly we had signed up for, what we were about to or how it was all going to end, especially as each new treaty whizzed past us and new member states joined. If we were coming along for that big Brussels road trip to *Ever-Closer-Union*-Land, we were perhaps only ever doing so like a confused, small-bladdered granddad in the passenger seat, reading the map upside-down, moaning about the temperature and asking every five minutes if we could be dropped off (just as an exception) for another wee.

Adding to our general befuddlement, we were in the EU but not the Schengen Zone. We were in the customs union but not the monetary union. We wrangled our very British opt-outs for some things, like the euro and the eurozone bail-outs, but we were definitely an integral part of the *European Economic Area*, which presumably caused a lot of cognitive dissonance for us, what with our long-standing reluctance to acknowledge ourselves as being part of a continent at all. No amount of Ever-Closer-Union would ever stop us, when asked where Europe *is*, from pointing at Belgium and saying, "over there!"

What I'm saying is this: it's confusing being British, so maybe we shouldn't judge ourselves too harshly when we ask ourselves a simple question and get ourselves into a bit of a muddle when a complicated answer comes out. And for any foreign readers wondering how these superficial and abstract-sounding layers of identity can intrude into everyday life, just imagine trying to find your nationality in one of those drop-down menus of websites. E for England? B for Britain? G for Great Britain? U for United Kingdom? E for European? I for Identity Crisis? We can't even buy a flight without browsing half the planet's phone-book. It's a nightmare, wrapped in a Union, wrapped in a constitutional monarchy, wrapped in a Commonwealth, wrapped in the crumbling trappings of an empire that died.

The Delusions of Grandeur

Then there is the gold-plated elephant in the room: the British Empire, which didn't so much die a dignified, elderly death, but popped out for milk one afternoon and got hit by a bus (or, indeed, a string of them.) Once upon a tea-time, it used to cover the face of the Earth – an empire upon which the sun never set ruled by a people the sun always burned. Yet now Britannia's faded dominion looks ever more like the acne on Earth's face – a light smattering of red island dots, strategic enclaves and tax havens, causing occasional but only minor irritation to the surrounding areas.

And yet, while the British Empire is now well and truly the *former* British Empire, one occasionally gets the impression that not everyone in the country has fully absorbed the memo.

Perhaps they're still looking around at the groggy morning-after clues of the decadent all-nighter we threw about a century ago – a seat on the UN Security Council, our expensively useless nuclear submarines, Australia's and New Zealand's flags – but it's been hard for some Brits to adjust to their new place in a world gone mad, i.e. going from GLOBAL SUPERPOWER with MORE BOATS THAN EVERYONE ELSE to a slightly damp and slowly sinking rock near Belgium, which a Russian spokesman at the G20 Summit in 2013 called "a small island that no one listens to." (Ouch.)

What's more, some British people don't seem to have adjusted to the country's post-imperial status at all. It's nowhere near as difficult as it should be, indeed, to find people from all walks of life in modern Britain – from confused chavs to posh twats – who are still talking about the country like they haven't noticed the last 100 years have happened. (Many of them have even been elected to parliament, which should tell you something worrying about the broad appeal of their nostalgia-tinged optimism, unrestrained as it is by our total lack of boats.) When dealing with these people's increasingly wacky views of Britain in a world of Americas, Europes and rising Chinas, I like to imagine a Chihuahua barking at a Doberman, i.e. it doesn't seem to matter that the outside forces of natural selection have crafted us into an increasingly sweet and harmless little shape, inside us – like all dogs – we still believe we are a wolf. It's confusion, yes, but it's also quite adorable confusion.

Luckily, these delusions of grandeur have never stopped us

noticing that modern Britain remains a very desirable place to live. (It is, of course.) However, they may have occasionally gotten in the way of us remembering that Europe is also – rather famously – full of desirable places to live. During the refugee crisis, for example, when the most hysterical amongst us seemed all but certain that "swarms" of migrants (David Cameron's phrase) were comin' over 'ere to sink poor, beleaguered Britain with their combined weight, we barely seemed to notice as those migrants quietly shuffled, instead, towards Germany, Sweden, Austria and all of the other desirable places in Europe (that also speak English as well as us.) Britain's biggest fans, it seems, have sometimes struggled to conceptualise the E.U. project as 500 million people with the freedom to live and work anywhere — from Venice to Vienna, Barcelona to Budapest, Marseilles to Munich. Instead, perhaps, they mostly saw 500 million people with British passports.

An Inferiority Complex

Of course, this kind of rose-tinted, singing-the-national-anthem-through-a-traffic-cone patriotism can be found in almost all countries and cultures (which should give you a rough indication of what it's worth.) If all of the world's nations were loutish blokes at a speed-dating party, you would rightly expect a lot of bragging, self-promotion and pomposity, with each country's patriotism taking a slightly different form but nevertheless being expressed with equal enthusiasm, righteousness and total lack of contextual awareness.

Mr Switzerland would be politely offering you cheese, security and a morally dubious bank account, slipping in secure, marriageable references to his 200 years of neutrality; Mr

United States would be flexing his muscles in a tight vest, buying you shiny things and offering you freedom (under the watchful eye of a thousand drones); Mr Spain would be changing the subject whenever the topic of 'jobs' came up but convincingly pitching you a laidback future of sunshine and fiestas – a dream life that could be yours (as long as you don't mind living with grandma for a while.)

And then you would get to Mr Britain, the cheeky chappy loudmouth underdog nostalgia-merchant of the room, lunging on tip-toes from table to table with a puffed-out chest, accidentally letting out a little fart and then pretending that he didn't.

Mr Britain would be polite for the few first hours, no doubt, and might even make a reasonably compelling case for his historical credentials while throwing in a few funny little jibes at Mr France's expense (*"do you know why the French have so many different kinds of cheese? Because they never invented cheddar!"*) But, as the evening wore on, a slow and gradual unravelling of sense might start to take place, with every confidence-summoning drink and each envy-inspired glance at Mr United States (with all his bloody boats).

Eventually, Mr Britain might turn sour, increasingly grumpy from booze, and unable to hide a mounting resentment that some Japanese tourists had fainted at the feet of Mr France instead. Before long, poor old Mr Britain would be mumbling and ranting ever more incoherently about irrelevant former glories, folding his arms belligerently and refusing to participate further, like a sad, ignored man in a corner who has just been reminded (by ten units of alcohol) that he hasn't been recently thanked for something he did twenty years ago.

"I didn't WANT TO brag," Mr Britain would slur at the end of the night, alone in an empty room, standing on a chair, "but I am LITERALLY at *the centre of the map*, so, yeah… you know what I mean, right? I had a whooole empire once, you know? What did France have? Like, *half*? *Pft*, keep it! I basically

DISCOVERED America, give or take. The USA was MY IDEA, so *la de da* Mr "OH LOOK AT ME, I'VE GOT SO MANY AIRCRAFT CARRIERS" PFT! *Bloody stupid America.* Well, so what? It was ME who invented the sandwich, and democracy, and playing rugby without all the girly pads. ME, ME, *ME.* And what about GREENWICH MEAN TIME, huh? *HM?* Time was my idea... *MINE!*'

The Psychological Crutch
of Nostalgia

The important thing to notice about modern British patriotism, anyway, is that a fair share of it often comes out expressed in the past tense, with a lot of our more recent confusion stemming from the fact that we are a society of people – of all ages, genders and ethnicities – who've all been told by the generation above us that we were all at least one generation late to what was once a really great party.

Oh it was glorious back then, whenever "then" was. A Mars bar only cost a thruppence! A house was only three shillingpence and a tupney farthing! You used to be able to buy them back then. Imagine that now! Houses! People knew their neighbours, you know? Music had words. Words had sounds – you used to make them with your mouth instead of with your thumbs on a smartphone. All playing with their computer games now, the kids are. Never won a war, have they? Never even seen a book, have they? Nope. Oh, and the economy. The economy! Booming back then. You could lose two jobs in the morning and have three new ones by the afternoon. Children were quiet. Respectful! Knew their place. And they could run faster. They lived in trees and only ate apples. News was only charts and graphs and facts read by professionally boring people who had had their personalities lobotomised especially by the BBC for television. The weather was mild, yet in different and exciting ways. Ah, those were the days!

Except they weren't, obviously, were they? No. Everyone died all the time, no one knew what the bloody hell was going on, all food came in a tin, every marriage was a loveless slog through seven decades of passive-aggression and spam, nothing ever happened, and the only time you ever met anyone from a culture other than your own, it was in the context of a battlefield. It was a world of polio and corned beef sandwiches and fascism and sad housewives crying into gravy, and bloody hell thank god it's over.

Good riddance to it, I say. The past was mostly rubbish. Still, I think it remains safe to say that many of our countrymen are still warmly nostalgic for this grand ol' time that maybe never was; wistful for a glory that they had only ever read about in storybooks written by dicks.

A Heavy Case of
Historical Amnesia

I can't help but feel that the British education system might have a little something to do with all this. In my old school, for example, I remember British history covering some ancient Kings and Queens for a while, then a conspicuous absence of data about what the British were up to, until the story suddenly picked up again some time around 1939 with a bit more vigour.

Unlike some other modern countries I could mention, Britain seems to have escaped relatively unscathed from the historical self-reflection game, and therefore still contains more than its fair share of people with a relatively rosy and one-sided view of "their"/"our" past. We look at the map at the height of the empire, all coloured in British, and more than a few of us still seem to think, "well... lucky ol' planet, I say!"

Indeed, the British Empire, despite containing the word "empire," is mostly not regarded as an imperial kind of pursuit at all (what with all the negative connotations that implies), but more like a widely misunderstood Outreach Programme for cricket. If this Outreach Programme is remembered through the lens of its occasional missteps – the famines, massacres and rather coincidental resource-exploitation – it's mostly with a lackadaisical shrug and an accompanying non-apology: "well, you know, you can't make an omelette without breaking a few eggs, can you? Ho ho ho. Still, never mind, eh? What's done is done. Onwards and upwards."

We are therefore a chronically nostalgic people and it's hard to blame us really, given that we have all had to grow up *in Britain*, constantly surrounded by the spangled pageantry and oldy-worldly, magic-looking relics of a past we don't always understand and are not always taught how to evaluate evenhandedly. Have you been to modern Britain? It's a pompy place. Our actual current institutions look like life-size replicas of models of institutions you might otherwise find in a history museum. We grow up marinating in a stew of ancient nonsense.

Our judges wear wigs, gowns and capes as if the judicial system is run on the same logic as *Alice in Wonderland*. Ask *any* British person who owns all the swans and they will reply, "the Queen." What? *Why?* Don't ask. Look at our parliamentarians some time – they debate actual current topics like "child poverty" and "permanent austerity," literally inches away from a golden sceptre. It's the world's longest-running democracy and it shows. MPs vote for things by shouting "AYEEE!" or by walking down a corridor to have their heads counted. The rest of the time, the debating chamber looks and sounds like the naughty classroom of a doomed supply teacher who has lost all semblence of control. Pubs close by ringing a bell. The Royals often move around by horse and cart (although, admittedly, that's better than by tax-funded helicopter.) There's castles. There's furry hats. There's people chasing fast-moving wheels of cheese down a hill. My passport has a unicorn on it and I have no idea why.

Then there's Guy Fawkes Night, where we stream out of our houses mid-winter in order to burn an effigy of a man who tried to blow up the Houses of Parliament in 1605. It's hard to imagine

241

a more top-down idea than 'Guy Fawkes Night,' incidentally, given the curious reality that every 5th of November, the entire country – children with sparklers, sweet grandmothers wrapped up in blankets, eager parents with an earnest handful of rubbish rockets – venture out into the cold winter's night to be reminded, with officially organised explosions, that *YOU DO NOT FUCK WITH HER MAJESTY'S GOVERNMENT*.

Sometimes, indeed, living in modern Britain feels a bit like being casually taken hostage by a load of institutions beamed in from a *Downton Abbey* DVD and the *Dungeons and Dragons* dimension. What's more, most of us still don't seem to mind all of this cartoonishly fairytale stuff draped over our First World country like a sequinned doily on a toaster. According to a 2015 survey by polling organisation YouGov, for example, 68% of Britons are still in favour of the monarchy (which makes you wonder if they haven't yet heard Darwin's great news.)

Better yet, one can go to YouTube and seek out the BBC's coverage of the Queen's birthday parade (also known as the 'Trooping of the Colour') except lovingly over-dubbed with the BBC's commentary on a North Korean Cult of Personality military parade[1]. It's uncanny and hilarious. As one watches great swathes of the British proletariat cheer and wave overpriced tea-towels at their unelected god-chosen overlords, one cannot help wondering if a national version of Stockholm Syndrome hasn't set in for the British.

This wouldn't exactly be surprising, given that we are a nation of people who are forced to spend our lives literally licking the Queen's back side. (By which I mean, of course, that her face is on the front of every stamp.)

[1] https://bit.ly/1NOX7x4

A Light Case of
Stockholm Syndrome

The Queen is our country's Head of State. I know that. You know that. Everyone knows that. She is literally one of the most famous Homo sapiens on the whole of Planet Earth. But let's just allow that one small fact to sink in a little moment longer. It's the 21st Century – the age of the self-driving vacuum cleaner – yet the United Kingdom is still fundamentally structured on the same level of sophistication as an ant colony.

Her name, her face or her crest is etched onto currency, carved all over post-boxes, painted on pub signs, embossed on government letter-heads, printed on tax documents, and gleaming gold on our passports' covers. On paper, too, she is the Head of the Commonwealth, Defender of the Faith (sort of like a mini-Pope for the Church of England), the Commander-in-Chief of the UK's Armed Forces, and – on top of her sprawling Rolodex of grand, jewel-twinkling titles – our prime minister must pop in once a week for a cup of tea and a chat with her.

And while it's all increasingly ceremonial (she's more like our country's version of *Tony the Tiger* than our country's version of Kim Jung-Un), British parents nevertheless find themselves in the awkward position of having to explain this all to children when they ask us questions like, "daddy, why do those people get to live in castles and wear very sparkly hats, but you and mummy look like everyone else and only have a two-and-a-half bedroom house in Borington-upon-Bland?"

"Well, honey," we must answer them, if we're being honest with ourselves and them, "some people in Britain are just better than others, you see. It's in their blood. Hundreds and hundreds of years ago, way back before we knew anything about anything, their "bloodline" was deemed to be "holy" by peasants like mummy and me. So, you see, even though we *now* know that everyone is just a cheeky little naturally-selected space-monkey like you, we all just sort of keep going along with it, because it helps the country sell souvenirs or something."

I mean, don't get me wrong: I'm no ideologue. If you're going to have a Queen, you can't do much better than *the* Queen, can you? I mean, look at her: she's a bloody diamond, Her Maj'. She's been in charge since the days when black-and-white television had literally just become a thing, using a single facial expression all the way to Netflix, and to this day she still doesn't have a single embarrassing gaffe to her name. She has made literally thousands of public speeches and appearances, without even so much as a single word misspoken. It's a truly extraordinary record.

Indeed, when researching that last statement to double-check if it really was true, I typed into YouTube "queen gaffe" – nothing. "Queen bloopers," nope. "Queen falls," nothing. "Queen trips," "Queen slips," "Queen bumps head," "... misspeaks," "... mumbles," "... fumbles," "... grumbles." There's *nothing*, I'm telling you. Do you know how that happens? You've got to be programmed from birth to efficiently fulfil your singular purpose of being a Queen. Yes, I really think she is *that* amazing (and yes, I am also sort of saying she is a robot.)

Probably the closest thing to a misstep in the line of duty I could find was the time that a hot mic caught her saying that some Chinese officials were – ready for this? – "very rude." And that's only *really* a scandal, in my view, if the aforementioned Chinese officials had in fact been "very polite" and the Queen was lying – in private – to slander them. And you know what? I don't think she was lying. I think she was right, and, despite not knowing what those Chinese officials did or said or who they are, I think they should bloody well apologise. Because let's face it: if there's a Politeness Radar in the land that can be trusted, it's the one whirring ten-thousand revs a minute inside the crown-component of Her Majestroid Queen-o-matic Elizabot 2.0.

I know it might sound like sarcasm, but it's genuinely hard to overstate just how impressed I am at this total lack of gaffes.

Think about it: cameras have been pointed at her basically *non-stop* for almost her whole life and yet somehow she has glided about in front of them (and her colony) without a single malfunction or noticeable glitch that people could point to and say, 'aha! Look! She is a human, after all!' I've fallen over twice today. Every other word I speak is a stuttering, mumbled fudge. How does she do it?

Well, I would be a subpar humourist if I didn't at least have a theory (to answer my own questions.)

Type "Prince Philip gaffes" into YouTube and you'll soon notice 'gliding inoffensively through the world' is not a sexually transmitted character trait. If the Queen is the embodied personification of Britain, Prince Philip is like an enteral symbol of the country's slightly racist granddad, yet there's no way for any of us to top him up with sherry until he goes to sleep. He's just out there, in the world, driving his car, meeting absolutely everyone, saying whatever the hell pops into his head. It's chaos.

I warn you, though: if you do type "Prince Philip gaffes" into a search bar, clear your calendar first. There's pages and pages and pages of results. There's compilations, Top 10s, there's "five decades of Prince Philip gaffes," there's 'best ofs,' 'worst ofs,' old ones, new ones, mash-ups, remixes, take-downs and tributes… it's almost dizzying, the breadth of output from his muddled mind. He's an industrial strength gaffe-factory. Every time he opens his mouth, it's like a wormhole opens to the opinions of a car mechanic in the 1950s.

My theory, therefore, is that Her Majestroid is outsourcing all of her gaffe functions to an external husband device. He is her buffer; her bulwark; her bumper. There's even a fantastically believable theory that Prince Philliptron is proactively acting like a gaffe-magnet on the Queen's behalf, i.e. that when the two of them are in a room together, meeting and greeting the worker-drones, he spots any potentially troublesome characters in advance (comedians, republicans, idiots, anarchists), then jumps in front of them like they have opinion-bullets meant for the Queen. He once asked one apparently high-risk candidate, a novelist, this question: "so, does a novelist... write books?"

There's *no way* that's not a diversion, right? Think of all the media training he's had; all of the life-long exposure to high culture, courtesy of an aristocratic heritage; all the things he would have to believe about his worth to society in order to feel not feel ashamed whenever trumpets play because he is entering a room. *Does a novelist write books?* I'm telling you: he's a shield.

As for me, I've only had one personal encounter with a member of the royal family thus far: Prince Edward, who graced my friends and I with his presence after we had completed a 24-hour climbing challenge of the three highest mountains in England, Scotland and Wales. After he had arrived by helicopter (which, we feared, may have cost more than every single person at the event had raised for the intended charity), Princebot E-droid came to our table and said to us, "well, don't you chaps look suitably tired."

"Well, yes," I replied, suitably tired, "we didn't arrive by helicopter."

My eyes widened suddenly. *What did I just say?* I hadn't meant to be rude to him; it's just that I was, as he had so astutely noted, "suitably tired" (or *fucking knackered*, as I would have put it in poor person-speak.) Immediately after the words had left my mouth, I saw first-hand that ancient flash of fear past behind his face – the DNA-encoded warning sirens inside all aristocrats wailing, "peasants! peasants! Bolt the gates!" – and the draw-bridge went up.

"Oh, fuf fuf fuf," he laughed, pretendingly, before quickly moving on to the next table.

Later on, it's worth reporting too (while I get the chance), he would *skip the queue* for the buffet, which you may remember from earlier in the book is not my absolute most favourite thing ever, especially not when I am *suitably hungry*, which I bloody well was. (This infringement we caught on camera, by the way, accompanied by our chavvy commentary: "the [treasonous expletive removed] thinks he's royalty! Why does he get to go first? I'm hungry and the [treasonous expletive removed] hasn't done anything!")

Anyway, for now at least, Britain seems to be not-unhappily stuck with its ancient dynasty of tax-funded, bling-wearing, self-replicating robot overlords… and that may long continue yet, or at least until we learn to deal with the topic of our monarchy as modern Germans apparently do. When the Queen visited Berlin in 2015, I must admit that I was actually pretty shocked by the casualness (and typical German directness) of anti-monarchy rhetoric splashed across the front pages of newspapers. Even *Der Spiegel,* which I had previously regarded as one of the more sober voices on the German news-stand, had a giant picture of her Majesty's face, captioned only with two unambiguously antagonistic words, "DIE QUEEN." *Yikes,* I thought, *steady on.*

A Casually Crazy Democracy

The most highly cited reason that British people gave for voting to leave the EU was to "take back control" and have political decisions made "at home" i.e. to cede back elements of the UK's sovereign democracy, especially on the topics of law and borders, which it had increasingly pooled with those of the other EU nations in Brussels. This is a concern that can be understood, even by people who might not agree with it. What is also slightly amusing about it, though, of course, is that Britain's "sovereign democracy" is also a synonym for an inherited rag-tag of mostly undemocratic insanity. We are not even *technically* a democracy at all, if you want to get all pedantic about it. We're a constitutional monarchy. We *have* a parliament, but it's not sovereign. The Queen is.

Continental Europeans – being only the mildly reformed tyrants, communists, anarchists and fascists they are – might not know, for example, that the United Kingdom has an almost entirely whimsical electoral system called *First-Past-the-Post (FPTP)*. Don't worry, I won't bore you with the details, but the main thing you need to know about FPTP for now is that it is almost exactly as modern, fair and inclusive as it sounds. It is the golf of governance.

Put it this way: if "democracy" was an ideal you liked, you probably wouldn't design one where voters' votes were worth wildly varying amounts depending on their geographic location and where all non-winning votes are taken out the back and shot. In the end, the amount of votes cast for a political party (of which there are basically two) have little correlation with the amount of MPs from that party that end up ruling the UK for the next five years. For example: the last election in 2015 was, according to the Electoral Reform Society, the least representative election in British history. The winners (and the current group of folks in charge as of this time of writing) won 50.8% of the seats with 36.9% of the votes. Without proportional representation, this meant they formed an all-deciding *majority government* from 24% of the electorate. (A lot of people in Britain also don't vote, of course, probably because it sometimes seems needlessly embarrassing to admit you participated.) Nevertheless, by the codified rules of Great Golf-land, these are now the people able to exercise 100% of the winners' rights.

As for the Upper House, whose role is to balance out the elected government, that's called the House of Lords, the name of which might already give you one small clue about where this is going. Democratically speaking, the House of Lords is an institution that will mostly never contain you.

On its seats, people investigating Britain's "sovereign democracy" will find the comfy bums of 26 bishops (!), four dukes (!) and 92 "hereditary" peers (please note: *men*.) The remaining members of the chamber – Lords, Baronesses, Earls, Marquises and Viscounts – are a slew of amazingly titled characters that sound like they were beamed in from a *Game of Thrones* flashback. This bizarre layer of magical-sounding tweeness is staggeringly entrenched in our political system. A few of my personal highlights include the Baroness Bottomley of Nettlestone, the Lord Palumbo of Southwark, and the Baroness Nicholson of Winterbourne ("Hodor!")[1]

These bastions of "sovereign democracy" are appointed to their life-long positions, of course, by something called "a Queen." *Oh, please remind me, what exactly is a Queen again?* you ask. Why, that's an elderly lady in a very sparkly hat who is elected in another fascinating exercise of "sovereign democracy" called "who is the human that came out of the vagina of the previous lady in a very sparkly hat?"

If you want to see how all this ties together into a surprisingly solemn explosion of bombastic nonsense, look no further than the state opening of parliament, which features hats being driven around in cars, horses dressed as wizards, ceremonial hostage-taking, 'the Cap of Maintenance,' 'the Great Sword of State,' a character called Black Rod (who literally gets a door slammed in her face, on purpose), the 'Yeoman of the Guard' searching the cellars for gunpowder (then getting paid for it with a glass of port), and, my absolute favourite touch of polite British passive-aggression, the death warrant of previously beheaded *Charles I* hung up in the monarch's robing room as a gentle reminder to the widely beloved Queen of the United Kingdom that *YOU DO NOT FUCK WITH PARLIAMENT*.

Again, I'm no ideologue; I'm not saying I have a plan for a better system tucked up my sleeve, nor do I have anything especially against this way of doing things. I don't care. Sure, it might *seem like* a weird, silly or outdated way to run a modern

---

1 If you want to know the fascinating history behind these ranks, crests and land titles, here's a quick summary for you: some people stole lots of stuff ages ago and then – here's the clever bit – never gave it back. (Congratulations! You're all caught up!)

state, but I'm also totally open to the idea that it might be as sensible, workable and valid a system as any other. I don't bloody know, do I? The world's a silly place.

All I'm trying to point out is this: there's a little bit of irony involved in the British saying we can no longer handle being partly run by unelected leaders who are somehow detached from the ordinary reality of our lives. It is, after all, the only thing we've ever known.

A Multiple-Personality Disorder

So, after that gentle analysis of our recent past, we return again to our muddled present, where our uncertain future is struggling to be born because of what 52% of us suggested a tenuously mandated government do one Thursday afternoon in 2016 – June the 23rd to be precise – the day when an almost exactly medium-sized howl soared up from the otherwise gentle-minded British masses, like a one-winged seagull emerging from ketchup, and declared defiantly: *WE* don't want to be ruled by *YOUR* unelected lunatics... *WE* want to be ruled by *OURS*.

Personally, I think that Brexit was a pivotal point in the history of BROKEN BRITAIN, because it was, rather ironically, the moment that the British may have actually *broken* Britain.

I'm not even, by the way, talking about the breaking up of the United Kingdom – of one, or all, of England (Leave), Scotland (Remain), Wales (Leave) and Northern Ireland (Remain) deciding to go their separate ways, although that too seems a plausible outcome at this time of writing – but about the breaking up of 'the British' into two parallel groups of British people, who had previously been able to co-exist relatively peacefully on the island because they were mostly unaware of each other (and because of politeness, splitting-the-bill and rounds.)

You see, there was a rather unhelpful problem at the heart of the EU referendum, built right into the very premise of it, and therefore the concept that the "will of the people" (or a coherent set of instructions) could emerge from it, no matter however clumsily, lop-sided, flapping, squawking and covered in red sauce.

It is well understood in political science that a democracy only works when you can draw some kind of line around some kind of people, in order for those people to be "the people" of that democracy. These people must be similar enough to each other to share some form of coherent identity (Britishness, anyone?), yet varied enough to need a majority vote system to peaceably resolve the potential conflicts posed by their differing values. Where and how and around whom these lines are drawn is famously tricky business, which is why your home-town can't hold a referendum for independence, but Scotland can, but only if the United Kingdom says so.

In political philosophy, this is called "the problem of the *demos* (people)". And it is mostly an *unsolved* problem, to put it rather mildly, as you may well notice every time you watch the news (over your friend's shoulder in the pub) and see the endless fighting it causes across the globe. The world is on fire because of exactly this problem. And many modern Brits – having lived together inside roughly the same lines and borders since 1707 – hadn't paid that much attention to this problem until it arrived, in June of 2016, with all the subtle charms of a powerful magnet swinging through a piercings convention.

"Our people," to Leave voters, were British. They felt betrayed by successive years of their political representatives about the direction of the European project, as what was originally pitched to them as a common trade area seemed destined, as if by the inevitable drift of its own logic, to become an increasingly federalised entity, with its fingers in ever more pies but not necessarily the democratic legitimacy to match. Unprecedented levels of mass immigration, too, were having a whole array of effects on the most unheard corners of the country (atop of the financial crash, the bail-out and austerity), with no signals coming from either the UK or the EU that any brakes could be pulled, let alone trusted. Some people wanted off what felt increasingly to them like a runaway freight train, before it threatened to take their sense of control/sovereignty/national identity off a cliff-edge with it. *You have one chance*, they were told, and, well, they took it. Their choice was understandable.

"Our people," to Remain voters, were European *and* British – as the first and second lines of their very passports told them they were. Everyone born after 1973 and every "Pro-European" had either a different "people," or *two peoples*, and so the whole Brexit "mandate" of 1.89% of one smaller population tipped over the 50/50 mark felt weirdly illegitimate to them, especially as a democratic justification for stripping away something so fundamental as *rights* and *freedoms*, not least of which because all EU citizens in Britain and many Brits in Europe weren't able to vote at all. What's more, literally millions and millions of people had built their lives under one set of arrangements, dutifully following the rule-book that society had laid down for them, yet were now told that those rules might radically change overnight, and not necessarily in a way that respected how much of a U-turn this would be. Their choice was understandable too.

Brexit, in other words, was "the will" of some people's people but not of other people's people, because we had all, rather unhelpfully, drawn the lines in our heads around different places. It felt perfectly democratic to some and perfectly undemocratic to others – and that's a bad recipe for what's supposed to happen in a democracy going forwards, and why everyone's been wrestling over the word 'democracy' ever since. 'Winners' and 'losers' hardly quite captures the full flavour of the problem this time. We're in a serious bloody pickle.

52% of Britons gave away something that the other 48% felt wasn't theirs to give away: their birth-rights (or, at least, heavily baked-in privileges) as citizens of Europe. (And if the result had gone the other way, it would have been just as bad, except reversed: Leave-voters might have felt they'd lost something irredeemable to a supranational institution they didn't trust, and/or got locked in to a *status quo* that felt ever-shifting, promised *more of the same* at a time when *more of the same* felt, to them, like a threat.) It was an impossible situation for a population of people, or indeed *peoples*, to be put in. Many Brits are now angry with the other "side"; there's bad winners, bad losers and only bad options for compromise between them; and yet we must also continue to live, work and get along together, otherwise Christmas will be ruined.

To people who live inside the bigger line (and probably, let's face it, are more likely to own a cafetiere), the "winners" of the referendum are trying to re-draw their line right through the middle of the more important one; between them and their friends, between them and their customers, between them and their partners, and, perhaps, between them and their pants. *It is the will of your people*, they say, *but not of ours.* They have much to lose from Brexit, on a very, *very* personal level, and it rubs unfriendly salt in the wounds to brand them all as "Remoaners" or "snowflakes" by default.

To people who live inside the smaller line (and probably, yes, I ain't afraid to bloody say it, might even prefer a cup of tea, thank you very much), the "losers" of the referendum often seem totally out of touch with the lives and concerns of ordinary people, especially on tricky topics like immigration. It is working people, after all, who have lost jobs and had salaries eroded as a direct consequence of the unrestricted, and mostly unrestrictable, influx of unskilled labour from within the EU's growing borders. They are, and have always been, at the sharpest edges of the single market, and it rubs unfriendly salt in the wounds to brand them as "racists" or "little Englanders" by default. You might also be less enthusiastic about the European omelette, too, if you were one of its eggs.

And I think, my dear friends of either political opinion or neither, that's the position we are going to be stuck in for a while. It is a pretty irreconcilable difference.

Unfortunately, it had to happen first, before the British could notice the troublesome reality that they had for decades been living in two different countries, one on top of the other, a Britain that was European by choice, and a Britain that was European increasingly begrudgingly, reluctantly, even angrily. There were two peoples on some islands, friends and families alike, who thought that they were one people, then realised they were wrong.

Britain, a crack through its middle, broke.

The End

(... well, Almost.)

The British Europeans and the European British

So, to my European readers and my fellow countrymen alike, I say thanks for reading as we reach the end of our time with the bloody British, both in this book and in this Union of Europeans.

To readers from Britain, I offer also my apologies, not for anything in particular, but, you know, just in case something (or, indeed, everything) in this book has been the cause for embarrassment, distress or awkward feelings of any kind that could have otherwise been avoided: I'm sorry. It's just a joke (book), and I love you really. So, yes. Sorry, sorry, thank you again and sorry. (Sorry.)

To readers from the Continent, I must say slightly more. Firstly, of course, I must applaud you for your patience and perseverance in making it this far. You have swam valiantly through the murky waters of passive-aggressive politeness, ridiculous understatement, little problems, big compromises, impossible double-think and universal disappointment, yet arrived here, on the other side, with your sanity left intact. My hope is only that the public service information presented in this mildly vengeful little booklet will help you deal with us in the future: to spot (or hear) us in restaurants, to sympathise with (or side-step) our stag-dos, to banter with us (without taking offence), to drink with us (without dying) and to effortlessly predict, as confidently as any modern Briton, the outcome of our next Sparkly Hat election. (Spoiler alert: *Charles.*)

Most of all, I hope this little book will help you look past any frustration you might feel towards us as things get Brexity, and to remind you of what will always be there when you come to visit us on our island home: an easily embarrassed people, a very, *very* funny people (no need to question that) and a fundamentally good-natured, well-meaning, fairness-fuelled people, cheerful and chipper in the face of the everyday awkwardness of having to be ourselves. I hope that when you look at us in the future, you see us not as enemies across a negotiation table, but also as innocent hostages of ourselves and of our culture, of our old, slightly mad institutions and of our own omnishambles of roiling political ironies.

I know it is not always easy to deal (or do deals) with us, especially as all the complexities of our bonkers old system spill over the borders of Britain and become your problems too. However, I hope that, in time, you will come to accept us once again in your European hearts, as wide as the massive and terrifying landmass that birthed them.

Lastly, my dear European friends, I have one small favour to ask. While I would understand if it feels a little trickier than usual to summon the prerequisite sympathy, compassion and generosity towards the British at this particularly juncture of history, I must make this slightly cheeky request of you anyway: would it be at all possible (but only if it's not too much trouble, of course) that you, I don't know, *offer me amnesty maybe*? *Please?*

I know it's a big ask, but I must at least suggest it, not just for myself, but on behalf of all my fellow countrymen, at home or abroad, who have become innocent bystanders to the Brexit process, but fear it is they who must become the token sacrifice made upon the altar of it. Half the people on our island, it would seem, are getting Brexited against their will, de-Europeaned against their wishes, yet the most valuable thing they stand to lose – that cocktail of international citizenships – is the thing they themselves voted to keep and the one thing that Europe could still offer them, perhaps, even if the UK no longer can.

European citizenship is derived solely from the European level, of course, and yet it is the United Kingdom that must, as the price of Brexit, revoke it from the Scottish, English, Welsh and Northern Irish, wherever they live, however it might affect them, whichever way they voted and whatever they believe. That decision was outside of the EU's control, of course, but what might still be inside the EU's control is how it defines that citizenship in relation to those who might still want it but are trapped inside the closing net of a departing member state. Is it opt-in or opt-out? Temporary or permanent? This is new territory; untested waters. The treaties only specify how people attain their European citizenship, but not how, or even if, they must lose it. If the primary goal of the European project is, by its own definition, one of promoting peace between historically dreadful neighbours – then it might not be crazy to imagine a form of European citizenship that is above and beyond national citizenship, not downstream of it, and one which could now be retained by citizens to whom it had already been granted, especially those presently in the process of using it like, for example, (*ahem*) me. There is, I think, a moral high-ground for the taking but also, just maybe, a long game to be won.

Germany, apparently, has a rapidly ageing population and a ticking pension time-bomb to disarm. So do Italy, France, Spain and Poland. Germany, according to some economists, could need up to 500,000 inbound migrants a year just to balance its books. This means, probably, that there will have to be more inbound immigration into the EU anyway (in order to fund the increasingly long lives of all the people who will be most grumpy about it), whatever European society generally thinks about that… so, well, why not some more Brits? We're nearby, we're nice (mostly) *and* we already have the right passports. An amnesty could be in everyone's interests.

Oh sure, some cynics might say of this idea that I'm just biased because I don't want to leave my flat, fill out loads of boring forms, deal with reality or be compelled to shotgun-marry my girlfriend in some spectacularly unromantic Brexit-fuelled proposal, and those cynics would be right. But, also, hear me out.

While broad, strange coalitions of voters made their choice in the referendum for a broad, complex spectrum of reasons, certain demographic trends did, nevertheless, jump out of the wearyingly complicated Brexit fog. The Leave-voting camp, for example, tended to skew older (70% of over 75s were for Leave) and included the vast majority of the country's retired people and more of its home-owners. The Remain-voting camp, on the other hand, tended to skew younger (73% of 18-24 year-olds were for Remain) and included the vast majority of those presently in higher education (students were 6 to 1 for Remain) and lots more city dwelling renters. People of non-voting age, meanwhile, are (or would have been, at least) the most pro-European demographic of the lot, whereas, on the other end of life's Brexit spectrum, Leaving the EU was most strongly supported by those who are also – let's face it – the most likely to have Dexited the material plain of reality since the vote took place. (And, lest any young folks think I'm wailing "old, dead people stole your future!", I gently remind them that they were also the least likely age-group to vote.[1])

Anyway, what I *am* trying to say is this: if Europe was at all worried about the UK becoming a new rival on its doorstep, it might potentially look at that topsy-turvy demographic breakdown, and see a potential future work-force of quite pro-European British people, ripe for import. Perhaps Brexit need not be a disaster for the Continent, but an unparalleled opportunity to poach some friendly British immigrants for itself. What's more, the raging Brexit culture war might even do the heavy lifting to help separate the younger, freer, tax-paying

---

1 One poll estimated only 35% of voters under the age of 24 turned out.

wheat from the older, more settled tax-draining chaff: Leavers will want to remain and Remainers will want to leave!

In terms of assimilating fresh waves of British migrants, Brexpats and Brefugees, though? Well, I'll be the first to admit that we might be a bit of a high maintenance bunch at first (and we'll probably need you to speak English to us for a decade or two, at least…) But, on the whole, I think you'll find us to be relatively harmless and agreeable creatures should you invite us to remain, unilaterally, within the family of European citizens, even if the UK, unilaterally, does not extend that same invitation back.

Sure, we *might* act a little bit like we own the place for a while (sorry) and we might clog up your bureaucracies with our crippling inability to make decisions, but, other than that, you probably won't even notice we're here as we settle down across the Continent and begin dutifully contributing to the local economy (of pubs, bars and breweries.) We'll queue, we'll make jokes, we won't have strong preferences and we'll be easily impressed when you show us all of your wonderful, fancy, exotic European things, like *renting, cuisine, expressing your opinions* and *noticing your feelings.*

"Brimmigation," as I call it, could be a policy hit across the entire political spectrum (as long as we ignore all of its obvious flaws.) Indeed, even the most far-right, most anti-*different-people* people would have a hard time spotting us from afar (apart from the sunburn, perhaps.) Meanwhile, just think of the opportunities that continued *free movement of British people* could offer! What kind of British Europeans would you like to fill those human-sized holes in your economies and societies? Some agreeable engineers, maybe? Some friendly freelancers? Funny women? Modest men? Polite families? What about some well-mannered, mop-topped musicians? We're pretty good at that! Oh yes, let the *Brain Drain* begin!

As young Britons and radicalised Remainers flee the post-Brexit Britain of their nightmares, desperately swimming across the channel on makeshift boogie-boards and bails of hay in the hope of getting their *28-countries-for-the-price-of-one* passports back, the EU's PR department could be there to rescue them with an aluminium blanket and a warm flask of tea, before taking a quick selfie and then quietly ushering them away to start paying some taxes. Not only would it be a *win-win* for the EU – as the Continent lovingly absorbs grateful, useful people at the expense of their newly declared competitor, the UK – but pulling hypothermia-ridden liberals onto the shores of France, Belgium and the Netherlands could be a great propaganda victory for the EU in its upcoming *Mildly Cool War* against Britain.

EU 1 – 0 UK.

I, for one, am ready to accept. So, what about it, Europe? Offer us amnesty? *Please!*

It is ~~2018~~ ~~2019~~ ~~2020~~ the future.

The United Kingdom has left the European Union.

Today, millions upon millions of despairing young Britons and radicalised remainers are fleeing their troubled homeland, making the perilous journey east across the channel for any slim hope of getting their 28-countries-for-the-price-of-1 passports back.

Europe, too, is in crisis, as hypothermia-ridden liberals wash up in unprecedented numbers on the shores of France, Belgium and the Netherlands. It is the world's busiest shipping lane and the waters can be rough, yet still they arrive in their thousands; some on makeshift boogie-boards, others on bales of hay. Many of the new arrivals speak no other language than English.

One exhausted Brefugee (or Brexpat, as he prefers) was asked upon arrival why he had taken such great risks crossing the 21 miles of salt water by stolen swan pedalo: "In my land, there is problem, many troubles," said 26-year-old James, in English, "but my people – people who voted remain, I mean – believe that here, across the great sea, there is... *hope.*"

As the EU struggles to cope with the sudden influx of moist Britons, some of its critics have questioned whether it is doing enough to help integrate the swarms of desperate newcomers. "We are struggling," said one EU volunteer, handing out cups of tea and phrase-books, "it's like Dunkirk backwards."

In an effort to stem some of this criticism, the EU has produced this official, illustrated *Integration Guide for British Refugees*, in the hope of accelerating the assimilation of post-Brexit Britons into European culture, so that they might finally begin their new lives on the Continent.

Integration Guide for British Refugees and "Brexpats"

Respecting Boundaries

Hello... and welcome to Europe. Did you know that Britain is *in Europe*? It's true! This is why many Europeans find it odd when British visitors talk of "going to," "being in" or "visiting" Europe. Show the locals your keeness to integrate by openly acknowledging that you share a continent.

Free Speech

In Europe, preferences are allowed, and even encouraged. Feel free to tell your new continental hosts what you think, feel, want or need (even if doing so might risk causing reality to be affected.) You need not worry about "being a burden" on European people, as they are also able to say no.

Integration Guide for British Refugees and "Brexpats"

Variety and Choice

Don't be afraid to leave old British habits at home. Instead, why not "do as the Europeans do"? There is much that is new to discover. Indeed, thanks to the safety-proofing of good English spoken across the Continent, you'll be better placed than most to enjoy this bountiful new variety immediately.

Rights and Privileges

Remember, too, that all of Europe's Europeans are *equally European* in Europe. There is no "British exceptionalism" here. If *you* want to reserve a sun-lounger (hangover permitting), you have the exact same right to do so as every other human and towel. Just get up early enough: it's first-come-first-served!

Integration Guide for British
Refugees and "Brexpats"

Conflict Resolution

In Europe, it is considered normal to acknowledge the possibility of conflict (in order that the conflict might be resolved within a decade.) You can help your continental hosts by expressing any negative feelings you might have outloud (rather than, for example, hiding them in a passive-aggressive joke.)

Effective Communication

In Europe, *what people say* and *what people mean* are often closely related. (This is no accident.) To communicative effectively with English-speaking Europeans, be mindful of over-using meaning-muddying politeness, understatement, confusing idioms, meaningless platitudes and false modesty.

Private Beliefs

Europe is broadly secular and one's religious beliefs are considered a private matter. Not all Europeans, for example, may share your enthusiasm for the earthly dominion of elite, god-sanctioned overlords ruling all people and owning all swans. It is most polite, therefore, to keep these beliefs to yourself.

Faith-Based Religion

On the topic of fantastical beliefs that are almost entirely unsubstantiated by real world data, Brits Abroad need not take offence if their European hosts fail to share a sense of optimism that *"football's coming home."* (It is merely that the Continental worldview is more restrained by reality.)

Integration Guide for British Refugees and "Brexpats"

Appropriate Dress

In Europe, it is often acceptable to keep your shirt on, even after it has passed 18 degrees. Flag-based swimwear and patriotic garments are not forbidden, but should be considered carefully: while they *will* help advertise your country of origin, they may also impede somewhat your ability to effectively "blend in."

Cultural Norms

Try to embrace the exciting diversity that life on the
Continent can offer. Nothing is 'weird,' just 'different.'
Don't forget, certain British norms and customs may
also seem like curious eccentricities to Europeans too
(such as the All-Weather BBQ.) Don't be discouraged;
this is all part of the fun of cultural exchange.

Integration Guide for British Refugees and "Brexpats"

Local Cuisine

In Europe, it is quite normal for restaurant food to be crafted with specific ideas inspired by a rich history of culinary tradition. Menus, therefore, should *not* be regarded as the beginning point of a negotiation, but a list of options. Why not ask for a recommendation? (Or an English menu.)

Alcohol Consumpion

While alcohol is widely consumed and enjoyed across the Continent, there is also a parralel culture of people being able to say no to alcohol as well. In Europe, this will not offend anyone, cause them anxiety or invite their judgement. Feel free to enjoy this relaxed attitude towards drinking in moderation.

Integration Guide for British Refugees and "Brexpats"

Gender Roles

In Europe, men and women are free to socialise and celebrate together. Informal gender mixing is even encouraged. Men can drink white wine. Women can drink beer. Don't worry, no one will witness either of these legitimate beverage choices and give you an embarrassing nick-name.

Civic Life

In time, we hope that you will come to appreciate Europe less as an exotic holiday backdrop for banter and more as a normal place where normal people do normal things like live, work and drive ambulances under a common rule-book. Thank you for your partipation and good luck in your new life!

Also by the Author:

Avoiding Adulthood
Irresponsible Advice for Begrudging Grown-Ups

"Ridiculously entertaining!" - Christopher Shevlin, *Author of Amazon #1 bestselling 'Johnathan Fairfax' series*

Are you terrible at life?

You're not alone. But the problem isn't you: it's **adulthood** - with its ridiculous expectations, soul-sucking admin and casual threats of prison.

What if you could get all the perks of being a grown-up without having to throw your inner child under a bus? You can!

With *Avoiding Adulthood*, it's now possible to opt-out of life's most nagging problems... for the price of mere dignity!

So join bestselling author **Paul Hawkins** today and learn to:

· Do a whole weekly supermarket shop in just five seconds!
· Pull a sickie so convincing your employer will beg you not to come in!
· Become instantly and undeservedly rich (just by moving somewhere scary)

Avoiding Adulthood is packed full of anarchic British silliness, impractical advice and a serious plan to become a Somali warlord. It's the perfect gift for that chaotic and ridiculous "grown-up" in your life (especially if that chaotic and ridiculous "grown-up" is you.)

Life is hard, so why not cheat?

About the Author

Paul Hawkins is a British author and illustrator from (almost) London, England.

While he participates begrudgingly in the world economy as a humourist – the minimum viable job – he prefers to spend his time faffing, drinking, apologising and/or traveling the world in search of an elusive and undeserved retirement. To this end, his life-long pilgrimage to avoid a "proper" job has deposited him in the Holy Mecca of Delayed Responsibility-Seekers: Berlin.

His books include the *Der Spiegel* bestseller *Denglisch for Better Knowers* (Ullstein, 2013), *iHuman: a User's Guide* (C.H. Beck, 2014), *Avoiding Adulthood: Irresponsible Advice for Begrudging Grown-Ups* (C.H. Beck, 2016), *The Bloody British* (Goldmann Random House, 2017) and *How to Take Over Earth* (Ullstein, 2017). The latter title is forthcoming in the original English.

You can follow his "work," read mind-bending articles and find out more about him at:

www.paul-hawkins.com
or
www.hencewise.com

If you'd like to tell him about everything he got wrong about Britishness (preferably politely), then you can contact him directly at **paul@hencewise.com**, or via **@hencewise** on the usual social media channels, or, for any more sensible requests, via his literary agent at **Landwehr & Cie**.

Printed in Great Britain
by Amazon

63990200R00166